D0555752

THE EARTHBORN

THE
EARTHBORN

PAUL COLLINS

A TOM DOHERTY ASSOCIATES BOOK
NEW YORK

THE EARTHBORN

Copyright © 2003 by Paul Collins

This book is printed on acid-free paper.

A Tor Book
Published by Tom Doherty Associates, LLC
175 Fifth Avenue
New York, NY 10010

www.tor.com

Tor® is a registered trademark of Tom Doherty Associates, LLC.

ISBN 0-765-30307-8

First Edition: April 2003

Printed in the United States of America

0   9   8   7   6   5   4   3   2   1

ACKNOWLEDGMENTS

I'd like to thank the following friends for their invaluable input: Meredith Costain, Sean McMullen, Gwenda Smyth, Cherry Wilder, Cathie Tasker, Randal Flynn, Dmetri Kakmi, Nick Sandalis, and Noel Harman.

THE EARTHBORN

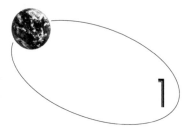

1

Fourteen-year-old Welkin Quinn glanced at the bulkhead. The time dial showed that he was five minutes late for his duty shift. The captain would probably have him tossed in the ship's recyclers and inquire as to his tardiness later. He finished tugging on his boots, checked his uniform in the tiny mirror his ensign's quarters barely warranted, and exited at a run.

As he dashed along corridors and charged recklessly around corners, he regretted that humans were restricted to sub–light speed, otherwise he could have been at his duty station on the bridge *before* he even got his boots on. If subatomic particles could do it, why couldn't he?

The final elevator ride up three levels was sheer agony. He'd never noticed before how *slow* these things were! He checked himself in the mirrored surface of the elevator doors. Everything *looked* okay, but Captain Sobol was notorious for finding fault. Rumor had it that Elder Sobol—as he was known off the bridge—possessed scanning electron microscopes instead of eyes. How else could he spot a speck of lint the size of a chlorine molecule?

Welkin slammed to a stop outside the bridge entrance. He quickly polished his brand-new ensign's insignia—since he figured he wouldn't be keeping it for much longer!—tugged his tunic straight, and walked in with the pretended nonchalance of an old spacer ready for anything.

The bridge was a hive of activity. Nevertheless, Captain Sobol's eyes flicked across at the recently promoted ensign, and he frowned.

That look alone was enough to turn Welkin's legs to jelly. He cleared his throat to deliver an elaborate excuse, but the captain beat him to it.

"Man your station, Ensign!" Sobol turned away, fixing his attention on the forward view screen where a blue-green planet, shrouded in brilliant swathes of cloud, hung like a Christmas bauble in the inky depths of space.

Old Earth! The unforgotten, almost mythical homeworld.

Sobol took up position behind the conning tower. "Prepare for orbit."

Welkin moved quickly to his station, joining his friend Harry Soames.

Harry shot him a look. "Are you begging to be a cadet again?" he hissed under his breath.

Welkin ignored him, got to work setting up spatial vectors for their insertion into orbit around Earth. He could see from his board that Harry had been covering for him. He gave his friend a grateful look, then concentrated on the job at hand.

Time passed, and before he knew it a brief cheer went up. It was such an unheard-of thing on Sobol's bridge that Welkin was startled, but the captain seemed to be in a rare good humor. He also seemed . . . well, almost wistful, even sad. Welkin had a sudden insight that left him feeling uneasy. The captain's job was over. The skyworld known as *Colony* had finished its long, excruciating journey to the stars and back, and after this there would be no more journeys among the stars. And no more need for star captains.

Because everything was about to change. Forever.

Welkin found Harry in the officers' mess hall, wolfing down rehydrated stew. Welkin dropped in the seat beside him. Harry studied him for a full twenty seconds.

"What? Did I grow another head?" Welkin asked.

"That'd be a help. It might triple your brain power! Are you suicidal? Or just plain bored with life? Any other time Sobol would have sent you to work on one of the vacuum crews!"

"That's not so bad."

"Naked!"

"Okay! You're right, I messed up," Welkin agreed, irritated. "I slept in. Won't happen again."

An impact vibration shook the mess hall and the adjacent galley. Several kitchen utensils clattered on the floor.

"What in Space was that?" Welkin asked.

"One guess."

"Lower deckers! Maybe the rumors are true."

"Guess they're not happy about something."

Welkin looked at his friend oddly. "You sound like you're sorry for them."

Harry shrugged. "Don't you ever wonder why a third of *Colony* has been 'discarded'?"

Welkin quickly looked around before turning back to his friend. "Harry, what's got into you? You want to be discarded yourself? They catch you talking like that and the heavies will be paying you a visit."

Harry lowered his voice. "All I'm saying is they're people, too."

Welkin's mouth dropped, horrified. "They're scum, Harry! Worthless freeloaders who want nothing better than to destroy everything we have! Don't you see? They're jealous. We're the pinnacle of civilization. The results of three hundred years of ongoing genetic engineering. We're superior to them in every way, and they can't take it." He looked pleased with himself. "Look, I'm not unsympathetic. They're genetic throwbacks. No different from the primitive lowlifes infesting Earth. Is that their fault? No. Is it ours? Space, no!"

"So what happens to the Earthborn when we land?" Harry asked glumly.

"What always happens, Harry. History is full of examples. Forty thousand years ago our ancestors ran into the Neanderthals. The result? No more Neanderthals. It's our job to make the planet fit for civilized human beings!"

"I don't understand why we have to exterminate them. It's a big planet."

Welkin stared at him, genuinely puzzled. "They're primitives.

They carry *diseases*. Parasites. And worse, they're genetically inferior. Do you want them polluting our gene pool? You want to marry one of them? I sure as Space don't. We don't have any choice."

"You sound like a vid, Welkin."

"So? You think the elders don't know what they're doing?"

Harry paled. "Of course not! I'm as loyal as the next person. Don't get me wrong. I just wonder, you know? Like maybe there's another way—"

"There is no other way. What we're doing is humane. Putting them out of their misery."

Whatever Harry would have said next was cut off as a giant vid screen covering one wall flickered to life. Captain Sobol moved into view. Behind him, on the bridge view screen, was Earth.

The entire mess hall fell silent.

Sobol cleared his throat. "Skyborn, I greet you." He paused and smiled. "The day we have looked forward to since the Great Disappointment when our ancestors gazed upon the worlds of Tau Ceti and realized that our dream of colonization could not be fulfilled, has finally arrived. Behold Earth!"

He stepped to one side. The vid screen zoomed in closer until the blue-green orb filled the frame. An inset picture of Sobol appeared in one corner. A stern expression settled on his face.

"Three hundred years ago we set forth from this world to plant our civilization upon another. Sadly, it was not to be, and the ancestors decided, for right or wrong, to return home, a decision made easier by the knowledge we gleaned from the final Earth message transmissions one hundred and eighty years ago. Global war had broken out and civilization itself had crumbled!"

Welkin glanced around the galley. Every face was mesmerized by Sobol's speech. He looked back, not wanting to miss a word.

"And so our revered ancestors asked themselves: Did we not journey across space to bring civilization to the stars? How could we then neglect the very world that gave us birth? What would we have history say of us? That we abandoned them? No. That we did not care? No! That we lost our humanity among the inhuman stars? NO!"

Every throat in the mess hall joined in Sobol's emphatic denials, Welkin as wholeheartedly as the others.

"We are human," Sobol said with a simplicity that was almost moving. "And so it was decided to bring the gift of humanity back to the world from which we sprang. It was our duty."

Sobol's face suddenly darkened. "But it was a close thing. There were those who disagreed, who felt that we should pursue an idle dream and quest on into the darkness of space, perhaps for eternity. Those were sad days, when families were torn apart, loyalties tested. But we came through the civil war and became stronger. The rebels were vanquished to the lower decks where their genetically inferior descendants scheme and plot to this day, making our lives difficult. But they will scheme and plot no more.

"But enough of the past! We return not to the Earth our ancestors left, nor to a world full of thriving superior humanity. No! We return to a planet infested with a degenerate species that once was human, a species that is little better than animal, possessing a dangerous cunning. Our mission—and it may take years!—is to cleanse the homeworld, restore civilization, and rebuild the supremacy of true human beings!"

An enormous cheer drowned out his final words and reverberated through the ship, bursting forth from every corridor and community room. When it eventually settled, Sobol resumed.

"We have entered orbit. We have begun atmospheric braking. *Colony* will touch down in twenty-four hours. It will not be an easy landing. This skyworld—like the others sent off to different destinations—was not meant to endure three hundred years of cold, hard vacuum and cosmic radiation. The outer hull is riddled with fatigue. Our propulsion systems are weakened. But we will land tomorrow. Of that I assure you. So now, Skyborn, go about your duties with the flame of destiny in your heart. For we are going home!"

The silence in the mess hall continued long after the vid screen snapped to black.

Despite the uplifting words, a chill feeling sleeted through Welkin. He recognized it was a dull surprise. He was scared. Scared of something he'd rarely thought about before. The future.

. . .

Welkin and Harry hurried into the briefing room and took their seats. Elder Tobias was at the lectern, looking grimmer than usual. A low buzz of conversation filled the room as ensigns and other low-ranking officers—all about Welkin's age—discussed the latest events.

Tobias rapped for silence.

"Settle down! Last time I heard this much squawking was in the henhouse on farming deck!"

A titter of laughter snaked around the room. "Let's get down to business, shall we?"

He hit a switch on a console. The lights dimmed and a vid screen lit up. The scene showed a prison cell somewhere on the detention level. A long-haired youth was strapped to a chair. His clothing was ragged and he had a wispy beard. His eyes were wide with fear.

There was a loud click, and something went *whump* through the boy's body. He arched back, his mouth agape, his paralyzed diaphragm muscles preventing an agonized scream from escaping his throat. Just as abruptly, he slumped back, barely conscious.

A stern voice addressed the boy in the chair. "You are from the lower decks, correct?"

The boy nodded feebly. Saliva dribbled from his slack lips. All his muscles were flaccid.

"Repeat what you said before!"

The boy blinked, trying to concentrate. He licked his lips. Haltingly, in a voice slurred by electroshock, he answered. "Planning— surprise attack . . . this time tribes united. Tired of lower decks. Not fair!" He regained more muscle control. "Not fair! Our destiny, too! We're human. Just like you . . ." He started to laugh. The click came again and his back arched in a bone-wrenching spasm.

Tobias shut off the vid. The lights came up.

Welkin noticed that Harry looked slightly ill. He didn't feel good himself, but the boy was a lower decker, after all. What could he expect if he was caught? Welkin had no illusions as to his own fate should he ever be cast down to the lower decks. He might live a whole minute, possibly two, before they tore him apart and carried pieces of his carcass back to the tribal cooking pots!

"Welkin! Are you daydreaming again? What did I just say?"

Welkin jumped to his feet, confused. Harry whispered something that sounded like "go to bed hurt."

"Sir! All wounded will retire to quarters for bed rest!"

The class erupted in laughter. Welkin swallowed.

"Interesting interpretation, Ensign," said Tobias. "I think your shipmate needs to articulate more clearly next time. What I said was, we shall shortly 'go to red alert.' I think that's clear enough. Now sit down and pay attention!"

Welkin sat down, trying to shrink into his chair. He gave Harry a quick but blistering "Thanks a lot!" look. Harry shrugged, barely containing a smile.

"We shall remain on red alert until *Colony* has landed, at which time new duty stations will be assigned. As you saw from the vid, we are expecting a breakout from the lower decks. Steps have been taken to neutralize this threat and I believe the danger has been contained. Nevertheless, we cannot allow ourselves a moment's respite! And it is with great sadness—and disgust!—that I broach a subject that until now has been a closely guarded secret known only to the elders."

A tense but expectant silence enveloped the room. Welkin found himself actually leaning forward, along with all the others.

"It has become known to us that lower decker sympathizers are among us!"

A collective gasp sprang up. Welkin stared in disbelief at the elder.

"You see the danger? What before was merely a dangerous turn of events regarding the degenerate criminals on the lower decks is now part of an ugly, treasonable conspiracy!" He paused. A vein throbbed in his temple and he stared at them with an implacable malevolence. "Mark my words, Skyborn. Rebels are among us, and we shall root them out and destroy them all—starting right now!"

The rear door burst open as if on cue. Four burly heavies, carrying stun rods and neutralizers, shouldered into the room. They came straight for Welkin. He froze, shocked into numbness.

But the security guards pushed past him and grabbed Harry, dragging him from his chair.

Welkin stared at his friend, whose face had drained of all color. "Harry?"

Harry looked back at him expressionlessly.

A sudden fury welled up in Welkin, and as the other officers hurled abuse at Harry, he found himself joining in, becoming part of the mob and its ugly, barely restrained violence.

A gloved fist slammed into Welkin's jaw, snapping his head back. A trickle of blood appeared. He wiped it away, sat up straight, teeth chattering.

He was in a portless, nondescript room, containing a chair bolted to the floor and equipped with leather straps for wrists, ankles, and throat. The heavies had come for him soon after Harry's arrest, dragging him from his duty station. Harry must have accused him of being a lower decker sympathizer—maybe to save himself . . .

The man in front of Welkin, Harlan Gibbs, was head of security on board *Colony*. He was thin, ascetic, almost emaciated. He believed in little other than order. Order at any cost, and obedience as the rigid path to that goal. In a previous era he would have made the perfect Gestapo commandant. Right now he was smiling a thin, dangerous smile that made Welkin's skin crawl.

"Harry told us everything, Welkin, so why not confess? Cleanse yourself of your sins. Be free of the awful guilt. I know what a terrible burden such secrets can be. Let me take them from you. You'll feel better for it."

Welkin knew he would like nothing better than to end his interrogation, except he had no secrets to reveal. Indeed, if this went on much longer, and if some of the rumors of Gibbs's tortures were true, then he would desperately be making up secrets to divulge.

"Sir," he said weakly. "I have nothing to confess, sir. Harry was my shipmate, but I didn't know he was a . . . collaborator!"

You would have denounced him if you had, wouldn't you, Welkin?"

"Yes, sir! I would have. Sir."

"Good boy."

Welkin started to relax. Suddenly the fist shot out again and caught him on the temple, rocking his head sideways.

"I believe you," Gibbs said in his oily tones. "But I have protocol to follow. One must be absolutely certain, don't you think? This is an infection after all. And it must be rooted out!"

"But, sir, I'm innocent!"

"You might well be. But there is value in punishing the innocent along with the guilty."

"Sir—?"

"Ever since the Age Plague when everyone over the age of twenty died, except for the chosen few, the elders, we've understood that social diseases are like those of the flesh. Slow and cunning, moving from one healthy organ to another, destroying from within. I'm afraid that once you have been exposed . . . well, I'm sure you understand, Welkin. It's for the good of *Colony*."

Welkin took up the refrain. "For the good of *Colony*." But he didn't understand at all.

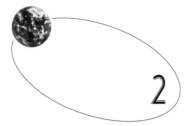

2

Klaxons blared. Welkin recognized the code, even though he had never heard it before. It was one that had not been heard on board *Colony* for one hundred and fifty years, not since the terrible days of Tau Ceti. It meant *planetfall*.

Welkin steadied himself against a bulkhead as the skyworld tilted. He could picture what was happening. Indeed, he should have been a part of it, would have been, if it weren't for Harry!

But it was no good thinking about that now. Harry was either dead or cast down to the lower decks, which was worse than being dead. Welkin's fate was more complicated. Even a few weeks ago he would have followed Harry in quick order, but Harlan Gibbs had intimated a different fate. A possibility of redemption. The word was tantalizing. Even coming from the cruel, thin lips of Gibbs, Welkin had found himself feeling dizzy, feeling . . . hope.

They would need cleansing teams once they landed, Gibbs explained, to exterminate the Earthborn vermin. It would be dangerous work—many would not return. But it was for the glory of *Colony*, and for Welkin it held the faint chance that one day he might work his way back into the good graces of the elders.

After all, what else was there?

He had heard of Skyborns, condemned to the lower decks, who curled into a fetal position and died. No physiological reason, they just died. They were *Colony*, born and bred. Without it, there could be no existence, no continuation, nothing . . .

"Let me out of here!" he screamed.

His voice went nowhere. He could scream forever in the cells and no guard system would hear. It was useless banging on the cell door, but he staggered around the wall and banged anyhow, in a panic reflex. He had never been claustrophobic in his life, but locked inside a prison cell on an aging skyworld about to make planetfall somehow overcame the genetically engineered suppressive mechanisms that normally protected him. He yelled again. Better than most he knew how dangerous this landing was. The entire skyworld could crumple like a tin can!

The light panels dimmed and flickered as the power source drained.

Welkin murmured his mantra for keep-calm:

I call upon the center of silence
Calm my senses
I call upon the center of the birth of light
Dispel the darkness of this time
So it be . . .

Repeating the mantra over and over, Welkin slid onto his bunk.
I'm going to die in here, he thought with a morbid kick. *Our shields won't last for long. They used to blow out regularly just in normal cruising mode.*

Then the floor plating shuddered. A deep basso profundo rumbling grew in the bowels of the gigantic ship, grew into a full throated roar, and somehow seemed to crawl inside his head and make his skull ache. He put his feet to the floor and felt the trembling under his grip-contact boots. *Colony* was going down, descending toward planetfall.

You couldn't strictly call it landing. A skyworld didn't land—it was more like worlds colliding.

Welkin watched as the metal plating buckled like a living thing. The walls crumpled in around him as massive g forces came to bear on the ship.

That's how the surface will look down there. All uneven and corrugated.

It'll be hard to walk around. But the Earth vermin manage okay. And if they can do it, we sure as Space can!

Colony had drifted between the stars far too long. It had been programmed to land on Tau Ceti III when it was a much newer skyworld, in its prime. Now it was a run-down rusting hulk that had barely made it back to the solar system.

Welkin had heard the old, sad story—about the elliptical orbit of Tau Ceti III and all the data on why the prime colonists decided to abort the mission and return through the darks of space to find another planetfall. There had been other plans, other systems and planet projects.

But landing wasn't suicide. He reminded himself that Systec— Systems and Technology—had calculated the stresses and forces facing *Colony* during planetfall. If they shunted all power into thrust resistors, they could achieve touchdown with minimal damage. *Except for the lower decks*, Welkin thought, with a twinge of guilt. Just as a man falling from a height can cushion the landing by letting his legs shatter, absorbing the impact energy, so too could *Colony* enhance its chances of survival by using the lower decks as a kind of giant shock absorber. Of course, at least half the lower decks would cease to exist in the blink of an eye as they pancaked together on landing. But as the elders pointed out with unimpeachable logic, that merely solved the two problems at the same time.

An elegant solution, except that Welkin had a momentary pang about Harry.

Welkin felt the slowdown from orbital speed as *Colony* plummeted through the stratosphere. He tried to stand, was thrown flat on his back. He dragged himself into the bunk alcove.

The ordio cut in: "All personnel are instructed to keep strictly to emergency-landing procedures. This is not a drill. Repeat: This is not a drill. Planetfall: twenty seconds and counting . . ."

A handhold, something to hang on to . . .

Colony abruptly bucked, flinging him out of the bunk, slamming him into a wall. He tried to grab hold of the waste unit.

"Eighteen seconds . . ."

Welkin lost his footing and tumbled across the floor, banging his head on the bunk.

"Sixteen seconds . . ."

He scrabbled back to the waste unit and clung to it in white-knuckled panic. Pain shot through him in a torrent.

"Fourteen seconds . . ."

The air suddenly became stiflingly hot. Power to the aerators had been siphoned elsewhere.

"Twelve seconds . . ."

A slow, rending noise sliced through the ordio voice.

"LET ME OUT!"

Welkin heard the echo of his own voice, screaming.

Colony juddered.

He felt a moment of weightlessness as power to the gravity plating missed a beat. Simultaneously auxiliary thrusters cut in.

"They've done it! We're reducing drive speed." He could imagine the frantic hum of activity on the bridge right now. Captain Sobol would be standing in the center of barely controlled chaos, the one still figure in the storm. Quick shouted commands would be flying back and forth. "Fuel cells go!" "Shields at maximum!" "We are go for landing, Captain!"

"Seven seconds . . ."

Welkin's mind went into a tailspin. *Colony* had been spying on Earth from as far away as fifty light-years out. It was no longer a planet on those database RMVs. There were no "thriving megacities" anymore. And no "rapidly expanding technology." The whole place looked like what used to be called the third world, but where were those international organizations and caregiving agencies?

Earth was beautiful. It was all there on the monitors, the green grass, the blue hills, the oceans, even the people. Humanoid, better than that, genuine human, blood sibs, products of the gene pool . . .

He knew the history of Earth, he thought he knew the face of Earth. Now in these last seconds he gave himself up to pure fantasy. It was not his past life flashing before his eyes but the past life of his ancient homeworld.

Can't wait to smell the fields! See the colors! Feel the breeze—the breeze! Strong enough to knock you down sometimes! And the sea. Huge waves—so big they pick you up and throw you down. And animals . . .

And dancing. He could see the Earthborn dancing—black skins, brown and white, throwing their arms everywhere and kicking the air . . . He had found dancing listed as a pagan ritual in databases.

He thought fleetingly of his sister, Lucida, and wondered if she was all right, or if Harlan Gibbs had paid her a visit, too. How far does a "bacterium of treason" spread? Or a "viral conspiracy"? Welkin didn't know. Perhaps he never would. Families were no longer the unit of childhood maturation as they had been on Earth centuries ago. Mothers, fathers, brothers, sisters—outdated modes of thinking, *dangerous* modes of thinking! *Colony* had done away with such sentimental and socially corrupting concepts. There was only one family that existed now: the family of humanity. And by definition that was to be found only on *Colony*.

Hysterical screaming broke into his thoughts. The lights dimmed, flickered, and went out. Welkin almost screamed himself. For all his officer training, for all the endless neural simulations he'd experienced, *darkness* was still the most dreaded cataclysm that could befall the Skyborn. A thousand souls screamed as one in a darkness blacker than space.

Colony hit. It plowed into the Earth with vast and implacable inertia. Nothing could possibly stand in its way. Welkin was thrown across the room. Somewhere deep in the ship the thrust resistors screamed as more power surged through their overheated circuits and they died. But before they expired in a spectacular shower of sparks and smoke, they did their job, the last that would be asked of them. They brought *Colony* safely home.

Almost immediately, a frightening cacophony of noise filled the ship in all directions: tons of hardened plastisteel twisting and buckling as the ship warped under gravity, fractures spiderwebbing through bulkheads and decking . . . Farther still, on the edge of hearing, Welkin could make out a cascade of *ping*s and *crackling*s as the mighty hull cooled.

Despite his fear, he knew he was high enough up in *Colony* not to get crushed, although he could feel the vessel tilting as more lower decks folded in on themselves.

He prayed Lucida was somewhere safe, and he prayed that the lights would come back on.

This was worse than any nightmare. *Colony* was like a living organism, and like any organism it was susceptible to disease or, in this case, contamination. Bulkheads would be ruptured, portholes smashed. If all duty stations were still functioning, then danger spots would be quickly sealed off. Under no circumstances could they permit the skyworld to be contaminated by the insidious disease-infested environment of Earth.

Colony's last massive groan, as it settled into its final resting place, almost drowned out Captain Sobol's last ordio announcement:

"We are down. We are home."

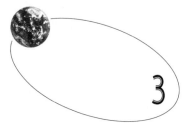

3

The multitiered *Colony* would have burned out high in the atmosphere were it not for its shields and antigravity stabilizers. Even so, it struck Melbourne, a city in the southeast of what was once called Australia, at sixty miles an hour.

Colony's shields took the brunt of the collision, then dissolved as *Colony*'s power overloaded and shorted. The lower levels collapsed like trodden cardboard as thousands of tons of extruded titanium concertinaed on impact.

The resulting shock wave toppled tall buildings in a five-mile radius. A cloud of dust shrouded Melbourne's skyline for forty-eight hours.

The pallid sun broke through on the third day.

Elder Jamieson, in charge of Earth reconnaissance, pursed his lips. Now was as good a time as any to make an initial foray. They'd need to establish safe territory from the earth scum and construct a barrier around *Colony* until its massive damaged infrastructure could be sealed from outside contamination. But first they needed to know what was out there.

"Leeson," he said, without turning. His subordinate, a short, thickset man, responded. "Sir?"

"We need a foraging team, to get the lay of the land. I doubt whether the Earthborn will have much food. Supply the scouts with scanners; there might be some ancient food vaults that haven't been desecrated by the heathens."

"Yes, sir, Elder, sir."

"And Leeson."

"Elder, sir?"

Elder Jamieson turned slowly. His voice was crackly and held no pity. "Expendables, Leeson. I doubt they will last long out there. Wire them up for telemetry. I want continuous readings for all possible contaminants, infectious agents, and background radiation." He waved his hand dismissively.

"As you wish, Elder . . . sir."

"One more thing. If any of them make it back to the ship, throw them down below."

Welkin was among the fifteen-strong party that was dispatched outside. The team comprised several suspected lower deck sympathizers plus those, like Welkin, who had had the misfortune to be exposed to the "contagion." There were also three army personnel who had volunteered for this mission. One thing *Colony* would never be short of was dedicated zealots!

They fell about like bowling pins at first. On board *Colony*, where corridors were perfectly flat and even the farming and recreational areas were designed for safety, few Skyborn had ever developed the need to learn about rough terrain. They coped as poorly as Earthborn might if confronted with weightlessness.

"Take it easy," a voice rasped loudly in Welkin's headset. "All of you. Get a puncture in your suit and we're leaving you out there."

Welkin swallowed, fighting a moment of panic. Nothing could be worse than to be left in hostile territory. It was certain death.

Wearing heavy-duty work boots and a gray contamination coverall with *Colony* in black letters embroidered on the upper right arm, Welkin gingerly picked his way through the skeletal remains of a building. He ducked beneath twisted girders and more than once lost his balance on jagged outcrops of concrete and tangles of sharp metal.

The vid sims on *Colony* had said that it would be bad, but this was worse than he had imagined.

There was nothing here, just a desolate wasteland and a never-ceasing wind that keened eerily through the ancient buildings. Even the broiling, sullen sky bore no resemblance to the smog-laden atmosphere he had expected.

Could the entire planet be like this? Maybe somewhere—on another continent—it was different. Either way, it was hard to imagine that this was the birthplace of humanity, that his ancestors had evolved on this desolate speck of mud. He looked back quickly at the quietly rumbling ship, squatting on tons of smoking rubble. Even stronger in his mind now was the silent thought that Harlan Gibbs had placed there. Redemption. Hope. A way to rejoin *Colony* . . .

Welkin knew then that he must prove his loyalty to the rest of the Skyborn. He must win his way back into the folds of the only family he had ever really known. With a sudden chilling resolve that he had never felt before—that was somehow *adult*—he knew he would do *whatever it took* . . .

But right now he had to concentrate, had to stay focused. He pushed those other thoughts away. He knew why he had been sent on this mission. He was an expendable, a "discard." It was either this broken, tumbled hellscape, or the lower decks. He almost laughed, which was a strange thing in itself. From where he was standing, he wasn't quite sure which was worse.

He tried to block out the excited voices on his headset. He felt more sadness than excitement. He felt resentment tear through him. He hadn't even been given a chance to farewell Lucida. It was just so—

"For crying out loud! Quinn!" shouted a voice. "We're under attack!"

Welkin jerked from his thoughts.

Over to his left, three of his party had broken rank and were stumbling back to the ship.

"I don't see anything!" Welkin shouted. Panic swept through him.

"Go to ground!" their group leader snapped. Two of them followed the order. The other kept going. He had almost made it to the gaping docking tube when bullets thudded into him. He crashed down and was still.

"Cover!" snapped a voice made tinny by the transmitter. "Sightings?"

"Glover here," came a cautious voice. "I've scanned them." He paused, but Welkin could hear his labored breathing. "They're everywhere," he whispered in a disbelieving tone. "Space demons above! The ground's crawling with Earthborn!" he shouted suddenly.

Welkin looked about frantically. Before he could see anything, gunfire sent him scurrying for cover. He hugged the ground so closely he could almost smell the dirt through his filters.

The others started fleeing through the rubble. Erratic gunfire echoed off the decaying walls. Welkin chanced a quick look and saw two make the ramp. He watched with horror as the doors closed. A third crew member barely touched the ramp when he suddenly flung up his arms and toppled to the ground.

"Flankers' report," Welkin said hesitantly. None of his training on *Colony* had prepared him for this. Welkin switched channels, frantically searching for voices. A white silence overrode the busy static from the field station. "*Colony*. Do you read me, *Colony*? Red Tag reporting."

Through his faceplate he saw the crippled craft tilted at an unnatural angle. Its solar shields were up. It may as well have been a blank wall of metal. *Colony* was maintaining radio silence. "*Colony*, do you read me?" His communications circuits cut out.

"Ohmistars," Welkin mumbled. "Ohmistars. Ohmistars." He wanted desperately to be out of here. He wanted space. He wanted the dull thready thrumming of *Colony*'s main drives as he slept. He wanted to look out of a viewer and see the comforting vastness of star-flecked space. Most of all he wanted his cocoon of metal. Solid, reliable metal.

He took a deep breath and trembled. He was going to die out here. He searched his mind for some procedural tactic that would get him back on board *Colony*. But there was nothing.

Welkin looked up bitterly at the towering citadel that was *Colony*.

The ship seemed to pierce the very sky. Even as he watched, cumulus clouds had swept in on the prevailing wind, enveloping the upper decks like cotton candy. He could barely make out the burnt orange and red COLONY lettering emblazoned on the ship's pitted hull. *Colony* was a mass of twinkling multicolored lights dotting a shark-gray carapace that loomed above Melbourne like a mechanical monster. Eyes winking from every surface; an omnipotent being that would be tracking him this very moment. But he was simply too insignificant—and too contaminated!—to retrieve.

Welkin was just getting up when suddenly he was jerked backward. He tried to scream, but the grip on his throat almost made him gag. He kicked and thrashed, but whoever had him was immensely strong.

His assailant twisted him about. The world blurred.

Welkin expected to feel the jaws of some hellish Earth beast bury themselves in his throat. He already had his eyes closed to shut out his death. When, after what seemed a harrowing few minutes, nothing happened, he snapped open his eyes fearfully.

He was shocked to see a human female standing in front of him. Her face was weathered and deeply tanned. Her black, gray-flecked hair was cut close to the scalp; her eyes were a glittering green. A strong jawline, rounded nose, and taut cheeks gave her a fierce appearance. An Earthborn primitive. Rough, tanned, and—he snagged on the word—*hard*.

Welkin lashed out with his foot, but she was too quick, too *trained*, he realized with a start. She spun him about again and pulled him backward like a cat dragging a wounded bird.

Then she was still. Her arms held him immobile for a moment before she ripped off his faceplate.

"NO!" he tried to scream, but she clamped a callused hand over his mouth.

Welkin squirmed, holding his breath for as long as possible before he was forced to exhale. His bulging cheeks deflated like a burst balloon. He knew he was going to die a terrible death, his lungs hemorrhaging as they tried to extract oxygen and nitrogen from the poisonous atmosphere of this world. It was either breathe—and be poisoned—or faint and maybe die anyway.

His face went red, his eyes bulged with the effort. His captor peered at him quizzically as if she couldn't quite work out what he was doing. Welkin gasped a few times before realizing that he could breathe. But how was that possible? The elders had assured them that Earth would have to be terraformed before the Skyborn could live there again. It would take years to heal the damage caused by the Earthborn vermin. Yet this air actually smelled nice. It smelled . . . he hunted for the word. Fresh. Unrecycled. He had a sudden understanding that left him dizzy. The air on *Colony* had been manufactured and recycled for three hundred years. Three centuries of endless human respiration, clotted with stale esters and chemical by-products. Why, this Earthborn woman might well believe *she* was asphyxiating if she ever got aboard *Colony*! What a strange notion, as if *Colony* were somehow . . . abnormal.

He turned frightened eyes to his assailant, but she held a finger to her mouth and demonstrated slow and easy breathing.

Welkin's heart was yammering so hard his body was rocking with its urgency.

"*Youkeep reel quiet, ki',*" she said, then drew a finger across her throat. There was no mistaking *that* gesture.

Her pronunciation was drastically clipped, but he had little difficulty understanding her. The purely functional components of a language were the last to change, and judging by their surroundings it didn't look as if the Earthborn had much high art or literature.

Welkin's throat constricted. His short, staccato whimpering sounded like that of a trapped animal. She seemed to understand this.

The only other noise now was of bricks being dislodged, the sound of scurrying people. Sibilant commands. Something heavy being hauled across the ground.

The Earthborn woman looked down at Welkin. "*They'r strippen you' bloke. Gor ani foo withem?*" Welkin frowned with the effort of trying to decipher her words. They might have been, "They're stripping your blokes. Got any food with them?"

Welkin shook his head. He dared not speak. His mind was screaming crazy things at him. *Zedda and Efi—they had made it back safely. But Glover and a few others hadn't. They're being stripped like when they're dead!* He felt sick. *I'll be dead soon. I can breathe this air for now, but I bet it's full of slow-acting poisons!*

The woman's eyes closed to slits. She indicated with her chin. Welkin followed her gaze. "*Feras-scumma-the-eart.*"

Welkin nodded as he tried to decipher her words. "Ferals. Scum of the earth." Clothed in all manner of cloths and dangling trinkets, they were like prehistoric creatures. Furtive rodents scurrying about like frenzied atoms. Suddenly, long-bladed machetes rose and fell in rhythmic blows. The creatures grunted with the effort. Blood flicked from the glinting blades like ragged crimson ribbons.

Welkin shuddered and his mouth dropped wide. Then he ducked down, his head close to the earth, hyperventilating.

"Your *Colony* tapes didn't tell you about ferals, did they?" the woman said brutally, dragging his head back up. "They soak their hair with water and crushed chalk—clogs it up and makes that god-awful color. S'posed to scare their enemies. If you ask me, it's lucky they don't have mirrors."

But Welkin wasn't listening. He uttered an involuntary cry of distress, and before he knew what he was doing, he had launched himself forward.

"Oh, no you don't, young fella!"

Welkin swung clumsily at her, but she deftly deflected his punch and wrapped her forearm around his neck.

"Lemme go! Lemme go!" he screamed. The woman's hand clamped over his mouth, muffling the words. After a long moment, he subsided. She took her hand away but kept it poised, ready.

"You're cannibals!" He spluttered the unfamiliar word. It triggered a series of flashbacks from *Colony*'s video archives. "Argh!" he screamed and bit down hard on the woman's palm.

"Mongrel!" She yanked her hand away and grabbed him roughly by his tunic, jerking him forward. Welkin's face collided with hers. He could smell the earthiness of her skin, her sweet-sour breath. It was nothing at all like Lucida's fresh breath and crisp smell. Thought of his sister propelled him backward, but the woman's fingers drove deep into either side of his jaw like steel clasps.

"Listen, you little . . ." With an effort she loosened her grip, and the ferocity in her eyes faded like a passing shadow. She flicked him backward and he fell back on his elbows.

The woman went to drag him up, but something held her in check. She knelt down beside him, clicking her tongue, and shook her head disapprovingly.

"Don't ever call me a cannibal! Got that, spaceboy? 'Cause if you want to meet real cannibals, I can introduce you. Any time you like!"

His stomach began to constrict, and before he knew it he was vomiting.

"Oh, shit," the woman swore and jerked backward. After a moment she said hoarsely, "You done now?"

Welkin nodded miserably. He couldn't control his body. It spasmed with fright, and for long moments he felt as though the foul-tasting air was killing him. He had to let her think that he was cooperating. If her attention glitched for one second, he'd be dead.

"Take long, deep breaths," the woman said and illustrated her instructions. She glanced about furtively. "We're running out of time, kid. Do it now!"

Welkin sniffed and wiped a cuff across his face to clear it of vomit. He tried to follow the woman's instructions, but he barely had the energy.

He looked anxiously around. The "ferals" were ripping packs from around their victims' waists. Pocketing whatever they could. Ever watchful. Distrustful—some fighting over bounty. Shoving one another. Wrestling on the ground.

Welkin whimpered.

With a yank the woman snapped his head around sharply. "Pay attention!" she barked. "They're dead. We're alive. There's nothing you can do to help them.

"Ferals," she repeated. "Run for your life when you see them." She shook him roughly. "Stay awake, kid. You need your wits about you out here. Name's Sarah." Her voice softened, but it still had an urgency about it, a tenseness. Like she had something on her mind that she would rather discard.

Welkin swallowed hard. His throat was parched. Confused thoughts crowded his mind. He was on Earth and he could breathe the air. He pushed hard at all the counterproductive thoughts that tore at him. The elders had said the Skyborn would die out here without oxygen. *Colony* personnel had been told the Earthborn had plundered the Holy Earth, and redemption by genocide was the only solution.

Sarah quickly checked their position. "I asked your name," she snapped. "You people talk another language now or what?" Her patience was thin edged. "Maybe now you're all a bunch of uncivilized barbarians, huh?"

Welkin was momentarily too shocked to answer. The idea that this . . . primitive *creature* . . . could regard the Skyborn as uncivilized was so staggeringly ludicrous, so far outside the narrow box of his thinking, that for a brief instant he thought he was misinterpreting her.

She prodded him and spoke to him as though he were a moron. "Me Sarah. You Spaceboy."

"Welkin. My name is Welkin. And I'm Skyborn," he said proudly and with enough adolescent conceit to draw a slight smile from Sarah.

"That figures." Sarah was contemplative. "Old Earthspeak. Not tainted like ours. Something about a plum. A plum in the mouth," she muttered to herself. "Well, your lordship, my apologies for saving your life just now, but I reckon that if we don't get the hell out of here—*reckona t'we dung't t' hellouda 'ere*—we're gonna be on somebody's menu tonight. You reading me?"

He stared at her in sullen contempt, then nodded. *She's quite mad!* Welkin watched her carefully, waited for her to loosen her grip. But then something else occupied his mind. For the first time in his life he felt a cold wind rushing at his face. He touched his cheeks and worried at their numbness. It was how he'd imagined being thrown into deep space might feel. Cold and desperate. With a knowledge of certain death.

"You're an odd one," Sarah said meditatively. She watched him with fascination as he wiped sudden tears that coursed down his grimy, unblemished skin. She clicked her tongue as though annoyed and with the dirty edge of her shirt sleeve wiped the last of the vomit from his face.

Sarah suddenly looked up at *Colony*, and her expression hardened. "Reckon they'll have us on infrared right now. What to do, what to do," she pondered. Her grip on Welkin was still viselike.

They sat there staring at one another until the crimson sky became darker and the shadows lengthened across the rubble-strewn street.

"It's time," Sarah said. She turned away but reconsidered. "I'm not with the blokes that just killed your comrades. All right?" His expression was blank. Perhaps he was having as much trouble understanding her as she did him? She talked more slowly. "There are dozens more gangs like them. But my people aren't like them. Understand that. Even if you understand nothing else." She looked down at his unusually thick thighs. Steroid injections? "You can run from me—you people are damn fast—but it'll do you no good. They're all murderers out there. See?"

Welkin nodded warily. On *Colony* she would be one of the degenerate renegades lurking down on the lower decks. Bilge fodder. Then an odd thought occurred to him. Maybe some of the lower deckers weren't degenerates. Harry had seemed normal enough, had even been his shipmate. Was he really "diseased"? It was very confusing. But right now he was on this woman's turf. Degenerate or not, it made sense to go along with her, learn as much as he could.

A vague idea came to him, something to do with Harlan Gibbs . . .

Welkin's stomach tightened and he gasped. It was a cramp reflex that occurred when he had what the elders warned were revolutionary thoughts. *Never have those thoughts!*

"You okay?" Sarah said. "Don't die on me, Skyborn."

Welkin nodded and cleared his head of the bad thoughts.

"Good. I hope that's settled. Stay close." She lowered herself and belly-crawled over the tumbled bricks.

Welkin watched in frank amazement. She reminded him of those eels he had seen on *Colony*'s viewbacks: a slithering thing that rolled from side to side across the bottom of murky water. Or a snake—a . . . sidewinder.

Sarah hadn't gone five yards when she looked back. "It'll be dark soon—you people don't like the dark, do you?"

When Welkin's face darkened, she said, "We've been watching your lot for days. No activity at nights to speak of," she mused.

Welkin hesitated. *Colony* was no longer an option. They'd put up a shield to prevent entry. The ferals—*feras*—would murder him for his suit. It was getting dark as deep space was dark. Darkness was a prospect that further churned his stomach. He tested his legs gingerly. Whatever malady had caused him to lose his control had dissipated. He scurried after her, mimicking her belly-crawl as best he could.

It took them half an hour to work their way across the broken ground and reach Sarah's destination. More than once Welkin tripped and tore jagged holes in his suit. Each new hole brought a cry of dismay to his lips—until he remembered he was already contaminated. He would never be allowed back on board *Colony*, even if the shield came down.

Sarah lay motionless, then poked her head up before quickly brushing away some loose rubble and unlocking a sewer grate. She paused and considered Welkin. "Now it's dark down there. They're Telstra's old communication underground service tunnels, but we have lights farther on. Close your eyes if you like. Makes no difference to me." She thought for a moment. "And the air levels aren't so good."

When Welkin made no effort to move she grabbed him by the shoulder and almost threw him into the opening. This time, however, he was prepared. He blocked her arms and they clenched. Their faces clashed, hers like hardened leather, his soft and yielding. She couldn't budge him.

"You're a tough'n," she hissed between clenched teeth, angling for better purchase.

He struggled with her and they remained locked. "We're stronger than Earthborn," he said tightly. Her stranglehold about his neck was nearly suffocating him. He, in turn, squeezed harder.

But for his youth, Sarah admitted to herself, he would best her. "Okay. Stalemate." She took a gamble and released him.

He pulled his arms back quickly and they both sat there, panting and glaring at one another.

"What is it with you?" she said. "A new super race like Hitler envisaged? Genetics gone wrong? What?"

He took several big breaths before answering. Earth oxygen was going to take some getting used to. And he could still only half guess her questions. "*Colony* had one-point-five g."

Sarah nodded in sudden comprehension. "So you were raised in a false gravitational field—half again that of Earth. Just in case Tau Ceti III was more massive than Earth."

"It's always been that way," Welkin said.

"Apparently," Sarah nodded. "Okay, Superman. What's your problem with going down there?"

He hesitated. "Why should I trust you?"

"I saved your life back there. Another minute and the ferals would have found you."

"I don't want to. It stinks. I'll die!"

"It's easier to die up here," Sarah said. She smiled a yellowed-teeth smile.

An eerie keening noise broke out a hundred yards behind them. A similar noise answered, this time from up ahead. Her expression hardened. "We don't have time to argue. I'm taking a risk bringing you along. Some of my people won't like it. Come with me and I'll protect you. Stay here and die. Your choice, *Skyborn*."

That said, she dropped into the gaping hole.

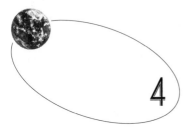

4

Welkin clung to the metal rungs. They felt grimy and disease-ridden, just like the fungus-covered walls. He had never seen such *filth* before. Did the degenerates who lived here ever get used to it? Would he? Maybe he was becoming a lower decker? The thought made him shiver.

Sarah touched ground and craned her neck. She could see the Skyborn kid staring incredulously at his hands. "Welcome home," she said. "A bit of dirt's not going to harm you, you know." She couldn't keep a slight sneering tone out of her voice.

As she expected, he stiffened. She was learning exactly which buttons to push.

Welkin glanced up at the war-torn rubble they had just crossed. He could flee back to *Colony* and throw himself on their mercy. Surely they would understand how his team had been ambushed. Indecision warred inside him. Maybe not a good idea. The elders had thrown them out here in the first place. Besides, darkness was falling fast—a giant black thing with wings outstretched, shrouding the sky with its enormity.

His jaw tightened. He wanted so badly to hit someone, *something*. It was all so unfair! He hadn't done anything wrong! He suddenly remembered the vid Elder Tobias had shown them the night Harry was taken. The boy from the lower decks who had been tortured for information. He had also said it was "unfair." But that didn't make any sense. The boy was a lower decker. That was how life was for a degenerate.

The rungs at his feet gave a metallic *ting!* and he realized Sarah had struck the ladder with something. Time to choose. Go down or stay up? He'd been thrown into an alien scenario with no rules, no safety nets, and no abort button. To survive, he'd need an edge. That advantage he'd always had in the simulators, simply because the faster your reactions and the more you used them, the better you became. But this was the real thing.

He had a sense that his presence among the Earthborn could make a difference; just exactly what, at this stage, he couldn't work out. But he knew with a dread certainty that his return to *Colony* would not make the slightest difference to anyone but his sister. *If* she was still alive . . .

Welkin swallowed hard. Out here on the surface of an unruly planet he was like a fish out of water. Well, what did Elder Tobias always used to say? If a fish can't swim, it better grow legs damn fast! And that was what he would do. Grow legs. But to do that he needed help. He needed an Earthborn! He *needed* Sarah.

Ting! Ting! Ting! Ting!

With his eyes screwed shut he descended until his feet touched solid ground.

"Took your sweet time!"

He felt Sarah beside him. Cautiously he opened his eyes. The light was dim and came from small bulbs hanging from a wire tacked onto the ceiling. The track of light wound its way down the darkening tunnel like cats' eyes. Cobwebs laden with scurrying spiders and husks of insects hung from the ceiling in gauzy hammocks.

Sarah looked back up at the vent they had come through, then studied Welkin. "Okay. We have to get a few things straight. So we know where we stand. You comprehend everything I'm saying, don't you? Just speak up if something's unclear. Misunderstandings get people killed around here."

Welkin gave a helpless shrug. "I understand most of the time."

"Good. For a moment I figured we were going to have communication problems."

"*Colony* will come looking for me," he said, suddenly defiant. He hated the way she sounded so authoritative. So much in command. She was nothing but a heathen—probably not more than one generation from a cannibal!

"Not after dark they won't," she said knowledgeably. "We've been watching your craft, see. Since the dust settled, anyway. Besides, if they'd wanted you back they had plenty of time when we were out in the open."

"Maybe you didn't come up on the scanners," Welkin said. *Otherwise the elders wouldn't have sent us out here!* There was too much to think about. How *had* they remained undetected?

"We could've been watching from a long way off," hedged Sarah. "Or maybe we know this place like the back of our hands and no amount of technology is as good as experience. Either way, we've decided you people don't like the dark. My guess is that you've been in space so long the lights have always been on. The only darkness was in space. Right?"

"Perhaps," Welkin said uneasily. Only nightmares contained the dark. "Are you going to kill me? We've heard—"

"Whatever you heard you can forget. Some turned cannibal. Mostly ferals." She gritted her teeth at some thought, then voiced it. "There'll be campfires tonight. A feast."

"*Colony* people," Welkin heard himself whisper. His eyes widened with alarm.

Sarah's steady gaze met his. "I lost two friends the other day. You learn to take death in your stride. I would've liked to have buried your people before the ferals got to them." She stopped abruptly. "But it's not worth the bother anyway. Ferals dig 'em up, see. We're not like that."

"*Colony* people haven't killed anyone!" Welkin blurted. "Just now was the first contact we've—"

"Save it, kid. Your guys have been on a killing spree for days. The old 'We come in peace' palaver was broadcast for at least a day. Reckon the whole of Melbourne town heard it."

"It doesn't matter," Welkin snapped, fear making him angry. "All Earthborn are degenerate scum. Genetic throwbacks!"

"Scheduled for extermination, no doubt."

Welkin tried to hide his reaction. He looked away guiltily, though why he should feel guilt puzzled him.

Sarah chewed on her lower lip. "We had a word for that once. Genocide."

Welkin met her gaze for a brief instant, then looked away again.

"You'd be surprised how much old history we remember. Of course, we're still degenerate savages. You Skyborn tricked a whole swag of locals. We lost an indispensable friend. Gimp by the name of Mundine—a true-blue friend of mine."

"What's a gimp?" Welkin asked, despite himself.

"A liability for the most part. Someone no one wants in his or her family. Gimps like their own independence too much."

She shrugged. "But they're handy to have around. They're sort of like, I don't know, hoboes in Old Earthspeak. Anyway, this gimp was a black fella who knew everything about living off the land. A gimp might be physically or mentally crippled. They tread their own path. It's no good trying to make them walk somebody else's."

Welkin rounded on her aggressively. "Then why kidnap me? Maybe I have my own path!"

"Maybe you do. And maybe our paths lie together for a time. The universe works in mysterious ways, my young friend." She touched the laserlite slung over her shoulder. "Right now, most of our time is taken up with food and weapons. But I figure there's got to be more. And that means finding a mekanic."

"A mechanic? You mean a technician?"

"Names don't matter."

He laughed. "Then you kidnapped the wrong person. You need my sister. Lucida's a top-rank techie. There's nothing she can't fix or improvise."

Sarah eyed him thoughtfully. "You got a ship full of Einsteins, yeah?"

"Stuff you Earthborn couldn't even imagine," Welkin boasted. He felt himself swell with pride. Here was something that *he* had: knowledge. Compared to him, these people were like children.

Sarah snorted. "We know a lot, kid. But right now life's too short and hard. Surviving takes up most of our time." She swatted a mosquito that landed on her shoulder. "If your sister can make surviving any easier, maybe we can use her."

Welkin stared at her like she was crazy. "You think she'd help you—you—?"

"Degenerate scum?"

"You don't know as much as you think. Not about *Colony* people. They'd rather die than come out here. And believe me, they don't want to save you."

Sarah actually laughed, a loud full-throated laughter that rocked her whole body. Welkin became even more puzzled. What if they were all insane? What chance did he have?

"Now you're wondering if we're crazy, right?"

Welkin flinched. Could she read his mind?

"No, I can't read your mind. But you're pretty transparent, Skyborn. We Earth scum are a bit more guarded. We don't wear our thoughts on our faces. Anyway, we better move. It's getting cold."

The mere mention of cold made Welkin shiver. Earth's harsh climate was another thing the elders hadn't taken into account. Or had they? he wondered.

She moved out and he reluctantly followed, stumbling over the uneven ground.

"So your sister's the smart one, huh?"

"Lucida once built a dynamic memory allocation unit out of old spares and cannibalized parts."

Sarah mulled this information over. "I guess if you're impressed, then I should be."

"Even the elders commended her," Welkin said. He noticed that Sarah chewed her lower lip when she was thinking; other times, the tip of her tongue poked out of the corner of her mouth.

"So who are these elders? They're the bosses? Or just the advisers?"

At this simple question Welkin tensed up as a flood of memories unspooled. Their mother, Magda, had died from a recurrence of the Age Plague. He didn't know how his father died, but the elders had always dissuaded him from prying. Under normal circumstances this wouldn't have worried most *Colony* children. But Welkin and his sister weren't normal kids. They had had more contact than was usual with their biological parents, whereas most children were raised in subdivisional nurseries and came to see the twenty or thirty subdivision parents as their own. Welkin hadn't ever really thought about the ways he and Lucida were different, except that they seemed to get into more trouble than other kids.

Their father's death had been a terrible blow to them. They grieved openly, which was politically and socially incorrect, even dangerous. "We've become nothing but uncaring animals," Lucida had screamed at her unit. The elders hospitalized her for that one—and warned that further outbreaks would require swift remedial attention. Both Welkin and Lucida quieted down after that warning. Freethinking radicals were either thrown downside, lobotomized, or simply vanished. Spending the rest of your life with parts of your brain missing didn't appeal to either of them. In fact, their change of attitude had been so marked that it had stirred further interest in them from the elders.

Their subdivision playmates shunned them, and they were officially reprimanded, a black mark being entered in their life files.

Black marks accumulated. None was forgotten. None was forgiven. His innocent friendship with Harry had been the final unforgivable black mark. And here he was, consorting with barbarians and freezing his butt off.

"Hello? Earth to Welkin? Tell me about the elders."

Welkin blinked. "They're the leaders on *Colony*. A long time ago, there was a plague. It killed almost everybody over the age of twenty. The elders were those who were genetically pure, who resisted the disease. It was natural that their children also became elders."

Sarah raised her eyebrows. "You've brought a space virus back with you?"

"Nothing like that. It was brought under control ninety Earth years ago, though there have been recurrences. The first time was the worst. It devastated *Colony*, wiped out seventy percent of the crew and almost all the astrogators. If it weren't for the few elders who knew the secrets of navigating the stars, *Colony* would have been lost forever in the void. After that, social structure changed. Young people had to learn to run the ship, just in case the plague ever mutated and came back stronger than before. But the plague hasn't been seen in years. The elders say it's been wiped out for good."

"So why'd you people come back here? We got our own problems—we don't need more trouble."

"We're not here—"

"Cut it. You're causing problems. What happened when you reached Tau Ceti III?"

"It was found to have a highly elliptical orbit. At its perihelion—"

"Closest to the sun?"

"Sorry. When it was closest to the sun it was too hot. At its aphelion—farthest from the sun—it was just too cold. The other planets were just as uninhabitable. Tau Ceti itself was smaller than Earth's sun and cooler. The ship couldn't last forever. Besides, war had broken out here. The elders met for a special meeting and in that meeting a miracle happened. Our true destiny was revealed."

"Your destiny?"

Welkin nodded eagerly. "Yes. They realized that it was no accident that *Colony* was sent to a dead star system. There was a great purpose hidden in this journey! Don't you see? We are the seeders! We are the new Noah's Ark. We were sent away into darkness so that Earth might one day live again and see the light of reason and civilization!"

Sarah's face was oddly expressionless. "You're going to *seed* a new civilization?"

Again the eager nod, the bright eyes.

"Once you get rid of ours?"

Welkin barely heard her, still lost in the vision of his ancestors.

This kid has been infected with a dream, Sarah thought. *And I must admit, it's the kind of dream that could inspire an entire people. Or create a race of murdering fanatics . . .*

"I wondered why they were sending boys out to do adults' work."

"I'm fourteen!" Welkin said hotly. "And an ensign!"

Sarah grinned. "Adult status on *Colony*, maybe—but here you're still a kid. You'll see what I mean when you meet others of your age. Refresh my memory. Why Tau Ceti?"

"Earth control detected a continuous signal indicating intelligence."

"So NASA picked up some beam back in 2010. The news made everyone happy. Just like when those guys first landed on the moon." She smiled at Welkin's frown. "You might think we're savages. But some of us have hoarded books and CRCs. Compact replay crystals. The *Colony* fiasco was well documented."

Welkin stared, perplexed. "Earthborn can *read?*"

"We can even tie our own shoelaces. Most people thought *Colony* was a myth, a way to make what was happening here less . . . awful. After all, if humans prospered around some other world, some new Earth, then maybe it didn't matter if this one died. A lot of cults sprang up. One bedraggled old visionary even said *Colony* would return one day and lead us from darkness. They stoned him to death. But I guess he knew something the rest of them didn't. Anyway, what happened to the aliens?"

Welkin shrugged. This was ancient history so far as he was concerned. *"Colony* discovered that the signal came from an automatic beacon left behind thousands of years ago by some unknown race."

"How come the ship crashed when you got here?" Sarah ducked beneath a low-hanging support beam. She was smiling.

Welkin thought she was being sarcastic, and pride flared within him. He wasn't going to let this Earthborn scum smear *Colony*'s reputation, no matter how badly they had treated him. He replied hotly, "We weren't meant to survive in space for that long! We were a *terraforming* project. Nobody expected us to go all the way there *and* come back. We barely made it. *Colony* was constructed to become a ready-made habitable city for us when we landed on Tau Ceti III. But the return journey deteriorated that facility. Major systems have been cannibalized to bring us home."

Sarah snorted. "Your ancestors' prime objective, Welkin, was to populate the galaxy. That doesn't mean colonize one planet. It means found an empire. The fact that Tau Ceti III was uninhabitable isn't an issue. Your people either hit a glitch in the cosmic program, or simply forgot their original directive and decided to hell with it, let's give up the ride and head on home."

"That's not true! This is our true destiny!"

"So you said. But pardon me for not giving a damn. The success of your 'destiny' seems to require the failure of mine," Sarah said.

Welkin wouldn't meet her eyes.

"I might be degenerate scum, Skyborn, but I'm not stupid. And I know something of your history that you probably don't. Can't see your elders broadcasting the fact that the majority of passengers who gained berths on *Colony* did so through subterfuge and murder." Sarah bit her lower lip as she dug into old memories. "Most of those assigned to travel never made it."

"My ancestors?" His voice was filled with momentary doubt.

"Some changed their minds, some had their minds changed for them. The world was heading rapidly toward global warfare. Earth wasn't a good bet back then. Berths on *Colony* were priceless and black marketeers killed and maimed to gain them."

"Anything else?" His lips were compressed in a thin white line. *Who did she think she was?*

"Don't get uptight. This country was founded on convicts and it worked out pretty well. It's just a shame that such a promising idea— a spaceship full of specialists in every field of earthly expertise— wound up taking more than its fair share of scum."

"Not everyone was bad."

"Maybe not, but it had enough bugs to make most of the barrel rotten."

"Degenerative genes have been bred out of *Colony* personnel," Welkin said firmly, though before he could stop it, a truly chilling thought intruded: *But maybe not out of the elders . . .*

"Seems like you got rid of morality at the same time." He was about to flare again. "Eyes open, Skyborn! We saw survivors of the crash escaping from the lower decks. Your people shot them in the back. Some of them were just kids."

Welkin wanted to deny her accusation, not because it was false, but because it made her despise the Skyborn. And for some odd reason her opinion mattered to him. "They're rebels," he explained. "We had a mutiny at Tau Ceti. Not everybody wanted to come back to Earth. They didn't understand our destiny. The mutineers that survived were confined to the lower decks. We've been battling them ever since."

"And crash-landing was supposed to wipe out the lower decks. Yeah?"

Her guess was disturbingly accurate. She didn't stop there, though. "You're a reject, too, aren't you? That's why they sent you out." She watched his reaction carefully. "They don't care if you live or die. They just want to know how dangerous it is. Am I right?"

"They'll take me back!" Welkin shouted. Tears of rage blinded him. *I'm Skyborn!*

"Nice try," Sarah said. "But your elders have fooled themselves about one thing. They're so bloated with arrogance, so convinced that we're completely vulnerable to their technology, that they've forgotten one of history's great lessons. Germs."

Lucida sprang to Welkin's mind. "We're healthy. Our hygienic drenches are fully operational."

Sarah shook her head. This kid was so raw it hurt. He'd be more than a handful to look after. In the pit of her stomach she knew she shouldn't take him under her wing. "I'm talking about viruses that Earthborn people are immune to but that your people probably have no immunity to. You ever heard of measles? It was a killer disease once."

Welkin brushed his face with his hand. It felt clammy, like it did when he was working in the hydroponic gardens. He kept well clear of the spiderwebs and the fungus-riddled walls.

Thought of hidden bacteria made Welkin squirm inwardly. This woman seemed so . . . so omnipotent. Like the elders. He wanted so badly to pull her down from her throne. "Maybe we've brought back something *we're* immune to that you're not."

Sarah tilted her head and stared at him. The look of wonder faded from her face. "That's one thought you'd best keep to yourself. The others? They're not so easy to get on with as me."

She smiled abruptly. "You'll be safe for the time being. Keep your mouth shut, Skyborn. And remember, eyes open!" She turned to go, then stopped. "One more thing, Welkin. I'm the only friend you have right now. Stay on my good side."

The tunnels wound around and around in an endless maze that made Welkin dizzy. The unevenness of the ground sprained his ankles, and he could feel them swelling inside his boots. He knew that taking the boots off would be a big mistake. Several times he banged his head on the low tunnel roof and felt blood trickle warmly down his face.

It was a nightmare that never seemed to end. He was more tired than he ever remembered feeling. *Spent.* His legs were leaden; lifting them, putting them down, lifting them again, was torment. All he wanted to do was rest. But he couldn't let this Earthborn show him up. He had to keep going.

Finally Sarah stopped. She raked her scalp. "Rest time. Pull up some dirt." She squatted to one side of the tunnel, out of the thin trickle of evil-smelling amber water that flowed down the center of the causeway.

Welkin sat down facing her. The wall fungus, for all its putrid appearance, was slightly phosphorescent. No doubt one of Earth's many new mutations. Sarah's face looked spectral and relaxed. He suspected she wasn't resting for her own benefit, but for once his pride took a back seat.

"When *Colony* left it caused worldwide problems. Now that it's returned it's causing more problems," she said. The subject was an annoying itch that she had to scratch.

"You're not *that* old," Welkin said. "You wouldn't remember—"

Sarah looked amused. "No, I'm not *that* old. Earth remembers history, too. *Colony* was built in space, orbiting Mars. It took maybe fifteen years from A to Z."

Welkin leaned forward. "What else do you know about *Colony*?"

Sarah laughed derisively. "A lot of things your elders wouldn't tell you. Like the corruption that I just told you about. The wealthy obtained berths all right. They knew Earth was going downhill long before *Colony* reached the planning stages."

"But not *everyone* was corrupt," Welkin insisted hotly. "You're just saying that!"

"You people have been gone a long time, Welkin. You've got a lot of Earth history to catch up on. Most of the gritty stuff would've been edited out of your texts."

"They wouldn't do that," Welkin said slowly. He tried to keep his voice steady, but doubt was crowding in at all angles.

"Have it your way. But it's a cert that if *Colony* passengers had been chosen from a good genetic pool, as they were supposed to be, you would've had a better chance up there. Instead you had inbreeding and more crooks than a convict ship."

Sarah slapped at her forehead in mock anger. "There I go again. Sorry. It's just that the world had so much false hope for that damn hunk of metal."

"We had hope for Earth, too. But as we got closer we picked up random UHF broadcasts." At Sarah's querying look, he explained, "We don't use radio anymore. We employ a variant of what's known as quantum entanglement. Simultaneous transmission." He kicked at a piece of rubble and it went bouncing from one side of the tunnel to the other until it clattered out of sight around a bend. At Sarah's inquisitive look he self-consciously rubbed his boot into the water-worn bluestone pitchers.

"You get a kick out of doing something like that?" Sarah wondered idly. "There's a lot more around. "Kick 'em all you like."

Welkin hesitated, then pulled his foot back and kicked at another piece of rubble. It too skittered off into the darkness. "Just wondered what it'd be like to kick something. Like they do in vids. And soccer."

"You've led quite a deprived childhood," Sarah said, a tinge of sadness in her voice. "You and everyone on board *Colony*."

"It wasn't all bad," Welkin said, momentarily forgetting not to show any weakness in front of this Earthborn woman. "Lucida and I used to play the neural sims a lot. Any Earth game we could find."

"Simulators? Like virtual reality games? Stuff in cyberspace?"

Welkin held his head up proudly. "*Colony* technicians advanced virtual reality's technology. You jack into a neural sim and you're actually *there*. Facing your opponent." He parted a small patch of hair behind his left ear. She peered closely, saw a metallic implant where an electronic jack would fit. "You can choose weapons, like swords or lasers or even no-holds-barred. The environment is as real as this." He waved his hand at the surrounding tunnel.

Sarah eyed him thoughtfully. "So you could be jacked in right now? Maybe everything that's happening to you here is a mock simulation. The elders could be testing you."

He reacted as if slapped, staring at her in genuine confusion. How *would* he know? There *was* no way to tell the difference between a neural matrix environment and a real one.

Maybe Sarah was right, maybe the elders were testing his loyalty. He could still be sitting in that prison cell where they questioned him after Harry was arrested. The thought chilled him thoroughly. For a moment, he didn't know what he feared more: that all this was real, or wasn't.

He looked down at his swollen ankles, at his hands scraped raw from feeling their weary way through the dimly lit tunnels.

"I don't believe it."

"Good for you. Reality can be lethal. Best you take it seriously." She changed the subject. "How much technical training do you have? Can you repair radio equipment?"

"I don't know. That's kinda prehistoric," Welkin said. "Besides, the last two years on *Colony* everything was pretty much geared to arriving here."

"Something puzzles me. I don't see how your people could've kept going with two halves of the ship in opposing hands."

He took a deep breath. "Military personnel commandeered the main cruise cabin. From there they diverted the power banks, activated the bulkheads, and sealed a perimeter around us. Then they systematically sought out individual pockets of resistance and—"

"Okay. I get the picture. But they didn't get everyone, did they? The people on the lower decks, what are they like?"

"Barbarians."

"Like me."

"I didn't say that. They eat people. Like the ferals."

"So the elders tell you," Sarah said.

"It's true!" Welkin pushed away from the wall and scowled at her. His hands were clenched into fists at his sides.

"Relax. You'll give yourself an aneurysm," Sarah said. A half smile played on her lips. She got up and with a casual flick of her head motioned for him to follow. "Let's go. I just needed a little time with you before you meet the others. Everything's going to be fine."

Despite her reassuring tone, she was worried. She wasn't quite sure how her family would react. She knew she was taking a risk. Leaders of families weren't voted in or out. Usually, they outlived the previous incumbent, though "outlived" could take on several meanings. This kid was potentially a boon, but just as likely could turn into a liability—a gimp. Too dangerous to keep. Maybe too dangerous to let go. That was one thought she would keep to herself for now!

She glanced at him as he struggled over a fallen drainage pipe. He was pallid, his skin almost translucent. She could see bright blue veins through the jagged tears in his suit. They had no sun up there. No doubt they had solaria, but why keep using them for three hundred years? Sun-replicating lightbulbs would provide vitamin D without the potential long-term hazards of UV radiation. Many earlier Earth cultures had also shunned the sun, had created elites who prided themselves on their pale superiority. Only the lowborn were tanned. Those who worked out-of-doors, who *labored* to support the pale ones. Perhaps that's what the elders planned for Earth in the long term. A comfy, cozy life for the Skyborn while the worthless Earth scum worked the fields to feed them.

She wondered why she had rescued him. Did she need him? Would the others resent his presence after Kenny-H and Bilbo had been killed by the colonists? Certainly the ferals would have killed him straight out. But then, they weren't terribly bright. Would the others accept him?

He presented a problem, all right. He was a walking contradiction. The product of a highly sophisticated, technological, and proud society but one whose frontier skills were lacking, who had become soft with time and easy mechanized living. Yet he possessed something that was more precious to Sarah than food and weapons: *knowledge*. And not just knowledge of technology. He knew better than anybody living among the Earthborn just what heights humans could aspire to. On Earth, such dreams had died out long ago. Many, like the ferals, saw themselves on some almost mystical level as no better than the animals that rend one another over food. Could a feral dream of the resurrection of humankind?

She didn't think so. Could the other families? The answer to all her tumbling questions was simply yes. She had a good feeling about the kid. And her hunches usually paid off.

Stumbling and at times barely saving himself from falling, Welkin let himself be dragged along. He refused to complain about his feet, about the tiredness that was even now gnawing at him like some squirming bug. He found that talking took away the stress from walking through the darkness and kept his thoughts away from his rapidly deteriorating worldview. "Why did you ask if I knew anything about technical stuff?"

"I have a plan to restore the TV towers in the Dandenong Ranges. Right now they're just a pile of scrambled junk. The two guys we lost the other night were our mekanics. They knew tech stuff."

"What are Dandenongs?"

"Hills twenty miles east of here. They used to house two of Melbourne's main water storage reservoirs. More importantly, we'd get a good reception of radio waves up there and put out better signals. We need to contact others, get the right kind of people together, so we can get things up and running. Carry on like we are and we're heading nowhere fast."

"They'll think you're building an army. They won't like that."

"I don't give a toss what *Colony* likes or doesn't." Her face was grave. "Earth is divided right now among dozens of tribes and families all warring one another. Each has its own turf, but resources are scarce, which means raiding someone's else's patch. But that doesn't have to go on. We can work together and rebuild."

"You've had a hundred and fifty years to rebuild. If it was going to happen, it would have by now."

"Ordinarily, I might agree. But you don't have all the facts. What brought down civilization wasn't the war or the radiation. It was what happened afterward. Nuclear winter."

"That's why the sky is like that?"

"Yeah. And that's what has changed. I noticed it about four years ago. There's more sunlight now, and it seems to be increasing at a cumulative rate. You see what that means? Earth is healing itself. We can plant crops again, build farming communities. For the first time in a century and a half, the human race has a chance!"

For a moment Welkin was caught up in her bold vision. Then he remembered. "Until we came."

She eyed him speculatively. "Yeah. Until you came." Her voice dropped. "You could have arrived as heroes, extending the hand of brotherhood, helping us to get on our feet. Instead, you're bent on exterminating us. Well, we don't go easy, mark my words. And for all your shiny advantages, you're the 'aliens' here, and you're on alien turf. *Our turf*. I wouldn't count us out yet."

Welkin was silent for a long moment. "Will your family hate me?"

"No. Well, not exactly. They'll just take some time getting used to you."

Welkin's face held no expression, though his lower lip quivered for an instant. "I'm not wanted by anyone."

All of a sudden it hit Sarah. For all his posturing and pride, Welkin was just a fourteen-year-old boy thrust into the rigors and demands of early adulthood. And he was very scared. She had to make this right, and quickly. For good or ill, he was her responsibility now.

"It's going to be all right, Welkin. I promise."

He looked stricken for a moment. At last he said quietly, "That's what my mother said. Just before she died."

Sarah sighed. The boy was an emotional minefield. She'd have to be careful. "Listen to me, Welkin. I know I'm just an Earthborn in your eyes, probably not worth spitting on. But I want you to listen to me. I pledge myself to you and your well-being. I will protect you and succor you to the best of my ability. You are my family, my family is you. Eyes open!"

Welkin stared at her. He didn't really know the meaning of what she said, but he recognized the simple powerful mantra of ritual when he heard it. For no reason he could put his finger on, he was immediately comforted. The lost, bleak feeling that had swept over him a moment ago was gone.

All his life he had belonged to some kind of social unit. Now he belonged again, even if it was just some Earthborn fraternity. Yet he didn't fool himself. These were primitive rituals; the Earthborn could not possibly understand the true nature of belonging, of family, of destiny. How could they? Perhaps one day he would teach them. For now, it was enough that he *did* feel safer. And that, he supposed, was just one more puzzle to file away for the future.

Welkin's stomach grumbled, reminding him that he hadn't eaten for some time. "What will you do for food in the mountains?"

Sarah almost burst out laughing. "Food? The ranges are full of it. Trick is to find it. Which is why we had a deal with Mundine, that gimp I told you about. He was teaching my kid sister, Gillian, all about food gathering. He's gone now," she said as an afterthought.

Mundine. *Another* Colony *victim!* "Food's usually in concentrates on *Colony*," Welkin said awkwardly. "Nothing like you've been eating, I bet."

"Neither is the Dandenong food like our usual food. You ever hear of Australia's Aborigines?"

"Not that I remember," Welkin said.

"Well, their diet consisted of large insects like cicadas and witchetty grubs, and root vegetables such as yams and water lilies. Had some once."

"Water lilies?" Welkin said incredulously, further confirming his belief that these people were barbarians. "Plants?"

"Sure. Tastes like celery. And their seeds can be ground into dough that you can bake like bread in the ground over hot rocks."

"Are there still birds and fish? You can eat birds' eggs," he said helpfully.

"Gimps aren't terribly good at trading that stuff with us," Sarah said. "But there are wild fruits and berries. Read somewhere that because of the volcanic soils and high rainfall, all that good stuff grows like wildfire. Should be bees up there, too. With any luck we could track them to their nests for honey."

Welkin gave her a faint smile. It was good the Earthborn still had plans in all this carnage.

"Tell me something of your lineage. Your parents." At Welkin's sudden distrust, she added, "Curiosity—that's all."

"The original Quinns, dating back to *Colony*'s launch, were neuro-cybernetics experts. The prime Quinn was responsible for the sky-world's techmates."

"Sounds like a dating service for computer nerds," Sarah laughed.

"Dating—?"

"Never mind. That's a thing of the past. Carry on."

"They were semi-intelligent plastiroids that maintained *Colony*'s communication system. My father, Howard Quinn," he said proudly, "revolutionized nanofiber optics." At Sarah's blank face, he added, "It made all the old wiring on *Colony* completely redundant."

"Just like us," Sarah said. "A wireless society."

"Nothing like—"

"A joke," Sarah said quickly. *Watch him. He's on the edge.* "A stupid joke."

"What were you doing when *Colony* landed?" he asked suddenly.

She turned briefly but kept walking. "Luckily I was miles away." Her voice became choked. "I was supposed to be with my two mek-anics, Kenny-H and Bilbo, working on a wireless. *Colony* crashed slap-bang on top of their dugout."

"They were your technicians," Welkin said awkwardly.

"You got it in one, damn them," Sarah spat. "Caused a bit of a bust-up with my team." She paused by a ladder and rested her foot on the first rung. "I've been collecting homeless waifs all my life. Street kids, really. You build a team, you know? Because some people need a family."

Welkin knew exactly what she meant.

"That's something I hope to achieve. Make ourselves available to anyone who needs us. But first, we need to get set up, stabilize our-selves. But a family needs the right ingredients. If you don't get it right, it'll fall apart just like that!" She snapped her fingers. "Without certain members the team's dysfunctional. Kenny-H and Bilbo kept the team even tempered. They counteracted the hotheads. Now I've got a few renegades who want to go their own way."

Welkin shrugged helplessly. "Why don't they?"

"Oh, I'd say they're biding their time." She looked up the length of the wall ladder and clambered up into the sewerage pipe.

Welkin wished he still had his faceplate to filter the dust Sarah disturbed.

She reached down and he gripped her outstretched hand. "One, two, three," she said and heaved.

His feet made paddling motions as they slipped on the rock face, then Sarah gave one mighty heave and he scrabbled up alongside her.

"It's okay to be scared, you know," Sarah said close to his ear.

Welkin said nothing. He *was* scared, but he wasn't about to admit it to this Earthborn woman, family or no family. Everything that was happening to him was new and shocking. He itched all over and felt dirty, as though every pore in his body was clogged with grime. His scalp crawled. Maybe because of bugs. He'd read about lice. The urge to scratch madly was almost uncontrollable. His armpits and back felt especially uncomfortable, as though tiny life-forms were wriggling all over him.

Sarah began shuffling forward on hands and knees.

Welkin sneezed a couple of times. On *Colony* a sneeze was considered to be a psychosomatic symptom left over from their ancestors rather than as evidence of infection. Welkin added it to his accumulating list of worries.

Despite his coveralls, he was also beginning to feel the cold. It was something he had never experienced. "I need warmer clothing," he said and was disturbed to hear his teeth chatter. It was a complete abnormality to him.

"You should've landed somewhere near the equator."

"I don't think we chose where to land," he said, disgusted. "We barely had enough thrust to come straight down." He sneezed again.

"Bless you. What happened to your shuttle craft? Skimmers?" She furrowed her brows. "Doesn't make sense you wouldn't reconnoiter before landing."

Welkin had to think about that. "I've never seen a . . . skimmer.

I've seen Earth planes, though. Things with big wings!"

"You're about a century out of touch," Sarah said. "Landing craft should've come down with advance parties. Maybe had a powwow with the Earthlings. Just to make sure everything was sweet with you people coming down here. Sort of got in our good books." She sucked her lips loudly. Her head swiveled around and her wide green eyes glinted at him. "But that wasn't part of *Colony*'s plan, was it? You came back as conquerors, not long-lost expatriots.

"What were you told, I wonder? That maybe you'd been shot down by Earth Defense? Something real wacky, I bet," she mused.

For a moment Welkin relived those horrifying hours in the prison cell as *Colony* plunged toward Earth from its decaying orbit. Before that, there were repeated fire drills, instructions for landing procedures. Rumor had spread that the lower deckers were planning a breakout, were cruising the boundary bulkheads looking for ways into the upper decks. *Looking for food!*

Suddenly she scuttled up into another pipe. Welkin pulled himself up after her. A rush of fresh air indicated they had reached the surface. He gladly heaved himself out of the grate. The cold air seemed to soak into him like water into a sponge. He never thought he'd be glad to suck in a lungful of Earth air, but the fact was he rather liked it. It didn't have that *canned* sour smell that permeated the air of *Colony*.

He took in his surroundings. They seemed to be in a street of derelict office blocks. He had seen vids of a street like this—busy with traffic and sunlight glinting on a thousand windows.

"It's our equivalent of a full moon," said Sarah, glancing at the sky. "Good for your people. Not so good for us. We'll have to be careful."

A laser beam arced down, cutting a brilliant swathe through the night. Sarah crouched. It wouldn't be long before the *Colony* storm troopers discovered the railway passages and sewer tunnels below the city. But it was still a maze down there. *Their* maze. Sarah turned to Welkin. "Could they be looking for you?"

"I don't think so," Welkin said hesitantly. It was funny how facing death and having your whole world turned upside down made you look at your past life differently. He knew with certainty that Harlan Gibbs had intended him for the lower decks, the same lower decks that had been flattened into the ground, crumpled like tinfoil. Planetfall may have saved his life. Not for the last time, he wondered what had happened to Harry.

Sarah spotted troopers patrolling a forty-yard spread about two hundred yards north of their position. Raised under 1.5 g like Welkin, and probably genetically enhanced, they were built like gorillas—not to be tangled with at close quarters. She beckoned him. Crouching, she sprinted for a doorway.

Welkin silently cursed her courage. She knew he had no option but to follow. And when she made up her mind, she just acted, seemingly without thought. It was unnerving.

"Quiet now," she said when Welkin breathlessly reached her. She pursed her lips and whistled. There was no corresponding whistle and Sarah frowned. "Stay here." Without warning she swung the laserlite before her and hurried across the antechamber and up a flight of spiraling stairs. When she reached the top she waved for Welkin to follow.

He took the stairs clumsily, falling twice. In the dark Sarah grimaced at the dull, echoing noise. She dragged him up the rest of the way. "Get with the program, kid!"

"We don't *climb* to different levels on *Colony*," Welkin said. He massaged his ankle. "I'm not used to all this," he wheezed. "And don't call me *kid*."

"That's the spirit. You'll need that and much more to survive on Earth." After a moment's reflection she said, "Despite your heavier gravity, they didn't keep you blokes very fit, did they?"

"There was little need," grated Welkin. "And if we're so weak, what are you so worried about?" He held his head up and looked at her defiantly. Inwardly his stomach cramped.

"There is need now, so get used to it. As for me being worried, don't think twice about it. I've lived with death all my life."

Sarah hefted her weapon and turned abruptly. She led the way along a corridor until they came to an open elevator shaft. She nodded to the rungs leading up the shaft. "Do you think you can climb those?"

Despite the shivers, Welkin could feel spasms racking his body. He'd never before experienced such fatigue. His knee joints and neck felt swollen, his eyes "snowblinded" by atmospheric light, his sneezing fit a grim reminder that he might already be diseased. He stiffly shrugged his shoulders, trying to shake out the tightness. "I don't know. I'll try."

"You first, then," she said. "I'll catch you if you fall." At his startled look she winked.

She helped him into the well and held on until he had a firm grip of the rungs. "It doesn't pay to look down. Not that you can see anything."

"Thanks," he said. His voice seemed to reverberate a long way.

It took them five minutes to negotiate the floors. On several occasions Sarah had to urge him on.

"My hands are swollen!"

"Soon it'll be so cold you won't be able to feel them," she grunted. She put her shoulder against his bottom and pushed.

Moments later Welkin collapsed on the floor of the third level. His face and hands were frozen, his breathing heavy.

"No more climbing," she said.

Welkin exhaled noisily. "I was just getting used to it."

"I'll remember that."

Sarah helped him to his feet and guided him across a vast floor strewn with yellowed paper and broken office furniture. She rapped three times on a steel door, then withdrew a heavy key from a pocket and opened the thick reinforced door.

Welkin stared at the black hole that gaped before him. He had the disturbing sensation that this was a doorway between life and death, yet nothing in his experience told him which he was leaving and which he was about to embrace.

"Why'd you bring *that?*—*Why'dy' brin'tha'?*"

Fanned out around them in a semicircle, almost surrounding them, was Sarah's family: a ragged, motley gang of Earthborn. *Degenerate scum*, came the thought before Welkin could stop it. He was shocked to realize that they were all aged between eleven and sixteen, though he had a feeling they were older than they looked, older in ways he couldn't quite grasp.

They were tanned, of course, and oddly *worn*. He'd seen story vids from Old Earth in which bright young boys went off to war and returned drawn and haggard, an unfathomable look in their eyes, the same look you sometimes saw in the faces of old men like the elders. These Earthborn possessed that strange, unnerving look. Instinctively, Welkin knew they had all passed some terrible rite of passage, otherwise they wouldn't be here, alive and breathing. He wondered if a similar rite awaited him. Or was he already in it?

Most of the family wore scuffed black leather jackets with cutaway denim vests that carried a motif on them. It looked like an animal's head, like maybe a lion or something, with huge saber teeth jutting out from a gaping mouth. Their leggings were shredded, as were their homemade boots. Most of them wore black and red bandannas tied around their foreheads.

The last thing he noticed in those silent seconds was that some of them had ornaments hanging from every feature. Pieces of junk metal tugged at their earlobes, cheeks, eyebrows, and lips.

Welkin shrank back against Sarah and blinked. He was suddenly all too well aware how much his life depended on this Earthborn. Anxiety almost made him run for the door. But Sarah had locked it. Jump for the window? But they were several stories from the ground. Nowhere to run. His hands clutched at Sarah's utilities. He suddenly felt as though he'd slipped into a horror virtual reality program, although unlike any he'd ever played.

Sensing his tension, Sarah shot Welkin a fleeting smile. "It's okay. You're among . . . friends."

The teenager who had challenged Sarah was taller than she and broader by a hand span. He stood facing Sarah with his feet planted wide apart, his thumbs hooked into his waistband. His posture was relaxed, even nonchalant, yet in a subtle way it was also provocative and challenging. The teenager had spiky mud-colored hair cropped short in places. Above all Welkin noticed his manic eyes. He'd seen them before in the faces of the elders.

"Why'd you bring *that!*" the youth repeated.

"Good to see you, Ilija. I missed you, too," Sarah said coldly. "I've made the rite of belonging with him."

A quick, gasping hiss shot around the room.

"You can't do that!"

"Can and did."

Ilija swung back to the others. There were seven in all; some of them peered at Welkin as though he were some new species of animal. And one was the fattest person he had ever seen. He was huge. Another wore *glasses!* He didn't think even the Earthborn wore focal glasses anymore. How did they stay on the boy's face?

"She's broken custom! You heard her! She can't make the rite without consent of the family!" Ilija took a defiant step toward Sarah. She stayed her ground.

Suddenly Ilija howled and danced across the room in a complicated but obviously ritualistic series of movements that seemed to act out the story of his displeasure—and something darker.

Sarah stepped in close. Her arm shot out, palm up. The heel of her palm caught Ilija in the forehead and sent him sprawling to the ground. He stared at her through slitted eyes.

"You have cursed us," he said.

"And you're a superstitious fool!"

The fat boy cleared his throat. "Act . . . ually, Il-Ilija, Sar-ah ca-ca-can make the rite with-withhh-out asking us first. It-it's not actually da-done that way, but in emer . . . gencies—"

"Oh, shuddup, Budge! They're the *enemy!*" He climbed to his feet. "Enemies must be killed. It's us or them!"

There was a murmur of assent. Ilija smiled, puffed out his chest. He had some support, but how much?

"Lay a finger on our friend here and I'll have you," Sarah said in a deceptively even tone.

Ilija looked at her sinewy, tanned body, the dark eyes that missed nothing, and the easy stance that could change instantly into a deadly fighting posture, and he realized that it would be a near thing. Too near, for now . . .

He shrugged and laughed derisively. "Fight you over one of your *pets*, Sarah?"

Sarah smiled and everybody relaxed. She reached out and touched a huge loop that swung from Ilija's left nostril. "Another kill? Good for you!"

Ilija jerked his head away but kept the easy grin on his face. His eyes never left hers. "While youse was pussyfooting it around out there, me and Green mixed it with the aliens."

"They're dangerous, Ilija. We need to keep our distance. They have advanced weapons."

"Yeah?" Ilija smirked. "We'll see about that."

Sarah gazed at her family. She indicated the Skyborn. "This is Welkin. He has been driven out from the sky ship and he is now one of us. His enemies are our enemies, his food is our food. Eyes open, family!"

They intoned back, "Eyes open!" Some of the responses were enthusiastic, some were noncommittal. Others were sullen.

"So that's settled? He's one of us and he is under my personal protection."

"For now," Ilija said. "But the spaceboy stays out of it." He pushed moodily past the others and paced the room.

Sarah said quietly to Welkin, "Get over there and don't make a sound. They need time to get used to you."

Welkin backed up slowly, hugging the wall to the corner. Any second he expected this pack to turn on him. And Sarah would be unable to stop them. Vague memories of wolf packs shredding their prey sped through his memory.

He kept very quiet and still as he watched his captors. He knew some of these Earthborn hated him. They resented his presence more than the threat of that huge spaceship that had crash-landed among them and destroyed their day-to-day existence. Because he was here, because he was *real*. He was something they could lash out against and hurt. Maybe he should have taken his chances with *Colony*.

He tried to banish these negative thoughts. He was alive and unhurt. And he was going to stay that way if he had anything to say about it! The thought that had come to him earlier returned, flashing into his mind with a cold and terrible brightness: *Whatever it took* . . .

It made him shiver, just slightly. It was such an adult thought—and ruthless.

"Only one thing cropped up," said the short, curly-haired youth with the impossible glasses. His curt, clipped voice drew their attention from Welkin, for which he was thankful.

"We've arranged a meet with Bruick. They have some—" He stopped to look at Welkin. Sarah waved him on. "Some equipment from the sky ship. They'll exchange it for food. I told them we couldn't trade ammunition."

"We've hardly got any food to trade either," another youth said.

"Okay," Sarah cut in. She held up her hand for silence. "What's this equipment they have, Con?"

"They don't know what it does," Con said.

"Give us a break," Ilija said from the back of the room. "What sorta fools do they think we are, the maggots!"

"We'll take a look at it, then make up our minds, shall we?" Sarah suggested.

Con pushed his glasses farther up his nose. "And him?" He glanced at Welkin. His question wasn't unfriendly, merely curious. Welkin knew right away that the boy with the glasses sided with Sarah.

"He comes with us," Sarah replied. She looked pointedly at Ilija. "Or does someone here have a better knowledge of the sky ship's equipment?" When no one answered, she said, "I didn't think so."

Ilija opened his mouth but shut it. He glowered at Welkin.

"Con, you're with me," Sarah said. "Gillian, you lead out. Budge, you check on Pedros and Green. Pedros might even be asleep—he didn't answer my call again, damn him."

After a rest and some food, the "bartering party" left by different routes and rejoined at a prearranged rendezvous. Sarah explained that they had several exits in case of fire or attack.

Even in daylight, most of the stairwells and tunnels would have been ill-lit by sunlight seeping through jagged fissures. Now, traveling at night, they carried cleft sticks containing the phosphorescent fungus. Sarah even had a working flashlight, but it was for use in emergencies only.

They moved quickly but with ever-vigilant caution. Con brought up the rear while Gillian was somewhere ahead on point. The others took flanking positions. Despite their caution, they moved efficiently and with purpose.

At one point, as they crept through a maze of broken corridors and collapsed walls, Gillian and the flankers rejoined the group, the terrain too dangerous for wide formation. Welkin kept sneaking glances at her as she glided around obstacles, climbed walls and debris with catlike grace. She was a waif of a girl compared to Sarah, yet she was tautly muscled, her movements fluid. Welkin guessed she would be a deadly fighter. But he found it difficult to think of her like that. She was pretty, with an elfin face, and black hair cropped short in the utilitarian fashion favored by the family. She had deep, dark eyes and a frank expression that hid nothing. With a start, he realized he was scared of her, scared of her . . . *girlness*.

"Keep up," Sarah said briskly. "Don't lag behind."

They slipped out of the building and merged with the night. Somewhere along the way Gillian left them. Welkin didn't ask where she went. These people seemed to do things as though by instinct. It was a bit unnerving.

Welkin looked longingly back at the building. He hated the open spaces, felt naked in them. Worst of all, there was no *ceiling*. It was almost obscene! He had an almost primitive desire to put his head down and run for cover like a rabbit bolting for its burrow, terrifyingly aware that *something* could drop from that big airy emptiness in the blink of an eye. Welkin understood the rabbit perfectly, even if he'd seen them only in vids. Right now, he wanted to be under something, *anything*. Nor was he aware that when he walked in open spaces he did so hunched over, shoulders clenched, as if waiting for a blow from above. It added to his abiding sense of unease.

Colony had been so *regimented* and safe. Everyone had his timetable and allotted hours in which to perform his duties, and everyone performed the tasks set him without question. Above all, they had had their training, their endless regimental briefings, their sessions in the recently developed neural sims that stimulated correct thinking and acting. On top of that, everyone on *Colony* under the age of sixteen was nominally part of the glorious and heroic Army of Resurrection. Day in and day out, in everything they did, it was drilled into them how to their generation had fallen the greatest honor of all, the reclamation of Earth, the rebuilding of an entire world, the social terraforming of Old Earth itself!

Apart from the micrometeor showers that sometimes got through *Colony*'s shields, Welkin always felt safe in the skyworld. Once, he'd been in the scanner cabin and had listened as a staccato of impacts rang clangingly through the ship as the space debris, traveling at colossal speeds, slammed into the hull. Standard drill was to exit all "surface" compartments, which were then sealed off in case of rupture.

Now, here on Earth, he never really felt safe.

Welkin stayed close to Sarah. He knew that despite his superior training and education he wouldn't last long alone out here. Everything was too hostile and barbaric. He tried to control the anger that was rising in him. Damn those stupid virtual reality games he'd played on *Colony*. His whole upbringing had been a pack of lies. Virtual games were nothing like the real thing. That's all they'd been— games. Games to keep the kids happy while the elders toyed with their future.

He forced these thoughts away. He had to stay focused. He was in this mess, and it would need all his superior ingenuity and resourcefulness to get out of it. His best hope was Sarah. She seemed to know what she was doing, and she seemed to genuinely like him. Unless that was a trick . . .

Sarah clicked her fingers. Three of them were huddled behind a firebombed vehicle. Its windows had been blown out and its doors were welded shut by corrosion.

Sarah held a finger to her lips until she was sure they were secure. "You keep your lips zipped, Welkin. The people we're meeting tonight are bad news. Let's not provoke them more than we have to." She thought for a moment, her tongue protruding. "If things turn sour, you hide out till morning, then head back to *Colony*." She pointed to a huge building, from behind which a glare spread into the night sky. She squinted. "You can't miss it. They've got the entire area lit up like a Christmas tree."

Welkin felt butterflies in his stomach. The moment for action was rapidly approaching. He had a presentiment: Somewhere in the next few hours he would be presented with a terrible choice. What he decided would rule the rest of his life.

A noise whipped his head around. He peered over the hood of the derelict car.

The night was filled with a low, clanking sound, punctuated by dull, rhythmic thuds. And something else, something Welkin had heard before but couldn't place for the moment. A mournful, wailing sound. The clanking grew louder. Metal on metal—ear-piercing and discordant squeals: *thumper! thumper-thump!*

A troupe of ferals, indistinct at first, came into view. Some carried pipes of various sizes and lengths in each hand, clanging them together as they walked along. Others had large tins and metal buckets hanging about their necks, which they beat with sticks. Over the top of the din came the plaintive wail of a mouth organ. Welkin had seen one in a blues hologram once. It was the saddest sound he'd ever heard.

He looked questioningly at Sarah.

"Not the sort of musos you'd listen to on *Colony*, I'll wager." She squinted to get a better view of the shadowy figures. "Shockers," she said, hoping to channel his anxiety. "A bit hard to play guitars and keyboards without electricity."

"Do they always do this?" Welkin's skin prickled as though he knew the answer.

"It's a ritual feast—" Suddenly Sarah tugged Welkin back down.

Several ferals charged across the wind-scoured street. They were chasing a tall screaming figure. Sarah kept her hand on Welkin's arm, felt his muscles tense.

"There's nothing we can do, Welkin. Everyone has his own path, even when it leads to death."

The other ferals stopped their playing immediately and joined in the chase. They darted through the broken landscape like rats streaking in for a kill. Before long, they passed from sight.

Sarah indicated an alleyway that ran between two buildings that slumped against one another like tired old men. Gathering themselves, they moved out, diving into the steepled tunnel formed by the leaning structures. The inverted V shape had an odd cathedral feel to it. Welkin reflected that in olden days they would have crossed themselves before entering.

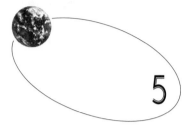

5

The meeting was held at an abandoned factory. Every skylight had been shot out, and most of the corrugated iron had long since rusted. The full moon, pushing in through barred vents, cast striated shadows that gave the meeting place the feel of a prison.

Bruick's gang had fanned out at the far end of the gutted building. Classic passive-aggressive deployment, ready for anything. They wore tattered clothing that wrapped their bodies as if years of grime and lack of soap had welded the material to their flesh. Their hair hung in dreadlocks. Some of them had garish tattoos etched on their faces.

"Jabbers," Sarah told Welkin. "One step up from the ferals. Smarter. More cunning. Stay real close. And say nothing."

"Looky 'ere," one of the jabbers called. "It's Sarah's Squirrels!"

Raucous laughter jumped at them from around the warehouse.

"Fagin!" someone said. "Kindergarten ma'am!" The voice was scornful.

"Asswipe," Sarah mumbled. Louder, she called, "What have you got?" Her voice had dropped an octave and her manner was distinctly hostile.

Bruick stepped forward. He had a ragged beard. Perspiration was a silvery sheen on his cheeks and forehead.

"It's more a matter of what *you've* got, love," Bruick said. His voice was a casual drawl. "Apart from the obvious, that is," he added suggestively.

Several of his gang laughed.

Con's face went stony blank; his eyes narrowed to slits behind the thick lenses. He withdrew several items of canned food from his flak jacket and threw them to the ground.

Bruick went to pick them up, but Sarah said, "I don't think so," and waved the laserlite.

"Pretty piece of merchandise," said Bruick speculatively. He had a curving blade tucked into the sash knotted about his waist. It glittered as though studded with jewels.

"And it works." Sarah's voice was deadly serious. "I said, what have you got?"

Bruick kept a respectable distance. "Don't get excited, Sa-rah," he said, mocking her name. He called something to one of his gang who fetched a long cylindrical item that seemed too cumbersome to be an efficient weapon.

"Worth its weight in food," Bruick declared.

"Con?" Sarah said.

Con inspected the item.

"Hey, Four-Eyes, got yourselves a paleface, have you?" Bruick quizzed. Someone tittered in the background.

Sarah maintained her silence. Con seemed oblivious to the taunt and returned to Sarah's side. "Wouldn't have the faintest idea what it is, Sarah. I'd say a weapon of some sort. A blaster, maybe. Much too heavy to be a handheld weapon. And there's a plug at the back. We'd need a battery or something."

"It's a laser lance," Welkin said. *Traitor!* His jaw tightened.

"And?" Sarah prompted.

"So what do youse reckon?" Bruick interrupted irritably. He had somehow moved closer. "We ain't got all night."

Agitated, Welkin shook his head. Loyalty to *Colony* froze his mind.

With a start Sarah realized that two of the jabbers were missing. She scanned the darker recesses of the factory, then made a sudden decision. "We're moving out. No deal."

Sarah had time to take one step back before shots rang out. Con took a hit in the shoulder and slammed against the wall, spun by the impact. He let out a startled grunt and fell.

"My glasses!" he squealed against the pain burning his shoulder.

A barrage of arrows hissed through the air, *ka-thunk*ing into walls and the floor, quivering like needles.

"Back! Back!" Sarah barked. She lunged for Welkin but missed him. Con began to topple, and she jerked backward to lend him support. He tugged against her grip and swore beneath his breath. The swift humming of arrows in flight tore past them as Con swooped up his glasses. Broken! Then she was dragging him out of there screaming for Welkin to follow.

It was on sudden impulse that Welkin ran forward and snatched a food can from the ground. He flung it with all his might at Bruick, who had closed the distance between them. At that short range the can landed with the force of a thrown brick.

Bruick's head rocked back and he fell. "I'll kill you!" he screamed. "HELL!" he cried in agony.

Welkin hefted the laser lance across his shoulders. This action sent the jabbers diving for cover. Welkin swung the weapon around and then fled after Sarah and Con.

He heard Bruick's shrill cursing. Seconds later he was close behind; Welkin could hear the heavy footsteps gaining on him and tiny sobbing noises as though the jabber was seriously hurt but wouldn't stop for anything.

Welkin had barely made it to the exit when an arrow thudded into his thigh. The impact buckled his leg and sent excruciating pain shocking through every limb.

"Sarah?" he called, dazed. He'd never been hurt like this. The pain was terrible.

Suddenly more gunfire spat in the factory. Bright flashes lit the black backdrop like bright posies. Bruick fell heavily. His outstretched hand almost tripped Welkin, who quickly utilized the laser lance as a crutch.

Then Sarah bounded into view. Welkin thankfully leaned against the wall and stared blankly at the gnarled wood that protruded from his thigh. In his dazed state, he wondered how something so small could have such a devastating effect on his system. He watched the blood spread across his contamination suit like a ferocious replicating virus.

Sarah swung her laserlite around the edge of the door and squeezed off several shots. She jerked back as jabber fire took away half the door jamb.

"That was a damn fool thing to do!" she snapped. Welkin's pain was nothing new to her. She'd watched hundreds of kids die over the years. But she needed this one badly, for so many reasons. In his own unique way, he was a radical—him and that sister of his, Lucida. Radicals with inbuilt longevity—a regular Adam and Eve who would add healthy genes to Earth's decaying gene pool.

And their technical skills! Their *knowledge*.

She bit her bottom lip hard. Damn! It tore at her heart. Was she being selfish? Her head swam with jumbled thoughts.

Sharp pieces of metal and plaster exploded about them. Sarah poked the laserlite into the doorway and pressed the firing stud twice before pulling back quickly.

"I've got Con back there in a dugout." She struggled to focus her thoughts. "He's wounded. Can you walk? Welkin!" She slapped him hard across his face. "You're dead meat if you don't snap out of it!"

The sting of Sarah's open hand across his face brought momentary relief from the pain raging elsewhere.

"It hurts, Sarah," he said numbly. His heart was pounding so heavily his torso was contracting.

"Hold on to the laser lance," Sarah said evenly. "I'm determined we'll rescue *something* from this fiasco."

She lifted Welkin and straddled him across her shoulders. At a forced trot she crossed the moonlit square.

Con winced as Sarah staggered over the ridge of the dugout. Ricocheting bullets followed her. An arrow flew overhead. She let Welkin fall off her shoulders and threw her head back against the rubble.

"Con?" Sarah wheezed. She gulped in great lungfuls of air. "You gonna make it?"

"My shoulder. Oh, Sarah, it's burning to hell!" Con's eyes had suddenly become feverish with shock. "My glasses—"

Sarah scuffed his head. "We'll fix your glasses." She swung her laserlite over the ridge. Even at low charge the weapon was fearsome.

Shards of red ice spat into the air. The tracers sent the jabbers diving for cover. Some didn't make it.

Gunfire exploded in the middle distance, and Sarah exchanged a worried look with Con. "That'll be Gillian. Giving us some cover."

Sarah tore a strip of cloth from her shirt. She glanced briefly at the blood-smeared bandanna that Con held to his shoulder. "Okay. Grin and bear it, Con." She bound the wound and tied a quick knot. She felt Con's pain but couldn't show it. Not now. *They meant to kill us all*, she thought. And felt icy anger course through her. She'd make Bruick pay for this.

"The bullet barely touched you." She managed to keep her face expressionless, her relief in check. "You'll live." She gestured toward Welkin. "This one's another matter."

She cautiously poked her head up, then down. "Looks like we've got them bluffed. Gillian's probably easier prey for them." She scrabbled to where Welkin lay sprawled. Even in the dark Sarah could see that his face had blanched.

"Listen to me, Welkin," Sarah said. "Depending on the arrowhead, this is either going to hurt a lot, or it's going to tear a lump out of your thigh and you won't know a thing, because you're not going to be with us. Okay?"

Welkin blinked, unable to understand her. His entire body was convulsing.

Sarah pushed a wad of cloth into his mouth. "Bite down hard."

Before Welkin could answer, Sarah pushed down hard on Welkin's leg and gripped the arrow shaft. "I *hate* this," she said and pulled.

Welkin's muffled scream was short. His body spasmed and then went limp.

Sarah held up the arrowhead to the meager light. "Wasn't barbed," she said to Con, tossing the piece of metal to him. They salvaged everything they could.

"He's lost a bucket-load of blood," she said. She tore more material from her shirt and quickly bandaged Welkin's leg. *Lucky he fainted*, she thought. *Bet he'll ache like all else when he comes to.*

She retrieved the laser lance and handed it to Con. "You can use this as a crutch. Yeah?"

He nodded. "You okay with Welkin? We can send somebody back for him."

Sarah hesitated. "No. If Bruick comes looking for us, he'll get him for sure. Best we clear out fast." Sarah pulled Welkin across her shoulders and scrambled over the ridge and down a steep incline. No one followed them, but back at the warehouse there was a long blast of semiautomatic fire. Sarah dived for cover; Con was a split second behind her.

Guttural voices grew louder. The sounds moved closer, then suddenly veered away. Distantly they could hear the ferals' monotonous drumming and the tinny shrieks of brass instruments.

"You don't think—" Con began.

"Gillian's too good," Sarah said, but the worry on her face betrayed the fact that her confidence was a facade.

"Yeah," Con said, looking over at Welkin. Even now the Skyborn was showing signs of waking. His wounded leg was twitching.

"Okay," Sarah said and scrambled up.

"The cellar?" suggested Con when the three finally slid into a small crater on one side of a vacant block.

"Good thinking," Sarah said breathlessly. Sweat lines ran down her blackened face. "We've stirred up a hornets' nest." She looked at Welkin. He'd woken up some moments before and had already vomited. "You must be freezing. We have utilities down there. C'mon, it's not far."

"It hurts," Welkin said quietly. If the Earthborn could voice their innermost thoughts, so could he. It was a welcome relief from *Colony*'s rigid social regulations. "I'm giddy." He was finding it hard to concentrate. The dull throb in his leg was the only thing keeping him awake.

"We're nearly there. Promise," Sarah added, her voice tired.

Welkin felt himself being lifted once more, and it was easier to sleep than to worry about things beyond his control.

It didn't take them long to reach their "safe house."

Welkin woke to find himself being supported by both Sarah and Con.

"You're with us again," Sarah said, relieved. Her breath was ragged, Welkin noticed. They must have come a long way.

As though reading his mind, Sarah said, "There are quicker paths leading to wherever we want to go. But the quickest path is often the most dangerous."

"Since *Colony* crashed, a lot of the tunnels down there aren't so stable, either," Con added.

"Here it is." Sarah held open a disguised trapdoor. It was a heavy wooden plank with jagged pieces of glass and red brick embedded in it.

Sarah descended into the darkness first, followed by Con who waited for a muted light to appear down below before gently helping Welkin down the stairs. Sarah reached up to lend support.

Sarah froze at a sudden noise. She had a quick look about, then pulled the plank back over the opening. She waited for a moment, listening intently. *Too jumpy by half*, she chastised herself.

Downstairs, Con had helped Welkin into a chair. He fetched a small crate for Welkin to rest his leg on. Welkin winced as he wearily sank into the chair.

Sarah wedged up a loose floorboard and pulled out a box of herbs. She rummaged around in it until she found what she wanted. "I'm no doctor," she said when she noticed Welkin watching her, "but I'm the best on offer."

"She fixes everyone," Con said confidently. "What she doesn't know about herb lore isn't worth knowing."

Sarah looked at Con. "Now *that's* a lie." She kneeled down beside Welkin and managed to control her anxiety. Blood had seeped clean through the bandage she'd applied. She went to the table and made a poultice. "I'm going to fix you up like brand new, Welkin," she said. *Another lie.*

Welkin craned his neck as Sarah began mashing the herbs. "What are you doing?"

"Mixing up a concoction." She thought a moment. "Comfrey leaves, thyme, and goldenseal, steeped in vodka. You've no idea how precious this stuff is. Jabbers would kill for it. But they'd drink it and let their people die of infection."

"They call it happy juice," Con said knowingly. "They've found our hidden caches a few times."

"It should stop the inflammation. If nothing else, it'll kill any germs down there." She wanted to keep well clear of the gangrene topic. The last thing she needed was for Welkin to believe he was going to lose his leg. If his wound began to stink in a few days, she would get him back to *Colony* quick smart. She promised herself that.

"Happy juice," Welkin said morbidly. "Sort of like witchcraft?"

Sarah frowned but kept crushing the herbs. "Bring that water to the boil, would you, Con? And careful. I'll tape those glasses, okay?" She restrained a laugh. Con had somehow balanced the dangling glasses across his nose.

"You're laughing," Con said.

"You look like such an *idiot*."

She turned to Welkin, suppressing her mirth. "I guess you Sky-born might well call natural remedies a kind of witchcraft." She gave Welkin a quick smile. "I've always had the theory that if the great witch-hunts of the Dark Ages had never taken place we would've all been at peace with ourselves and the Great Whiteout would never have happened. Instead of everything becoming mechanized we would've had a different history. One where Nature would have governed, and not the computer."

Welkin shook his head. "Computers are *everything*, Sarah." He was almost speechless with incredulity. "How can you say things would have been better without them? Technology got us to the stars!"

"I rest my case," Sarah said. She wrapped the crushed herbs in a tatty piece of muslin and immersed them in the boiled water. When the poultice was soft and mushy, she squeezed out the water and positioned it over Welkin's wound. "This is going to hurt. Try not to think about it."

"Hey, Welkin," Con said, getting his attention. "You see, when computers were invented, they took away a lot of jobs, because they were so efficient."

"What's wrong with being efficient?" Welkin asked. Again he

fought for words. The things these Earthborn were saying just made no sense whatsoever. "OUCH!"

Sarah winced. "Nothing's wrong with efficiency," she said, bandaging Welkin's thigh, "but it put a lot of people out of work. In the end, no one had jobs except a handful of computer buffs. The governments sold off everything it owned to get short-term funding, and within a hundred years everything the workers had fought so hard for over centuries, like free medical care, schooling, and social welfare, was abolished."

"Computers were actually the start of Earth's downfall," Con said earnestly. "You don't expect your *Colony* computers to tell you that, do you?"

Sarah nudged Welkin's chin. "End of history lesson. The poor guy's fainted again. Probably never seen his own blood before. Wouldn't need to up there on *Colony*."

"But *Colony*'s down here now, Sarah," Con said darkly. "Safe and sound on Earth."

"Snug as a bug in a rug, eh?" Sarah said. She washed her hands with a damp cloth. "You're up next, Con. Be brave." She smiled quickly. "Don't faint on me, too. One makes for a boring party."

Con grimaced as Sarah began cleansing his flesh wound. "He keeps staring at me like *I'm* the alien," he said. "Do you reckon he's never seen glasses before?"

"Nobody's seen glasses like those."

"That does it. I'm—"

"Ow!" she squealed when Con play-thumped her in the arm. "Hey, I've got an idea. You'll have to put your glasses on him when he comes to. Now that could be amusing."

"Wouldn't suit him," Con grinned. Suddenly serious, he said, "What's going to happen, Sarah?"

The question caught her off guard. She wrung the cloth out and reapplied the dressing. "With *Colony*?"

"Everything," Con said. "You've lived longer than anyone I know. You've explained about genes and the rest of it, about yours being immune to the disease, but what happens—"

"When I die?" she finished for him. "And now. Well, I write just about everything that happens in a journal, Con." She hefted herself onto the table and watched Welkin, not wanting to meet Con's pleading eyes. "That way, when the time comes, one of you lot can keep it going. I've nominated you, actually. You'll have to keep the journal, and all the books and CRCs we've stashed away. That way future generations will always have knowledge of our past—what we were and what we can become again if we avoid all the pitfalls."

"But *Colony* isn't going to let us live. They want Earth for themselves. Don't they, Sarah?"

"They've come back as invaders, Con. Sure. They don't want to assimilate with what they consider their contaminated inferiors." She considered for a moment. "Much like what Hitler did to the Jews back in the first Holocaust. I told you guys about it. Remember that story?"

Con nodded slowly.

Sarah spared him a quick glance. "The Jews survived, Con. And so shall we. It's just going to take a lot of thought and some good old-fashioned luck. That's all."

Sarah realized that Welkin's eyes had fluttered open. She shook her head. "If the jabbers call us 'Sarah's Squirrels,' I wonder what nickname they'll come up with now."

" 'The Walking Wounded,' " Con said. Then with a smirk he nodded to the laser lance on the workbench. "Welkin scored well."

Sarah ran her fingers fleetingly over the laser lance. "Where'd he learn to throw like that? Certainly not in the back corridors of *Colony*."

"Bruick went down like a ton of bricks!" Con said with glee.

"It was nothing," Welkin said distantly. He had come to moments before. The itch in his leg was driving him to distraction. "It's a game called bowling. We play it on a neural sim, but you still have to throw, even though you don't actually *throw* anything from your hand. You can skip things across the water by throwing sideways, or even target bottles lined up on a wall." Welkin's eyes were suddenly bright, his waxy face alive. "I sometimes beat Lucida!"

"Leave your leg alone. If it's itching, that means it's healing," Sarah said seriously. "Lucida was pretty good at bowling too, huh?"

"I miss her," Welkin whispered. His stomach suddenly cramped.

"I think I might be allergic to something," he said. He rubbed furiously at his eyes. "I'm bleeding!"

Sarah pulled his hands gently from his face. "You're not bleeding, you silly duffer," she said quietly. "These are tears. It's okay to show emotions. Let them come."

But Welkin fought the feelings inside him. He felt as though everything was toppling in upon him. He didn't need these Earthborn! If it hadn't been for them in the first place, he'd be safely on board *Colony* right now, probably asleep, or sharing study skills with Lucida!

Sarah regarded him with compassion. "If all this is about Lucida, then it's okay. We know you want to be with her. And we're going to do our best to make that come true."

He looked at her, surprised by her words.

She suddenly put her arms around him and hugged him. He tried to push her away, but for a brief moment tears blinded him and he thought of his mother, long dead. He sagged against Sarah, who rocked him gently for a few minutes before he gruffly pulled away, wiping his tear-stained face with his forearm. This was wrong. Skyborn didn't show emotion, especially in front of inferiors!

Sarah said nothing. Con busied himself with some minor chore. They both pretended not to notice Welkin's sniffles.

"I forgot. You said you were a bit cold before." She found an old flak jacket for him, then handed them both an opened Meals in a Can. "So we're celebrating, Con." To Welkin she said, "What does the lance do?"

Welkin knuckled his eyes to clear them. "It has a minifusion pak. They're outdated now—something we call raw power—but if the laser optics are sealed, and there's been no leakage, it's still a heavy-duty laser. The plug at the back is for more concentrated power, but its usage means greater loss of fusion life." He hesitated, then went on. "This model comes equipped with a solarbat for light use—should pierce a hole through just about anything at close range."

"You're of more use to us than any solarbat, and any other three kids, for that matter," Sarah said.

"That's for sure!" Con agreed enthusiastically.

Welkin reacted oddly. He was unfamiliar with flattery. A tingling rose on his cheeks. "I feel awfully hot all of a sudden," he blustered.

Sarah and Con were equally puzzled. They knew what was happening but not why Welkin didn't.

"You were saying the circuits are slightly damaged," Con said and turned to Sarah. "Welkin needs a sonic drive to fix it."

"A what?"

"A screwdriver should do it."

"Oh." Sarah withdrew one from her flak jacket. At the look on Welkin's face she said, "Stone Age version of a sonic drive. It's the best I can offer."

While Sarah prepared a splint for his leg, Welkin worked on the lance. It took an hour to connect the damaged optics.

The searing pain that throbbed in his leg was also a distraction that he fought to control. More than once he wondered how the Earthborn had survived without such basic equipment as medkits and sonic drives. It was beginning to dawn on him that he was *useful* to them. It was a strange feeling. He wasn't sure if he liked it.

Can I live among these people? Welkin wondered. *They're so different from . . . us. They're unclean, and they have no technology—they really are degenerates, just like the elders said. And it's so cold and I'm hungry all the time . . .* He forced himself to stop thinking. The Skyborn and the Earthborn were so different from each other that any comparisons between the two were bound to end in confusion.

Finally Welkin had the lance set up for a demonstration. He depressed a keypad, and a cobalt blue finger of light pierced a neat hole in the brickwork.

"All right!" Con said. He pumped the air with his fist.

"But leave the cellar in one piece," Sarah said good-naturedly.

Welkin switched it off. "You pull this bit down to disconnect the battery," he said, demonstrating. "Doubt that it will recharge down here, but in the sun it should."

"We don't get much sun anymore," Con said. "Though Sarah says it's getting better."

"If it had been worse, we'd have gone the way of the dinosaurs."

Con sighed heavily. "He knows all that, Sarah. Now Welkin, can we use this as a weapon? Does it always take a while to charge up?"

"With a heavy-duty power source it would be faster," he said, thinking. "But it's too slow for a weapon. *Colony* technicians made this model redundant before I was born." He paused to consider. "It must have come from the lower decks. They hang on to stuff like this down there."

"And I think we'd better hang on to it here," Sarah said.

"Ilija?" Con asked cautiously.

"Yeah," Sarah said. "Something's not quite right there. Can't put a finger on it. Not yet."

She turned to Welkin. "What's wrong with us, do you think?"

Welkin shrugged. "The sunlight issue is pretty major. There must be substantial pollutants as well, in which case you could speed up the process with catalytic converters." This was kids' stuff. "They eradicate the chlorine from the atmosphere and generate new ozone. It's easy."

Sarah and Con exchanged looks. "Jabbers make more sense when they talk," Sarah said, amused.

"Easy he says!" Con rolled his eyes. "How are you going to get these catawhatevers up there in the first place?"

At Welkin's consternation, Sarah laughed. "We're stirring you, Welkin."

"You wanna try on my glasses?" Con asked.

"No!" Sarah said, laughing in spite of herself.

Welkin reached out and took Con's glasses and gingerly placed them crookedly on his nose. He gasped. "I thought glasses were supposed to make you see clearer!" he said, bewildered.

"Oh, no! Con! You're a terror!"

Con took the glasses back. "I think they suit me better," he said, suppressing his mirth.

Welkin blinked his eyes, unable to see the humor. The Earthborn certainly had some strange customs!

"Here," Sarah said, seizing Con's glasses. She methodically wound some old duct tape around the bridge. "They'll never sit like they did, Con. If I could go to an optician and buy you a new pair, I would."

Con positioned them over his nose. "They never were perfect," he said.

"I promise never to make a joke about you being one-eyed about anything," Sarah said. Before Con could retaliate, she nudged him. "Truce!"

"Lucky," he joked. He put the lance away with Sarah's herb box. "It's not that safe here, but it's a damn sight safer than back at base."

"You're not wrong there," Sarah said. She gave a floorboard a heavy thud and it sprang up. Reaching down beneath the floor, she withdrew several cans and some green paper bags.

"We *are* celebrating," commented Con. "Good food. One can each." He held the can close to his glasses and read the label. "Peas. Swap you half-and-half for your carrots, Sarah."

Sarah smiled and handed Welkin a tin. "Dehydrated C rations. Braised sausages, braised steak and onion—we're out of Irish stew."

"And mouth-watering dark chocolate," Con put in.

"And milk powder," Sarah said with a quick smile. "Don't look so morbid, Welkin. Lives were lost fighting for this stuff." She heaved a sigh of resignation. "Gimps found that the old air base tunnels over at Tottenham were still loaded with caches of food. When the government sold the land, they probably figured it was cheaper to leave the stuff down there as landfill than pay to get it shifted."

"Very thoughtful of them," Con said, ripping into a can. He nodded to Welkin. "Get stuck into it, mate. You'll not see its like again."

"Condensed milk in a tube and freeze-dried rice," Sarah mused, obviously relishing the pictures these items conjured. "And remember the Vegemite, Con?" she laughed.

"And the dried soup powder." Con turned to Welkin. "You'll never know what you missed," he added.

"On *Colony* we had hectares of hydroponic units devoted to Earth food. Rhubarb, pumpkin, cabbage, and something called beetroot— but most of us don't . . . didn't get the real stuff." He looked up and found them both staring at him.

"You've got food on board that we haven't seen or eaten in years," Sarah said. "Stuff we even forgot existed."

"And animals, I'll bet," Con said. "Horses? Cattle? Antelope? Tell us what they're like, Welkin!"

"They're just animals," Welkin said. He sat back and shrugged uncertainly. He couldn't quite figure out if they were serious or not. "Sheep and cows mostly."

"Utilitarian," Sarah concurred. "Only animals that can be used for food or clothing. Certainly nothing kept as a pet."

"But in the storage vats, they have DNA samples of everything Earth had when *Colony* left." Welkin looked from Sarah to Con and back again. "And bioengineers even spliced a whole series of new species from old DNA samples."

Sarah and Con exchanged excited looks. "Got any dinosaurs, aside from the elders?"

Welkin gasped and instinctively looked about, as if expecting a heavy to materialize from nowhere and drag them all off to the brig to be brainwiped. Speaking badly of the elders was strictly forbidden. Indeed, it was the closest thing to blasphemy the Skyborn knew.

"A regular Noah's Ark," Con marveled. "The rebirthing of an entire planet."

Sarah eyed Welkin speculatively. "I guess that makes you Noah."

"Just like after it rained for forty days and forty nights," Con joined in. "Like in the Bible, Welkin." His voice had reached sudden fever pitch. "Don't you see—the return of *Colony* is how the Bible said it was in the beginning!"

"I remember bits of it," Welkin said slowly. "I never saw the animal bays." He dismissed their inquiring looks and concentrated on the canned food. He vaguely realized that he would have to take things slowly. There was such a thing as information overload and something else the elders had talked about. Culture shock. Though they'd meant it the other way around. Long, long ago, European civilization had decimated more primitive societies such as the Pacific Islanders and Australian Aborigines. These groups had had no protection against the culturally domineering Western countries. Elder Tobias once remarked that even without direct extermination, the Earthborn would become extinct within a hundred years, profoundly disheartened by their evident inferiority. Welkin wasn't so sure anymore; maybe it worked both ways . . .

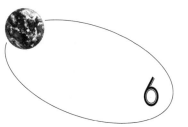

6

"It's odd, but I've just realized something," Welkin said. "Apart from you, Sarah, and Bruick, everyone's about my age. There aren't any elders."

"You're right," Sarah said. "We're anomalies—what you might call mutants. I used to think it was all the inbreeding—no new strains to vary the genetic pool. My latest theory is that some new strain of, say, autoimmune disease was unleashed during the war. Not many of us seem to mature past about eighteen." A wave of sadness came down upon her. "I'm years older than anyone I know. All my childhood friends have died." She frowned at a dark thought. "Not all naturally, either."

"And no one in our group can have children right now," Con explained. "It's too dangerous." He looked myopically at Sarah for confirmation. "If we wanted to, we could, couldn't we, Sarah?"

Sarah's smile was fleeting. "Too limited a gene pool, really. Which is another reason we have to get out of here. Meet more people. Get this wretched planet back on track."

"It's not something we talk much about, Welkin," Con said and was thankful when the Skyborn simply nodded.

Sarah threw the empty cans into a bag and stuck it in her utilities.

Welkin took several practice steps around the table. If not for his powerful legs, he knew the splint Sarah had tied about his wound would have totally immobilized him. He moved gingerly at first and realized with relief that his leg bore up reasonably well, all things considered.

"Walking like a local," Con said.

Welkin stumbled. Con caught him. "Just takes a bit of practice. That's all."

"I'm going to be a burden to you," Welkin said.

"Enough of that," Sarah said curtly. "If we felt that way we would've left you for Bruick. We're not a charity. Believe me." She replaced the floorboard and made for the trapdoor. "We're outa here and back to base. Con, you coming?"

"Yeah," he said distractedly. "You know, there's got to be a way of taking *Colony*—"

"Not right now there's not," Sarah said bluntly. Con acknowledged her suspicious glance at Welkin. "We've more pressing matters on hand. Like survival."

Welkin looked skyward. "Up in orbit you can see millions of stars. Clusters of them, just twinkling like bits of quartz."

"We haven't seen stars for a long time, Welkin." Sarah helped him up the stairs. Below, Con doused the light. "What with the pollution and dust, it's a wonder the moon comes through at all."

They pulled their jackets about them as the chill wind rushed them. Sarah smiled. Even a simple thing like the wind seemed to enthrall Welkin. It was like getting a baby and putting it in a grown-up's body and telling it to fend for itself. Just like that! And yet he'd acclimatized admirably. Or so it appeared on the surface. There was little doubt in her mind that there was a war seething inside him. She would have to watch him like a hawk. She guessed that the elders had systematically indoctrinated their people for genocide using the neural sims that Welkin had spoken of; if that were the case, Welkin might pose a grave danger that even he wasn't aware of.

Sarah suddenly realized she was fond of him, as if he were her own son. Now *there* was a thought—her first maternal instincts at the age of eighteen.

But she was already a mother to a gang of street kids who had been lost before they met her. A Nancy right out of *Oliver Twist*.

Con pushed the cellar door back into place.

Sarah snapped back to reality, eyes panning the area. "Hold on, Welkin. Not too fast." She was suddenly aware that he had moved off with more agility than he had displayed earlier. "This is where the fun begins. Shadow me, yeah?" she said, leading them into the chilly night.

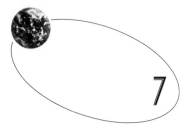

7

Even the slightest sound carried a long way. And the night was deadly
still. Welkin had been expecting the soughing of the wind through
the trees, the hunting calls of animals, night noises that he had heard
in all the vids on *Colony*. Instead, there was an eerie silence, as though
any sound was an intrusion, an anomaly that should not exist.

This isn't the way it should be!

"Quietly, now," Sarah whispered. She pointed to a faintly glowing
fire. Dancing amid its glow were shadowlike wraiths. The ferals were
still in a festive mood. To their right, the city skyline was lit by
Colony's floodlights. And somewhere in between, Sarah reminded herself, were Bruick's jabbers.

At a crouch, Sarah scrambled over some loose rubble and flattened
herself behind a crumbling wall. She reached out to give Welkin a
helping hand over the saw-toothed brickwork.

Welkin stepped over it clumsily and almost toppled, but Con
caught his arm. Sarah eased him to the ground. She winced at the
noise Welkin was making. Play all the sims you like, but nothing
prepares you for the real thing, she reminded herself. Her jaw tightened as she pulled him down beside her. "I know it's hard work."
Sarah's voice was whisper-fine. "But Sunday strolls aren't in vogue
anymore."

Aware of Sarah's agitation, Welkin pulled his arm back from her.
He rolled onto his back, his breath coming in short gasps. Con

crouched beside him, his glasses spookily reflecting the ferals' camp-fire.

"Of all the places they could pick," Sarah cursed, redirecting her frustration, "they had to plunk themselves right in front of Flinders Station."

"The stairs might've been a hassle for Welkin," Con said rumi-natively. "Maybe it'd be better to try Platform One?"

"I'm thinking of distance," Sarah said, deep in thought. "But okay. No way past the mongrels here. Platform One it is."

She got up and blended with the night. Con held on to Welkin until she gave a low whistle. "Not far, Welkin," Con said close to his ear.

But further comment was cut short. A brick exploded into a puff-ball. Welkin fell back in surprise. The next moment, a barrage of ballistic fire dug up the ground. Momentarily panicked, Con hugged the ground in a fetal position.

Welkin spun around uncertainly. There was a flurry of movement from the ferals' camp. Ululations filled the air. Bullets thudded into the ground so that small tufts of dirt sprung like magical weeds from the debris. Something clicked in Welkin's mind. He took flight to-ward the only certainty he knew: *Colony*.

His headlong limping rush into the night tore a curse from Sarah. But she had been spotted. The moment she pushed off after him, a fusillade lit the night.

Something thudded into Sarah's thigh, and for a moment she al-most screamed in agony. She staggered, wondering when the pain would strike. But it didn't. She scrambled to safety and quickly patted her utilities, seeking the telltale blood. "The cans," she realized. She pulled the bag of punctured cans from her pocket. "Thank you, God," she whispered.

"S-a-r-a-h!" It was Bruick's mocking voice. "You all right, girl?"

"Just great!" Sarah swore. "Con? You all right?" She sat up and swung the laserlite in an arc. The moment a blossom of light appeared from the jabbers she let off two shots. A bullet whipped past her ear.

"I'm here!" Con yelled. "I'm coming!"

More telltale lights winked in the night. Sarah squeezed off more shots. "Covering!" she called.

Con ducked and weaved across the short expanse of no-man's-land. A feral, face caked with white paint, appeared as though by magic. He screamed maniacally as he rushed at Con.

Sarah swung around and shot from the hip. Nothing. The laserlite was flat.

The feral ran smack into Con, and the pair tumbled to the ground. Sarah saw a knife rise and fall, and she screamed.

Welkin lay on his back in a hollow, swiftly assessing his chances of safely reaching *Colony*. In his panicked state he was sure he had heard pursuers. The ferals? *Cannibals!* Or Bruick's jabbers. Bruick's threat to kill him was still fresh in his mind. *Colony*'s perimeter had widened considerably. The elders had cleared a huge chunk of land around the homeworld. If only he hadn't been wounded!

He massaged his throbbing leg. Even if he could bypass the ferals and the jabbers, and avoid Sarah and Con, would the elders take him in? Or simply shoot him on sight? Surely they must know by now that Earth wasn't the cesspool of contamination they'd imagined? Or was he still failing to understand their true concern, the "social infection"?

But he *knew* things! Things the elders needed to know. Sarah and Con had filled his mind with lies and distortions. He felt ashamed that he had been taken in by it. All his training, all his beliefs, had come tumbling down. But now he would make amends. He would be invaluable to the elders as a source of information. He would return a hero. A survivor of the first conflict. A veteran fighter. Lucida would be proud of him.

With these doubtful thoughts in mind, Welkin clawed his way beneath a bone-dry water main and pulled himself up behind it. He listened for sounds of pursuit but found none. Somewhere close, sporadic gunfire smote the night like a drumroll. The ferals were still yelling war cries, or whatever those noises were. But he was sure no one was specifically following him.

Like a beacon, *Colony* rose up before him. Scarred and war torn, the colossus beckoned him home.

Sarah screamed and ran forward. Her own knife was out now. Oblivious to the gunfire that raked the ground around her, she slid into the tangle of human flesh. The jagged piece of steel in her hand flashed up and down, up and down, all the fury and frustration within her was behind the deep thrusts.

"Sarah! He's dead!" Con coughed. "He got shot!"

Sarah froze midthrust. Con's blood-spattered eyes opened. She stupidly wiped her cuff across his gagging mouth. The blood came away, thick and oozing. "It's not mine," Con said hesitantly. "I don't think it is."

Suddenly on automatic, Sarah dragged him up from under the feral. They returned to where Sarah had done the unforgivable: dropped the laserlite and momentarily lost all reason.

Con cleaned the blood from his glasses and readjusted them. "Something's up," he said, once he could see.

Sarah held up her hand for silence.

Voices rose and fell, and for a moment Sarah was indecisive. A high-caliber weapon suddenly spoke and they ducked. But the retaliatory reply came nowhere near them.

"The ferals and jabbers are at it," Sarah guessed.

"Or Gillian?" Con put in.

"We're out of here," Sarah said, making up her mind. She sheathed her bloodied knife and swung the laserlite across her shoulder.

"What about Welkin?" Con pulled her back. "Is he dead?"

"He may as well be," she said tightly. "He's gone home. Forget about him. *Colony* philosophies too ingrained. We'll never integrate with them, Con. It was just a silly pipe dream. That's all."

"Why would he want to go back to *that?*" Con wondered, smarting from the illuminated skyline.

Sarah snorted. "Why would he stay for *this?*"

. . .

The glaring artificial *Colony* light now forced the terrain into stark contrasts. Welkin kept to the deep etched shadows but knew *Colony*'s scanners would have detected him by now. Out in front of *Colony* lay an open expanse of land the width of a football field. He cautiously studied the desolation around him. The elders had stripped bare a boundary so clean, so meticulously, that not an inch of Earth influence remained. He could have as easily been standing on the moon as here on Earth. It wouldn't be long before they cleared their backyard, too. Then undetected approach would be impossible.

Now *Colony* would extend its influence. Outward, more and more, until the skyworld spread out like suburbs from a city, sending down its roots to gain strength, slaughtering everything in its way.

A morbid fear raged through him. His vulnerability was eating away at him. If either the jabbers or the ferals found him, he would die. Sarah and Con wouldn't take him back, and right now he doubted that they had survived the ambush. Sarah had been hit! He had no option but to walk on—and take his chances of being shot during that long walk across open ground to *Colony*.

He had taken two steps when he heard muffled voices. Recent events had honed his instincts and he ducked for cover. The heads and shoulders of two troopers appeared above a wall. Polycarbonated face shields open, reinforced armored suits, and heavily armed. Brashly superior, they stormed across the rubble as though invincible. They negotiated the uneven ground as though traversing the smooth corridors of *Colony*. But that wasn't surprising, Welkin reminded himself. Rumor had it that combat personnel had been training since birth for planetfall. Then he heard Gillian's voice. Not screaming for help, not plaintive, but authoritative. "I'm moving, damn you."

Laughter. The trio appeared at the end of the destroyed wall. One of the troopers scuffed Gillian's head and she stumbled. The other caught her by the scruff of the neck and hoisted her upright.

"Lemme go!" Gillian spat.

Welkin held his breath. He could go in with the troopers. He'd be safe then. His mind made up, he took one step into the open, but what happened next changed his mind.

The troopers exchanged words and suddenly changed course. Then one of them spun Gillian around and slammed her into a broken wall. She bounced back at him, but he blocked her with his elbow. Gillian's head snapped back and she sank to the ground.

Prickles of alarm tingled along Welkin's spine. Were they going to kill her? It made no sense to him. He hobbled along the brick face to get a closer look. Shortly, he was crouched on the other side of the wall. His heart was pounding.

Don'tletthemdothis . . . don'tletthemdothis . . . don'tletthemdothis . . .

"Stay down, scum," one of the troopers warned. "You won't need to get up!"

His partner laughed.

Welkin peered above the uneven wall. The troopers had taken off their helmets. One was unbuckling his battery pak. He slung it carelessly over the wall so that it draped tantalizingly close to Welkin's alarmed face.

"Keep watch," one of them said.

"Just hurry up," the other replied.

Gillian whimpered then.

What were they *doing?* Welkin chanced a quick look.

All reason left him at the sight of the man lowering himself over Gillian's writhing body. Without clearly thinking, and against all his ingrained beliefs, he unholstered the trooper's hand laser and pointed it.

The shot at this short distance drilled a clean hole through the trooper's head. He slumped forward.

Gillian's eyes went wide and she pummeled her assailant. Sensing trouble, he turned and had time to utter a curt exclamation before Welkin pressed the firing stud again.

"Get him off me!" Gillian hissed. "Snap out of it, Welkin. They're dead. You did right!"

Welkin stood transfixed. He had committed the worst crime of any Skyborn. He had taken not only one life, but two. The horror of his action swept over him.

Gillian heaved, and the body rolled off her. Frantically, she unbuckled the other trooper's battery pak and utility harness. She thought about the armor, but no, too much to carry.

A noise to their right sent a cold chill through Welkin. Cruisers. Their high-pitched whine was audible even at this distance.

Gillian grabbed Welkin and dragged him to the nearest doorway. The dark swallowed them.

Sarah and Con reached Platform One without further incident. Sarah had never thought she would welcome the ferals' presence, but on this occasion they had saved their lives. Bruick had lain in wait for them. Unfortunately for him, the ferals had reached the conclusion that his gunfire had been directed at them. She and Con had escaped during the ensuing gun battle.

The rest of the gang seemed to have gone out foraging, which pleased Sarah. Although it surprised her that Gillian hadn't returned after her flanking engagement. She made a mental note to remind her of their strategy. Always return home after incidents involving Bruick. He was a vindictive adversary, a forgotten character trait that had almost cost them their lives.

She and Con snuggled up together for warmth and slept for several hours until some inner mechanism woke her from a deep sleep. She pricked her ears and padded quietly to the defunct elevator shaft. Nothing but the faint thrumming of the taut elevator ropes. She cast about for intrusion. By design, this block had only two entrances and, therefore, two exits. The elevator shaft was a third option, open only in case of emergency.

Someone was climbing the stairs from the platform. "Con!" she whispered. She shook him awake, covering his mouth in case he spoke in alarm.

They acted in tandem, both skirting the room until they rested to either side of the fire door. Sarah figured there were two of them. Couldn't be her people. They stayed in safe houses if caught out in the night and returned at dawn, before things got hot out there.

Sarah held her knife out in front of her, ready to carve the first person through the door. Con would get the second. She nodded to him as the door swung open.

"Easy up in there!" Gillian called. "We're coming in!"

Sarah almost fainted with relief. "Where the hell have—"

Welkin's presence could have decked her. She covered her surprise admirably. "*Colony* didn't want you?"

"Don't start, Sarah," Gillian said. "He saved my life." She threw her arms around her sister. "And the idiot told me you'd got shot!"

Welkin was the first awake. He immediately limped to the window. During the night his leg had suffered a cramp, but apart from that mild discomfort, he was surprised at how well Sarah's poultice had worked.

He hadn't slept well. The troopers' brutality had shocked him. That sort of animal behavior simply didn't exist on *Colony*. That's how lower deckers behaved, not Skyborn. Clean, efficient extermination was one thing, but this was *uncivilized*.

Throughout their ordeal back to Platform One, Gillian had told him of many more *Colony* atrocities. His mind whirled in doubt. If he hadn't seen with his very own eyes . . .

Through the ever-present smog he could vaguely make out the sun low on the horizon. It was an uneven mass of pale luminance that barely smudged the skyline. Bold in daylight, *Colony* towered above the tallest gutted buildings. Its very presence made everything else seem insignificant.

Aware of his own confused feelings, he looked around him. Con had his back to Sarah's. He was snoring heavily, but Sarah seemed oblivious to the erratic snorts. Gillian had stayed outside on night shift.

Sarah's sharp voice startled Welkin.

"We don't linger by the windows."

Welkin moved back obediently. He had thought she was asleep.

"Sometimes snipers take potshots at anything that moves. Keeps us on our toes. What were you thinking about?"

"Nothing, I guess."

"Really?"

Welkin looked back to the square of sky. "According to the holographic records, there used to be planes flying overhead, birds making noises, traffic jams, horns blaring. People talking. It's weird that it's all gone."

"I guess technology got away, then. Did you know that from the Wright brothers' first aircraft to the first moon landing was about sixty years? Then another sixty years till interplanetary travel. Not long after that *Colony* was conceived. Fifteen or twenty years later it was a reality. But we didn't stop there."

"The war."

Sarah nodded. "Didn't last long. It was a pushbutton affair. Like three or four chess players stuck deep within mountains where they can't be got at. They kept playing till there wasn't anything left to play for."

"But I thought you had neutron bombs or something. Wasn't it standard practice to destroy the spirit of the people and leave the country in one piece? Otherwise there wouldn't be any point in conquering a country. Not if you demolished it."

"There's no such thing as a textbook war," Sarah said. "This was the granddaddy of them all. We never even found out what it was all about. The world just went crazy."

"All your lives you've lived like this." Welkin's mind rebelled at the idea. "On *Colony*, we're all the same. Everyone knows what has to be done, and does it. 'Everything is for the good of the whole,' " he quoted an elder maxim.

"That's all very well in a safe environment like *Colony*, Welkin, but down here on Earth it's a different ball game. We're too busy surviving. And holding on to a dream of contacting others and ending our isolation." Her voice trailed off.

"Others?" Welkin thought of space. "Extraterrestrial life? That was *Colony*'s secondary objective."

"I really meant other Earthborn, Welkin."

"Oh." Welkin shook his head. "There's no one out there, anyway."

Sarah looked skyward. "*Colony* made a big effort to find ETs, didn't it?"

"There's *nothing* out there," he snapped.

"What, you visited every planet from here to Tau Ceti?"

"*Colony* maintained a constant radiometric scan throughout the voyage. We were looking for any planet with a mean temperature of about seventy-seven degrees Fahrenheit, something with maybe twenty percent oxygen in its atmosphere, with an orbit not too elliptical and the planet's axis not too inclined."

"Textbook stuff," Sarah snorted.

"*Colony* tried," Welkin said.

"*Colony*'s part of the old world, Welkin. There's no room for it here. I'm sure we could use its technology to get us back on our feet, but with your elders in control, all we've got is another warring faction—a better-armed and -equipped one at that. A superpower, almost."

"It isn't really *Colony*'s fault," Welkin protested.

Sarah put up her hand for silence. "Forget it, Welkin. Eyes open." She went over to Con and shook him awake. "Time for a quick looksee."

Con jerked awake. He shook his head and got to his feet, rubbing his shoulder. It was itching like hell. They said that was one of the good things about being hit by laser fire. The beam actually cauterized your wound and stopped the bleeding. That is, if you were still alive after being hit!

"Sorry. Forgot about your shoulder," Sarah said. "Judging by your snoring, you slept well enough." She lifted his jacket to make sure the wound wasn't infected. "It was only a scratch anyway," she said dismissively.

Con scowled. "Next time you can get scratched," he said, bleary-eyed. "And you're right. I did sleep bloody well. Thanks for asking."

Sarah made a face behind Con's back. "It's called old age, Welkin. Hits you at fourteen or so. Blokes get kinda grumpy when they wake up in the morning."

"My sister's like that *now*," Welkin said. He blanched at the thought of her. He never thought he'd miss her snoring, either. Until he'd heard Con's during the night.

"Don't worry about your sister," Sarah said, obscuring any sign of their being there. She kicked at the rubble and messed up where they'd slept. "She's going to be all right."

They collected their few belongings and left the room.

"This is our fortress," Sarah said to Welkin. "It's got to be kept safe from outsiders. We often find gimps living in some of the offices."

"I thought you had a deal with them?"

"We try. Some of them are religious fanatics who claim God saw what we'd become and was displeased. So he, in his wisdom, wrought havoc to show his displeasure. Another Sodom and Gomorrah piece of fiction. Anyway, they're harmless enough, but we don't want them here. We need to protect ourselves and that means no freeloaders. And no, the deal is for food only as a rule—nothing else."

"So what happens when you leave? Will the gimps take over?"

Sarah and Con exchanged a smile. "I'm sure Bruick and the rest of them might say something about that."

"Then why hasn't he killed them all?"

"Because gimps will often ferret around in the daytime, while we're generally holed up. They don't give two hoots whether they're shot at—life means so little to them."

"Consequently," Con said, "they come up with some good stuff, which we barter for. Like food and herbs."

They met Budge five minutes later on the second floor. He was about Welkin's age but three times the size. Welkin had noticed him earlier when he'd first met Sarah's family.

Budge waved a beefy hand. His bulbous cheeks were flushed from recent exertion.

"No problems?" Sarah called.

"N-n-nah," he stammered. "Bu-but w-we got other . . . problems."

"Calm down, Budge," Sarah said mildly. "It's all right. Take your time."

"I-I'll sta-start again," he said and smiled sheepishly. "Rea-son Ped- Pedros di-di-didn't answer your call las-t ni-ni-night was that he'd taken off wi . . . th most of the guns and some other stu-uff, too."

"Like what?" Sarah asked icily.

"Trans-mit-ter equip-equip-equipment. Few tools. Prob-prob-probably every-thing he cou-cou-could car-ry. Ill-Ilija and Gree-en are miss-missing, too."

Sarah's facial muscles tightened. "That's going to set us back years. Damn!" She hit the wall hard with her clenched fist. "Damn them to hell. Why our transmitter gear, for chrissake? They wouldn't even know which end to stick in the bloody ground!" She spun from one to the other then, looking for an answer that didn't exist.

Welkin felt Sarah's anger wash over him. Looking at the holocaust about him, he still couldn't comprehend how Sarah's group had found all the equipment they had.

"May-may-maybe they'll tra-ade it?" Budge suggested.

"Who with? The jabbers? Ferals?" Sarah scoffed. "Bruick'd think it was some kind of rocket launcher, he's that thick."

"Steady on, Sarah," Con said.

Sarah shook her head angrily. "Did anyone see him go?"

Budge looked at the ground. "He ca-came up be-hind me last night . . . act-act-acted kinda str-ange. But I put it down to the fac-fact you'd had that argu-ment with him. He talk-talk-talked a bit, sound-ing me out, I guess, then sug-gested I go get some shut-shuteye. He said he was-wasn't feeling tired. That he'd take over from me ear-early, like." He looked up from his feet. "Look, Sar-ah, I-I-I'm real sorry 'bout this. I've been kick-kick-ing myself all morning."

"It's done now," Sarah said. "So . . . Ilija, Pedros, and Green. We can either go after them, or stick it out here until we find more gear."

Con kicked at the wall. "It's taken us this long to get the equip-ment we needed, Sarah. I for one don't want to hang around anymore. Not with the *Colony* people out there with scanners. We can't hide from them forever."

"Con-Con's right," Budge cut in. "They-they're not too worried 'bout us righ-t now; from what w-we know they got intern-al prob-lems. But when they get them fixed, they'll be out to solve us."

"Well, we don't have too many options," Sarah said with resig-nation. "How much food did they take?"

Budge puckered his lips, then smiled. "We were lucky on that count. Guess they were weight-weighted down with every-thing else."

"Probably had a stash somewhere," Con said. "Remember those

guys were always heading off together? It's no wonder Pedros was never around when he was supposed to be on duty. Sleeping, my foot! He was probably out with Ilija looting food."

"That's the way I see it, too," Sarah said. "Just as well they didn't know about all our safe havens." She bit her lower lip. "My fault. I knew we had problems." She turned to Welkin. "It simply means that all our plans have just been wiped out. We can't leave Melbourne without a purpose. The Dandenongs may as well be on the moon for all the good they're going to do us. Without the right gear we're in big trouble."

Sarah went to a cupboard and lifted it from its mooring. She began spilling gear from a hidden cache. Feeling she was best left alone, the others decided they had business elsewhere.

"C-come on . . . We-We-Welkin," Budge said. "I-I'll give you the roy-roy-royal tour."

"Thanks. But maybe there's some equipment here that I'll recognize from the history vids." He made a wry face. "Well, it *is* old stuff."

"Su-sure thing," Budge said and closed the door behind him.

Welkin started sorting through the various pieces of equipment that Sarah was pulling from the wall crevasse.

"What's the matter with Budge?"

"It's called stuttering. Some people can't help it. I found Budge out there when he was a kid. He'd been dumped by his family." She shook her head ruefully. "He's stuttered all his life. I've tried to help him, but it's too ingrained." She dropped a motherboard. "You never heard someone stutter before?"

Welkin shook his head. "I don't think so."

Sarah's eyes widened. "And I bet you people never had dwarfs, or disabilities, or, say, people with one leg shorter than the other?"

Welkin hid his contempt. "Of course not. Everyone's got legs the same length. And everyone's the same size. Sort of." He thought of Lucida. "My sister's a bit shorter than me—"

"I'll be a monkey's uncle," Sarah cut in. "So you've never seen someone Budge's size, either?"

"He must eat a lot."

"Doesn't that just beat all," Sarah marveled. "Either you've got genetic tuning down to a fine art, or those sons of bitches on *Colony* cull the imperfects." She shook her head in disbelief. "To keep the lineage pure. Like people once did with pedigree dogs and cats. They killed the imperfect pups and kittens."

"That never happened on *Colony*," Welkin protested.

"The sooner we get out of here the better," Sarah said and busied herself emptying the cache.

It was midafternoon by the time the others returned. Welkin had lost track of how long he had been slumped in the corner watching the Earthborn making an inventory of their few possessions.

"At least they left us something," Sarah said contemplatively.

"An-d we know . . . know why," Budge said.

"Hmmm," Sarah agreed. "Hard to carry three times your own weight. We're lucky they didn't have transport. Then again, there's no telling how long they've been stashing stuff, either."

Welkin got up and joined them. They seemed to have accepted him. Especially now that they knew he was useful. Saving Gillian from the troopers had clinched it. He was now one of them.

"Okay, listen up," Sarah called. "We can still make it to the Dandenongs. But there's little hope we'll have enough to rig a home transmitter, much less a TV mast." She shrugged helplessly. "There's just not enough gear for that." She looked thoughtfully at the youngest of their team, an eleven-year-old called Dario.

"And we have no chance if we stay in Melbourne," Dario said.

"You're right there," Sarah mused. "But I've been thinking." She turned to Welkin. "*Colony* won't exchange goods with us for our services, so what're the chances of our taking what we need—stuff your people wouldn't miss?" she added hastily.

"Get off the grass," Dario said. "We'd be dead within a mile of that craft. They've set up permanent scanners now!"

"You would never make the main cruise cabin," Welkin said slowly. "The mutineers tried that a couple of times. And they were better equipped than you."

Sarah shook her head. "Odds and ends," she said. "That's all we need. A hit and run. Preferably with no one being hurt. What do you say?" She glared at the others when they murmured dissent.

"Aft of the ship," Welkin began, "it's unstable . . . if you burrowed your way in—"

"Or used the laser lance and cut our way in?"

"Er," Welkin said. He shook his head slowly. "It won't be easy."

"Nothing ever is," Sarah said. "Didn't Gillian say they hadn't cleared aft of *Colony*?"

Welkin let the babble wash over him. He didn't think he could face *Colony* now. His thoughts were confused. Had the elders witnessed his defense of Gillian? Would they kill him as a contamination suspect? This was more likely. Or Harlan Gibbs might question him again. If he could prove himself to be a valuable asset, because of having lived among the Earthborn, they might hold him in some esteem. But that would mean betraying Sarah and the others.

He didn't realize that he was suffering from divided loyalties. The Earthborn were a ragged, motley lot, but they possessed a camaraderie that was addictive. These were *real* people, bowing to no one, individuals and rulers of their own lives. Not like his own people, who were so regimented. Those who disobeyed were dealt with as Harry had been, taken away and discarded to the lower decks or worse—brainwiped!

Then he thought of Lucida. She probably believed he was dead. He needed desperately to let her know he was alive.

The discussion went on around him. His name came up in the conversation several times. He knew he would be an integral part of any plan Sarah was hatching and that cold terrible thought returned: *Whatever it took* . . .

"Thanks to Welkin and Gillian," Con was saying, "we have two more laserlites and two hand lasers. There's not much else. We can recharge your laserlite now, though, Sarah—"

Welkin cut him off. "I'll do anything I can for you, but I want something in return."

The words drew immediate attention from everyone.

"What?" Sarah said brusquely.

"I want Lucida out of there. My sister." A plan was forming in his mind.

"That all? No one else?" Sarah said.

Welkin shook his head. "Lucida's a top-notch techie," he pointed out. "First class. She would be a great asset to you."

"I have no doubt," Sarah said thoughtfully. "What makes you think she'll want to come with us?"

"She will so long as she doesn't think she is fighting against *Colony*."

Sarah exhaled noisily as though a great burden had been lifted from her shoulders. "That's not so much to ask. You can't hope to tear down someone's entire worldview in one fell swoop.

"Okay, guys. Crowd around. This is what I've come up with."

Powerful quartz halogen beams sliced through the night. Welkin stood very still under their glare.

A stern voice boomed, "Name? Class?"

"Welkin Quinn." His voice sounded hoarse and nervous.

"Will you look at him?" a trooper joked. "Looks as though he's been through a recycler."

"He's been with the Earthborn," a second trooper warned. "Could be contaminated."

There was a loud automatic *click* that rang ominously in the night. Then a voice in an urgent, cautioning tone. "Hold on. The elders might want him alive. For questioning."

"I have vital information," Welkin called urgently.

There was scuttling movement all about him and blurred, confused whispering. Sarah had been right, Welkin realized. The troopers did doubt him. He launched into his rehearsed lines.

"The Earthborn are mounting a counteroffensive."

Bright arcs of light snapped on and stabbed the darkness in search of infiltrators. Welkin squinted into the steady arc light that stayed fixed on him.

"Are they here now?" demanded a harsh voice.

"I don't know where they are," Welkin said in a put-on, faltering voice. Sarah had explained that a too confident tone would raise suspicions. "I need food and water. I've been hiding from them for two periods."

"Better get him inside," said someone finally.

Welkin breathed a sigh of relief and cautiously followed the beam that trailed along the ground. He limped across the open field and stepped on board. The entrance closed behind him. Expressionless guards removed his clothes as one might handle a lowly animal. He was screened for bacteria and put through a filter to cleanse him. A team of medics lifted him onto a bench and murmured disapproval of his damaged leg. It was almost a relief to submit to their skilled ministrations. After a high-pressure shower and a change of clothes, he was ushered before a committee of elders who sat in a semicircle.

He stood nervously before the elders while they appraised him for what seemed an eternity. They were virtually gods on *Colony*. It was the original elders who had nurtured *Colony*'s existence since the Great Voyage began.

Welkin understood it was the highest of honors to be presented to them, but at that moment he would have given anything to be somewhere else.

"So, Welkin," said Elder Jamieson. "You have been among the degenerates."

"Yes, Elder, sir," Welkin said gratefully.

"You have been outside for nine periods—three of their days," said Elder Tobias. "What is your opinion of the Earthborn? Do they possess a rudimentary intelligence?"

"Could they be trained as slaves?" asked Elder Sobol.

"Sirs, they are truly degenerate primitives," said Welkin. "Some are cannibals, but they do have some intelligence. They sent me here as a decoy. They intend to attack *Colony* and steal our technology." There. He had done it. He had chosen sides.

Elder Tobias snorted. "I find it hard to believe that such primitive minds could conceive such a plan, let alone attempt to carry it out. Surely you are exaggerating their intelligence?"

Welkin didn't know how to respond.

"The boy is merely expressing his opinion, Tobias. He is not a trained sociologist," said another man, Elder Mahmood. He stroked a wispy goatee. "How did you survive three of their days without sustenance?"

"I was held captive. They fed me," said Welkin. "I think they intended exchanging me for food. But when *Colony* made no appeal for me they lost interest. I was lucky to escape."

"Oh?" said Elder Tobias. "It's a wonder they didn't kill you when they discovered you were of no value. It's well known they place little value on life."

"They spend a lot of time killing one another," Welkin agreed. "They're animals . . . Like the lower deckers."

"You witnessed bloodshed?" asked Elder Jamieson. His eyes never left Welkin's. He was the shrewd one.

"They kill one another with guns and arrows," Welkin said. "Life means nothing to them."

"Boy's been through hell," observed Elder Zecharia. She was the oldest in the room and was encased within a wheelchair elaborately festooned with a complicated web of tubes and hoses that sustained life in her. She controlled every movement of the chair via thought impulses. Welkin had never been this close to her before.

Elder Jamieson motioned for Welkin to take a seat. "How many of these barbarians would you judge there to be?"

Welkin appeared to consider the question. "I believe their numbers are greater than ours."

Jamieson glanced at his fellows and turned his lips down. "And why," he continued briskly, "in your opinion, have they not overrun us yet?"

"Maybe they wish to starve us, Elder."

Jamieson flicked his hand angrily. "Utter nonsense. If they are so short of food themselves, they could never lay siege to us." He raised his hands majestically, almost reverently. "This is a skyworld. Our farms and market gardens are indefinitely sustainable."

"I do not think they know much about *Colony*, Elder."

There was a brief silence in which the elders seemed to weigh his words.

At length Elder Tobias spoke. "You shan't have to worry about being held hostage again. We will find you work within *Colony* that will not necessitate your ever leaving the ship again."

"Thank you, Elder, sir," Welkin said quietly. "May I see Lucida? My sister?"

"Right away!" Tobias said. He looked to the others for confirmation. "This matter is settled?" he asked, as though concluding the conversation.

Two heavies entered the board cabin and escorted Welkin down the brightly lit corridor. Their air of unexpressed hostility made Welkin edgy.

"I am Systec Class," he said bluntly. "Levels eight to fifteen."

They were heading toward levels twenty-six to thirty-two: the heavies' quarters, an area no average citizen ever visited voluntarily. Or returned from once he had.

Silently they pushed Welkin into a tube. It swung on its cylindrical base and dropped swiftly.

"Level thirty," an ordio informed them.

The tube swung open and the heavies pushed Welkin forward. There was nowhere to run. No point in trying to elude them. They steered him to a door. One of them placed his palm over a lock and the door slid open.

Welkin was thrown in and the door closed behind him. It came as a huge shock to see his sister, Lucida, sitting bedraggled on a bunk. She looked terrible. Her long blond hair hung in knotted shapeless hunks, almost like the ferals' matted dreadlocks, and her clothes were stained and wrinkled as if they had been slept in for days. Her face was flushed and startled, just like the day their mother died.

"Welkin?" Lucida cried out in amazement. She rose halfway off the bunk, reached toward him, then abruptly stopped. The flush of happiness left her face as though wiped off with a cloth.

Welkin, dismayed, let his hands drop. He was swamped with disappointment. A disappointment he decided was wholly irrational. "You're supposed to say welcome home. Like they do on the vids." He put on a cheerful smile.

Lucida slumped back onto the bunk. "I'm sorry, Welkin. It's just that . . . just that everything's gone horribly wrong! And they told me you were dead!"

"I was captured by the Earthborn. I've been . . . living with them."

She looked at him with a tinge of horror. He quickly changed the subject. "What about Zedda and Efi?"

"They're dead, too. I think." Confusion edged her words. "The elders said you were all slaughtered out there. No survivors."

"I saw them escape!" Welkin gasped. "Only Glover . . . maybe three others were shot . . ."

"You're wrong!" Lucida said. "The elders—"

Welkin held up his hand for quiet—it was a Sarah mannerism. "Why are you in here?" He went to her, knelt and cradled her head. She clung to him, shaking. They stayed that way in silence for several seconds. "What's happened?" Welkin asked.

"What do you think happened? After they took Harry to the lower decks and questioned you, how long did you think it would be before they got around to me? It seems I'm *infected*, too, and the prognosis isn't particularly hopeful!" she said bitterly.

Her eyes were shadowed from lack of sleep, and fear. But his were shining.

"Look," Lucida said, awed. "You're *crying!*"

Welkin shrugged. "Earthborn cry whenever they want to."

Lucida touched his damp cheeks with her fingertips. "What have they done to you, Welkin?"

"Nothing. They treated me okay." In sudden remorse, looking around at his new prison cell, he said, "And I betrayed them, Lucida. For *this!*"

"I don't understand," Lucida said. "How could you betray them? They're just animals, aren't they? You can't betray a sheep or a cow!"

"They're not like that. They're . . . Oh, I can't explain it!" He clenched and unclenched his hands.

Lucida gazed at him. "You seem different. Older."

"And wiser," Welkin said. He smiled wanly. "You learn more than any tutor on *Colony* could teach you in a lifetime." She punched him playfully on the arm. "So what now?" he asked.

"It will be the lower decks for us," Lucida predicted, her voice shaking. "That's if there *are* any lower decks left since we crashed."

"We didn't hit too hard," Welkin commented knowingly. "They're still down there."

Lucida sensed his expertise. "Are they?"

"I have . . . friends on the surface, Lucida," Welkin said. "Though I think I've ruined their plans. Their leader is called Sarah. You should see her. She's so . . . I dunno. Top rank! Really tall and . . . bright eyes that miss nothing. She seems to know everything. She's terribly smart."

"Really?" Lucida asked cynically. "Then why did she let you come back here? She's as good as sentenced you to death."

"She had a plan," Welkin said. "Look, I know this won't make any sense to you, but everything the elders said about the Earthborn is a lie."

Lucida stared back at him.

"It's all propaganda," Welkin told her. "I didn't want to believe it. I fooled myself into thinking *Colony* would take me back with open arms. What an idiot I am!"

"That's *enough*, Welkin!" Lucida cried. She covered her ears with her hands and brought her knees up to her chest, like someone being attacked.

At last she said quietly, "You can't *say* things like that. It's *wrong!* You'll have us both brainwiped!"

Welkin was silent for a moment. "The Earthborn need us, Lucida."

"So what? We're going to be thrown to the mutineers. And you know what they do to 'softies' from the upper decks!" She suddenly looked down at Welkin's leg. "What's up with you? You're limping."

"I got shot," Welkin told her, surprised at the degree of pride in his voice. "With an *arrow*."

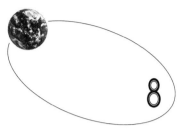

8

If the trial was a farce, the setting was most assuredly not. Only on rare occasions had the vast and cathedral-like General Assembly chamber been used for anything other than ceremonial events or the political deliberations of the ruling elite. The room itself was a perfect octahedron that rose in a series of cascading tiers, called galleries, for some twenty-two stories to a massive octagonal ceiling made of translucent plastisteel. Until recently this "window" gazed out upon the starry universe, but now it displayed a more modest view of the smoggy nighttime skies of Earth.

Sitting in the defendant's box, feeling very small and alone in this vast space, Lucida peered up at the galleries, searching for a friendly face. She found none. The audience was a cross section of *Colony* personnel, ordinary crew members, officers, former acquaintances perhaps, here to watch two traitors get their just deserts. Their faces were uniformly hostile, and the great Assembly space was filled with an angry buzz like a hornets' nest. Lucida shivered and looked across at her brother, restrained in a nearby but separate box.

Welkin avoided her eyes, but she could see that his face was puffy and bruised. He had been ill treated and looked dejected. Lucida tried to swallow her fear. How could this be happening to them?

The hearing was as brief as it was staged. Elder Jamieson, one member of a panel of elders, rapped for order. The chamber fell silent. Only the distant hum of air recyclers could be heard.

"Welkin Quinn, you are on this day charged with high treason in that you did knowingly and with malice aforethought abandon your brethren and your society, and did forge an alliance with the primitive beasts known as the Earthborn, and did further intend, with their assistance, to attack *Colony* and destroy her crew. How do you plead?"

"Not guilty, Elder, sir." Welkin's voice was almost inaudible.

"Let the defendant's plea be recorded thus. Let the proceedings begin, and may God have mercy on your soul, Welkin Quinn."

Elder Tobias spoke next. His voice was grim and tinged with disgust. "Tell us the truth, Welkin," he cautioned, without a hint of irony, "and justice will be served. Lie, and both you and your sister will suffer the dire consequences. Place the defendant in the decoder."

Welkin knew it was pointless to resist. He let a trio of heavies strap him into a limbic decoder. He had already survived two harrowing nights of decoding during which raw data was lifted directly from the glial cells of his brain that encoded his recent memories. He dully realized that the elders were going to use his own thoughts against him, presenting graphic evidence of his betrayal of *Colony* on the wetware display for all to see.

Welkin closed his eyes as a heavy placed metal tabs about his shaved head. He felt a sharp stinging as each tab sank its synaptic needle into his skull.

The screen above Welkin flared with white static.

Elder Zecharia leaned forward in her wheelchair. "Welkin Quinn, have you been informed of your rights? And do you waive counsel?"

Welkin nodded. It was useless to protest that he had waived counsel under duress. "I do, Elder."

Zecharia gazed solemnly around the gallery with steady, unblinking steel-gray eyes. "As is our custom, we shall display memories of your liaison with the Earthborn and allow the court to decide whether or not you are guilty as charged." She nodded curtly to the technician seated beside Welkin. "Proceed."

Welkin's head jerked as power surged through the tabs and into his nerve endings. Images downloaded. The wetware screen became a montage of shifting scenes: Sarah's kindly face, Con laughing at something Welkin had said, Sarah and Con offering him food, Tor and Simone being slain by ferals, Welkin seemingly fleeing. Welkin prayed feverishly that his most heinous crime had not been recorded—the killing of two troopers.

Welkin sensed rather than heard the gallery's collective intake of breath as each scene revealed one of their own—a Skyborn!—consorting with the enemy.

The images suddenly took on a darker hue, as if filtered. The resulting effect suggested a sinister, even maniacal intent. Suddenly, the two troopers appeared on screen. Welkin groaned, but to his mounting horror he realized the memory engram had been faked! The image showed Welkin sneaking up on the two troopers who were taking a breather, exchanging harmless jokes, wishing they were back inside *Colony* with their brethren. Without warning, Welkin leaped out of the shadows, snapping off two shots that dropped the troopers in their tracks, dead.

A horrified gasp sprang up in the Assembly chamber and quickly became an enraged howl. Welkin's head sagged. The elders had set him up, had edited his memories, and yet he felt obscurely guilty about the troopers. No matter what the circumstances were, lives had been taken. Taken by *him*. Somewhere inside the huge lie engineered by the elders there was, he realized, a kernel of truth.

"Enough!" cried Tobias theatrically. "I think we have seen enough. The elders will vote."

Each elder pressed a button on the table before them. Elder Jamieson gazed at a computer screen. After a moment he lifted his head and gazed at Welkin. His face was expressionless.

"Judgment has been rendered. Welkin Quinn, you have been found guilty of high treason. By the Law of Association, your sister, Lucida Quinn, shares your guilt. Together, you will be taken herewith from this place of judgment and banished to the lower decks, and there you shall remain for the rest of your natural lives, short though they may be. You are from this moment on stripped of your membership in our society, deprived of your former privileges, and dispossessed of your humanity, which is hereby revoked. You are thus cast out from the normal world; from this time on you will dwell in darkness! *Begone!*"

Welkin was too racked by pain to react to the anger that came thundering from the gallery. Shouts of "traitor" and "murderer" rained down on him from the gallery. The synaptic needles were yanked from his scalp and left dangling from the limbic apparatus.

He was unceremoniously dragged from the chair and, together with Lucida, was dragged from the courtroom.

Moments later they were in an elevator, descending fast. The ordio announced, "Level five."

Welkin gasped as it hit him. They were being discarded. He must have made a sound because a heavy suddenly spun around and slammed the heel of his hand in Welkin's face. "Shut up, traitor!"

Lucida whimpered, but she was spared a violent response as the elevator doors slid open and the heavies spilled out. Wearing riot gear and carrying snap guns they ran helter-skelter down a long corridor, dragging Welkin and Lucida like rag dolls between them.

When they reached the end, they trained their weapons on the bulkhead separating them from the lower decks. On the squad leader's signal, Welkin and Lucida were pushed to the bulkhead. The heavies crowded around while two of their number released the lock.

As the door opened, a dank smell wafted from within.

"It's *dark* in there!" Lucida cried. She pulled back frantically, but the heavies caught hold of her flailing arms and twisted them sharply behind her back. She cried out in pain.

"Let her go!" Welkin elbowed a heavy in the abdomen, then buckled as the butt of a snap gun thudded into his head.

"Welkin!" Lucida lurched toward him.

"Shove 'em in!" the squad leader ordered urgently, aware of movement in the darkness beyond the bulkhead. He stood back with his snap gun held firmly against his shoulder.

"In!" a heavy screeched frantically. "Move it!" He shoved Lucida so hard she stumbled against the door seals.

Welkin swung clumsily around, and as he did so something was flung out of the dark. The heavy behind Welkin cried out and toppled backward. Several chunks of metal then clattered against the doorway.

Welkin pulled Lucida down to the ground, but even as he hit the deck with her, they were pushed from behind. They tumbled into the blackness and were trampled as screaming mutineers struggled to get clear of the bulkhead before the door closed.

Welkin and Lucida curled into tight balls on the deck. Several bodies landed on top of them.

"It's dark. I can't see!" Lucida wailed. "HELP!"

Welkin dragged her firmly to him. *We're going to die*, his mind screamed at him. But Lucida's closeness cleared his mind. "Shhh. It's not like space . . . we can breathe . . . it's okay," he soothed awkwardly. *We're going to die and Lucida will never see Earthside. She'll die down here and it's all my fault!*

Lucida's body was racked with violent muscular spasms. Her throat convulsed and her mouth opened and shut involuntarily. "We're going to hell!"

"We're on Earth," Welkin whispered close to her ear. He held her tighter until her sobs were muffled against his shoulder.

Welkin and Lucida jumped as the door suddenly slammed shut.

"Hit the lights," said an authoritative voice.

Someone hot-rigged some wires. Pilot lights flickered, then became stable. The tension eased.

Ravaged faces with eyes as hollow as death peered at Welkin and Lucida. A group of lower deckers moved hungrily in on them. Some were clothed in rags, others seemed to have made a valiant attempt to maintain appearances. Most of them were kids no older than fourteen, though there was a sprinkling of older men and women. One man looked like an elder with a long, unkempt beard flecked with gray. The leader was in his early thirties. He held the others back with his outstretched hands and looked down at them.

"We've been convicted of treason," Welkin said quickly. "We're like you."

"Not like us, kid. You're a *softie* from the fat upper decks," said the older man. A scar cut a livid line from one cheek to the other. His nose had been hideously flattened; several missing front teeth muffled his speech. He looked worse than any Earthborn.

"I'm Lee. We can't linger here long. It's not safe. So we have to make a decision."

Lucida looked up. "A decision? What do you mean?"

Lee shrugged. "Nothing personal, kid. Scarce resources. Down here, we obey the inexorable laws of economics. So. You have thirty seconds to convince us you're worth preserving."

"Thirty seconds?!" Lucida stared at him, aghast. "You're going to *kill* us?"

"Twenty seconds."

"That's not fair!"

"It sucks," said Lee. He raised a makeshift crossbow loaded with a steel dart. He took aim at Lucida. "Ladies first, huh?"

Welkin stepped in front of his sister.

"Whoever said chivalry was dead?" Lee's cohorts laughed, and Welkin was immediately struck by the lack of malice. These people didn't hate them. This was just their life.

"My sister is a top-rank technician! She was first in her class and majored in primitive and obsolete technology."

"Like the kind we have down here?" Lee asked cynically. "Nice try."

"No, like the kind the Earthborn use."

There was a sudden raw silence. "Told you!" cried a ferret-faced kid. "We *did* land on Earth." He laughed. "I could *smell* it!"

Lee pursed his lips. "You think that qualifies you?"

"I lived among the Earthborn. I have friends there. They want to help us."

Somebody pushed through the crowd of onlookers and threw himself at Welkin. Welkin instinctively started to defend himself, then realized the newcomer was *hugging* him.

"Welkin! Space! I'm glad to see you!"

It was Harry.

Welkin stared at him, hardly daring to believe his eyes. Then they were hugging again and pounding each other on the back. Harry turned to the others. "This is my friend and his sister. I claim privilege!"

Lee lowered his weapon. He stuck out his hand and grinned. "No hard feelings, huh?"

Welkin found himself shaking Lee's hand and then several others as well.

"You can get to know the others as we go," Harry said. Without another word everybody moved out.

Harry stayed close and filled Welkin and Lucinda in on what had happened to him.

"The elders questioned me for several days and ran me through the decoder. I told them you had nothing to do with it, but they still didn't believe me. Or they did but they didn't care. Then they dumped me down here. I didn't even get a hearing!"

Luckily, he had fallen in with Lee's group, which accepted him when they learned he had some training in hydroponics.

"I can't see a thing," Lucida said. "Why are the lights so dim?"

"You get used to it," Harry told her. "We don't have a lot of power down here. As Lee said, resources are scarce."

They waded through puddles of stagnant water. The stench was worse than anything Welkin or Lucida had ever experienced. Several recently burst pipes leaked continually. Their boots, not designed for water resistance, made squelching noises as they picked their way along the companionway. There was a constant gushing noise from running water.

At times, the metal plating beneath them was so warped they had to jump across rents in the flooring. Huge sheets of plating had peeled back from the superstructure, revealing gaping pits of darkness.

"Careful, now," Lee called back as a kid called Wez squealed and slid a yard before being grabbed.

They reached some emergency stairs and climbed down. Once out of the companionway, they appeared more relaxed.

"It's no-man's-land back there. Anything goes," Harry explained, then looked concerned. "Things won't be easy at first. Most people need a period of adjustment, and some of them . . . well, some of them just don't make it. It's a kind of overload. They sit and stare at nothing for hours on end, then one day they're just gone."

"We'll be okay," Welkin said, confidently.

"Welkin lived on the surface for *three days!*" Lucida said.

Harry stared. "For real?" Welkin nodded. "Then we need to talk! There've been major ruptures in the ship's hull, and all the bottom decks are cut off. But I think there's a way out, only nobody will listen to me. They're scared. I keep trying to tell them that outside can't be any worse than in here, but it's got me beat. We've all been discarded, thrown out like refuse, yet most of the people down here still cling to the teachings and beliefs of the elders. Doesn't make any sense!"

"Maybe," said Welkin, "those things are more important when everything else has been taken away."

Harry eyed Welkin oddly. "I've never heard you talk like that before."

Welkin shrugged. "I've never been kidnapped by Earthborn, shot with an arrow, and condemned to the lower decks before. Guess there's a first time for everything."

Harry grinned. "Guess there is. And maybe I should just shut up till I get the whole story."

Welkin proceeded to tell Harry everything that had transpired from the moment Harry had been grabbed in the briefing session with Elder Tobias till he and Lucida had been shoved through the bulkhead door into the lower deck territory. At the end, Harry whistled.

"Wow. And I thought *I'd* been through a recycler!"

"I'm hungry," Lucida said suddenly.

Welkin grinned. "That's my ever practical sister! So Harry, what's to eat? And don't tell me leftover softie."

Harry said, "We're all out of softie. Sorry." Lucida shot Harry a horrified look, then realized he was kidding. Or hoped he was. He continued, "We've set up a protein lab. Sort of. And a hydroponic area, which I've managed to expand. Had to steal some power, but that's how it's done. You won't starve down here, but you won't turn into a heavy, either."

"Were you trying to break out when they discarded us?" Lucida asked.

"Oh, that!" Harry laughed. "No, we weren't trying to break out. We just give them a hard time whenever we can. Don't want them thinking they can take a stroll through our territory any time they like. Sometimes we even get a laserlite from them."

"Most of the bulkheads are locked from our side, too," Lee said. He had dropped back and was listening in on their conversation. "Tell us about outside," he said.

"Yeah, what's it like?" asked the ginger-haired Wez.

"The city is pretty desolate. A bit like this, I guess. It's divided up among warring gangs," he said. "Outside the city, it's different. There's no . . . *end*. It just keeps going, as far as the eye can see. Sarah told me that vegetation in the countryside has started coming back. Grass, trees. For a long time there wasn't enough sunlight for proper photosynthesis."

"Sunlight?" a woman in her twenties asked.

"Trust me, you have to see it to believe it!" He went on to describe what little he had seen of Earth, emphasizing the open spaces, the ruggedness of the inhabitants, and how cold it had been. Despite the list of negatives, there was also admiration, even longing, in his voice, which the others picked up on and puzzled over. A restless murmur snaked through the troop as they moved.

"The Earthborn have options," Lee observed. "We have walls."

"Walls can come down," Harry said pointedly. He turned back to Welkin. "This Sarah. Do you think she would help us, maybe even let us join her?"

Welkin shook his head slowly. "She can't do much without help from inside *Colony*. I was supposed to create a diversion in the main cruise cabin while some of Sarah's gang got on board to raid the food and equipment stores. She was going to take out some of the surveillance sensors. Then we'd all escape in the confusion."

The troop emerged from the stairwell, took up a new formation, and headed down a wide passage.

A stocky kid called Garth spoke up. "These other gangs," he said. "Sounds like this Bruick might be better suited to our purposes. More of them, for starters."

"They're worse than you can imagine," Welkin said. "You couldn't trust them."

"Maybe they wouldn't trust *us*," Garth said. "Anyway, why should we trust this woman? What's in it for her?"

A few of the others nodded, and all of a sudden everyone had something to say.

"*Quiet!*" Lee snapped. He didn't speak again until a hush had descended. "Right. Try listening, just for once. And keep your blasted eyes peeled! We're not back at home base yet."

Welkin tried to answer Garth's question. "Sarah has a . . . vision. She believes the Earth can be rebuilt. Rebuilt by people like us. And I trust her," he said simply.

Suddenly, a steel-tipped dart sliced the air and slammed Lee into a wall. His head smacked the metal hard and he slid to the floor.

"After him!" Wez screamed. His voice echoed in the narrow corridor.

Three of their party raced to the intersection. Warily they searched the darkness.

"Gone," Harry called back.

Lucida knelt beside Lee, probing the wound with her fingertips. She looked at the blood seeping from his shoulder as though it were something alien. "How do we fix this?" she asked anxiously.

"We don't call the medics, that's for sure," Harry said. He and Welkin lifted Lee between them. His head lolled from side to side.

"Gently," Lucida cried.

"Not to worry, he's tough." Harry grunted under Lee's weight.

They staggered off down the damp passage. The others formed a protective flank around them.

"Why did they do this?" Lucida asked, bewildered by the laws of the lower decks.

"They call it 'payback,' " Harry said. "We got two of their people when they raided our lab."

"But that's barbaric!" Lucida's eyes were wide with disbelief.

"You'll get no argument from me," Harry said with resignation.

They arrived at Bay View Dock. Lee was lowered to a chair and a girl called Kara tended his wound.

"Careless," Kara muttered to herself.

"Just another scar," Lee joked, then yelped when Kara dabbed the wound with water.

"Quiet!" she said.

Lucida looked about her. "We heard this part of the craft was in mutin . . . that is, in your hands," she faltered.

Welkin came to her rescue. "Which is why *Colony* couldn't send out landing craft."

"You got it," Harry said triumphantly. "They're all stored here. But the docking mechanisms are controlled from the bridge, so *we* couldn't leave *Colony* either."

"It's what's called in Old Earthspeak as a catch-32," Wez said.

"Catch-22," Welkin corrected politely.

"Catch-33!" Garth said.

"Enough!" Lee groaned. "Space demons above, argue about something that *matters!*"

Welkin stared up at the giant laminate window that had once been used to view the vastness of space. Right now a jagged rip down its middle made it appear like cheap glass.

"When we crashed, the shutters were closed," explained Kara. "But on impact—kaput!—they folded in and cracked the window."

Welkin shook his head with exasperation. "Then why aren't you digging?"

"Because not everyone wants us to dig," Lee said from his chair. "All the others are uniting against us." He looked down at the bandage Kara was wrapping about his shoulder. "They're too stupid for words."

"No one trusts anyone down here," Harry explained. He smiled ruefully. "If you think you can talk sense into them, go ahead. But I doubt you'll find a bodyguard."

Lucida glanced at Welkin and then turned to Harry. "What happens if you don't break through?" She nodded to the hole in the laminate.

"We stay here and fight. Until someone wins Bay View Dock, where there's a hatch to the outside already smashed in the landing."

"But the survivors may never even break through to the outside." Lucida shrugged helplessly. "Why can't you all work together as a team?"

Harry shook his head. "Because *that's* not how things are done. It's like . . . I don't know!" he broke off, exasperated. "You ask some funny questions!"

"I'll go," Welkin said.

"Not without me you don't," Lucida said firmly.

"Then you'll both be killed," Harry said. "No one *talks* down here."

Welkin looked at Lucida. He didn't want to risk her life. "I'll be better off without you." He felt a cold wave of emptiness.

Lucida turned to the others. "The outside is the *future*. You all know this!"

Lee waited to see if there were any offers to go with them. No one offered assistance. "We're too few to go with you."

"I guess that means you'll need my help," said Harry. "You'll probably trip over the first bump in the passage."

Lee fumbled around in his satchel. "Here. These might come in handy."

They were throwing stars, hunks of rusty metal laser-cut to fine, sharp edges. Welkin realized it was one of these that had wounded Lee. He fingered them gingerly. Vaguely, he sought the word *shuriken* but could only grasp *ninja*.

"Thanks," he said dubiously. He gave a couple to Harry.

"I don't believe this," Lucida said. She took a deep breath and followed Welkin and Harry through the airlock. It closed behind them, enveloping them in total darkness.

"I hope you can find your way back, Harry." Lucida's voice sounded eerie as it echoed and amplified in the confined passageway. They had walked for half an hour and Welkin and Lucida were completely disoriented.

"If we don't have any luck, it won't matter," Harry said simply.

They continued on in silence, stopping every now and then to listen. At one junction, someone stepped out in front of them.

Welkin recoiled. He fell into a defensive stance. The throwing star felt cold in his hand.

The man smiled. "You're a bit off beam here. Softies, aren't you? Who got you first? Lee? Cummins?" He was slapping a blunt instrument into the palm of his hand.

"Lee was waiting at his bulkhead when we were dropped down," Welkin said. He quickly scanned the area. Nothing but shifting shadows. A thousand places to hide. To ambush.

"We've got a proposition for you," Harry said.

"They're fair kill," said a voice from the dark. "I spotted them first."

They were surrounded. Voices rose in a rush, the manic whispers of a feral pack.

Suddenly the tunnel was alive with movement. Tentative at first, then confidently shuffling forward, eager for the kill. But the ambushers parted so that the first speaker had a vague view of Welkin and Lucida. "They're mine," he said.

"Harry's right. We came out to talk," Welkin said. He ignored the others and stared at one youth whom he assumed to be their leader.

In that split second one of them raised his hand to throw a star. He'd half completed the action when suddenly two blades sliced into him.

"Ambush!" a voice screamed.

"You're surrounded!" It was Lee's voice. "You there, moving to the back. Ease up or you're all dead."

"Steady," their leader said urgently. He looked ready to flee. But there was nowhere to go. He stood his ground. "Lee? Thought someone got you."

"Not today, Elab, and this isn't about payback," Lee called from the darkness.

Welkin noticed that the air was different, not as dank and stale.

"It's about the Bay View Dock," Elab said. "Even if you lot broke through, you'd be blinded. There's no hope for any of us out there. It's the upper decks or nothing."

"Blinded?" Lucida whispered from the shadows.

Elab stepped closer. His eyes were bloodshot slits filled with anger. "We've been down here so long we're as good as blind. Night vision only, see?" He looked about him, at the two gangs. "You'd all lose your sight out there."

"We mightn't," Harry put in. He still had his arm flung back in case any of them made a false move. "If we get control of the bridge, we'll have medicine and cloning kits to heal everybody," he said, pointing to his puckered, rheumy eyes. "From the outside we can *have* the ship."

"So what's on the outside that *Colony* doesn't have?" asked Elab. He turned to the others. "If it's Earth we've landed on, it's probably a radioactive hellhole fit for nothing."

"I've been out there," Welkin said.

"So you say, softie!" Elab scoffed.

"The air is clear," Welkin said, bluntly ignoring the other's taunt. He wished Sarah were here right now. They would listen to her. He straightened up as though the mere thought of Sarah lent him authority.

"Is that all?" asked Elab. "You want us to risk our lives for *clean air?*"

"They have *freedom*," Welkin added.

A strange quiet descended on Elab's group, as if they were mentally translating the word into something they could understand.

Elab stared at him, puzzled. "Freedom? Freedom from what?"

"Everything. Freedom from rules, freedom from *walls*, freedom from being shut in. They do what they want, go where they please, though there are turf wars among rival gangs. But nobody orders them around. And there are no elders."

A soft gasp ran through the group. No elders?

The uneasy silence was broken only by the rhythmic splash of water from fractured pipes.

"We need to unite," Harry said. "We're almost through to the outside. We just need backup. Elab?"

Before he had a chance to say anything, someone came splashing along a corridor. "Lee? That you?"

Lee went over to the kid. They had a hurried conference before Lee returned, ashen faced. "The heavies have broken through one of Cummins's bulkheads. In force!"

Then, as though to verify his statement, dull thuds reverberated throughout the corridors. It sounded as though they were surrounded.

Lights snapped on.

Most of them covered their eyes instantly; others fell to the deck in fetal positions, keening in agony.

"They've activated the mains!" Lee said. "Damn! I should have known that fresh air was coming from the ventilators!" His eyes were screwed shut. "Bay View Dock! Everyone."

Those who could see took hold of those who couldn't. Both Lucida and Welkin each took hold of two near-blinded kids and followed Harry, who knew the way.

"Here they come!" someone screamed.

A heavy appeared from a side corridor and lunged at Harry. He ducked to one side, and the heavy tripped on a buckled plate. Someone rushed forward and stabbed him in the shoulder.

There were muffled sounds ahead. The sharp, static hiss of laserlite fire was loud. Welkin removed the laserlite from the fallen heavy. Elab had reached for it too; he looked at Welkin through blood red eyes but let go.

Welkin fanned a firing pattern at a group of heavies. Two fell, another slipped and disappeared through the deck. Others scattered as the finger-fine photon bolts spat through the air.

The heavies returned the fire. Blue bolts bounced along the corridor seeking flesh. Wez dropped dead as ricocheting needle-fine beams seared though him.

Harry pushed Welkin and Lucida around the corner. "Up!" he snapped. He offered Lucida his cupped hands and helped catapult her up through a vent. Welkin needed no urging to follow her. He pulled himself up the rest of the way and helped Harry up.

Harry managed to drag his feet clear of the corridor as the heavies halted beneath them.

"Back!" he screamed as laserlite fire ripped into the shaft vent. Seared metal let off pungent fumes that burned their nostrils.

They crawled along an air duct, clawing at the smooth surface, slipping and cursing.

"They'll follow us!" Lucida screamed.

"Not up here they won't," Harry said confidently. "Too claustrophobic for them. Left here," he said and disappeared from sight.

Welkin and Lucida caught up with Harry as he kicked open a grille. It flew outward and clanged onto the deck.

They dropped through it into Bay View Dock.

"Why's it dark?" Lucida asked.

Welkin pointed to the ceiling. Someone had had the good sense to blast out the lights.

"*Vre kalostone!* It's the heavies, isn't it?" a girl said.

"Efi!" Welkin's mouth dropped. "And Zedda!"

"*Aye!* We thought you were dead!" Efi said, giving him a quick hug.

Welkin swung to Zedda and hugged her. "I told you they didn't die out there, Lucida!"

His sister was speechless. The elders had *lied* . . .

"Reunions later," Harry said urgently. "The others can hold them. For now," he said. He was still smarting from the lights; tears left dusty trails down his grimy face. He snorted, almost gagging on the acrid fumes from the vents. "How's it going here?"

"*Den ksero*—don't know—we think there is fighting outside," Efi said doubtfully. "There have been explosions. It might have been the main auxiliary going *teliose*—kaput! We had a cave-in near the hull."

Welkin turned to Lucida. "That could be Sarah. I was supposed to cause a diversion so that she could get to Hold Seven."

"She obviously thought you'd created your diversion when the fighting broke out," Harry guessed.

"Or the heavies think we've finally broken out and are attacking from the outside," Lucida suggested.

"Here comes Gemma," Lee said.

The girl belly-crawled from the gaping hole in the laminate. Despite her tattered appearance she looked overjoyed. "We're through!" she said excitedly. "The air—it's cold. But I didn't choke or anything." Coughing doubtfully, she added, "It's different."

Several kids jumped from air ducts onto the outer deck. It was getting crowded.

A dull thud shook the deck. "They're blasting everything," Elab said. "It won't be long before they get here. They've got scanners."

"The Earthborn," Lee said urgently. "Are you sure they're with us?"

"They need us as much as we need them," Welkin said emphatically. He prayed to the stars it was Sarah's team outside, and not the ferals or Bruick's jabbers. "They need food and equipment, so grab everything you can."

"Okay. It's now or never," decided Lee. "Efi, Marjel, Kaaron—sound the alarms. You're going through." He turned to Welkin, eyeing the laserlite with envy. "You'll need that outside. You've got to make contact with the Earthborn. It's going to be tight!"

Lucida looked apprehensively at the soil that had forced itself into the cavity.

"A bit of dirt's not going to harm you, you know," Welkin quoted, remembering Sarah's mocking voice when he had first dirtied his hands. Pulling her with him, he plunged into the hole.

Explosions rocked the ground. Sodden lumps of soil rained on the pair as they followed the short tunnel to the docking ramp. It felt as though they were negotiating a meteorite shower.

Shouting was interspersed with the constant reports of laserlites and ballistic gunfire.

"It's deafening!" Lucida yelled. She spotted a red firefly on her chest and screamed. Leaping out of the craft, she threw herself to the ground as a shot thudded into the hull beside her.

A dark-haired girl stood up and fired several shots into the dark.

"Gillian!" Welkin cried. So it *had* been Sarah's family outside.

Gillian grinned, but her smile faltered when she laid eyes on the blond beside him. "Got Ilija, by the way, but Pedros and Green are still out there somewhere. You'd better get a move on. It's getting crowded out here."

"This is my sister, Lucida."

She nodded, and her grin returned, bigger than before. "Sarah's over there. Move it!"

Sarah and Con were carrying a food crate between them. "That's some diversion," she said. "We owe you, Welkin." Her forehead crinkled. "What happened to you?"

Welkin wiped his hand across his shaved and pockmarked head. "Dark edge technology. You don't want to know."

She dumped the crate in a dugout several feet from the ramp and returned for another. Welkin and Lucida went to lend a hand.

"You're Welkin's sister?—*y'welking's 'ista?*"

"Sarah?" Lucida was staring at the woman with curiosity. "Welkin was right. You're . . . tall. And you do talk kind of funny."

Sarah grinned. "*Thasa complent, righ?*"

Lucida turned a bewildered frown to Welkin. "A compliment," he translated.

Con laughed. "Don't worry, girl. We'll teach you Earthspeak if it's the last thing we do."

"Ohmistars!" gushed Lucida. "You're wearing . . . eye focals—glasses!"

Con curbed his amusement. "So they tell me."

Sarah squeezed Con's shoulder. "Your leg, Welkin. You don't seem to be limping as much." She spoke as she ran, the others trailing close behind at a crouch.

"*Colony* fixed it," Welkin said, puffing. "Probably thought it was contaminated. Couldn't have Earth germs spreading throughout the ship!"

"I just don't see how they could—what the heck! You're fixed up. That's all that matters." The words were lost up ahead.

They kept moving, stooping below the level of the deck and carting crates of food that Gillian's kids had located. Lucida found the uneven ground easier to negotiate than Welkin had.

No matter what the Earthborn might think of the *Colony* softies, they were a lot stronger due to their high-gravity upbringing. He noticed with pride that he and Lucida had just carried a crate heavier than Gillian and Con's load.

"Isn't the cold funny, Welkin?" Lucida was saying. "It numbs your skin. Just like pressing your face against the viewport in space."

Welkin nodded acknowledgment. He knew how close to death they were right now. How just one stray piece of metal could cut them in two.

"And why's everything ruined? It's nothing like—"

Gillian sized up the spaceworn *Colony*. "*Your* home doesn't look so hot right now, either."

Sarah came up silently behind them. "Gillian? You got a problem?"

"Sorry," Gillian said quickly, then disappeared toward the gaping rent.

"That's about it," Sarah said wearily. "We can't carry any more."

There was an explosive burst of small arms fire from the ruins. Sharp spits in the cold air.

"That's not one of ours," Sarah said. "It means the others have arrived. Could be good, could be bad."

"Sarah," Welkin said. "A few people from the lower decks need help. They're probably scared to come out."

"How many?"

"A dozen or so."

Sarah turned to the others. "You all know where to rendezvous. Con and Lucida, you come with me. Let's move out."

Gillian and Budge covered them while they crept toward *Colony*'s crumpled hull. Eddying smoke began to rise as though subterranean caverns were spewing fire.

Harry emerged from the tunnel, followed by Efi. Others scrambled out; a few toppled at the first rock or depression that they encountered.

"Listen up," Sarah said. She had to raise her voice to be heard. Everyone seemed so excited. "Follow me closely." She looked at them. They were hyper but edgy, in awe of the planet. There was no time to explain anything to them.

"Where's Lee?" asked Lucida, standing on tiptoes.

"He's not coming," Harry said. "Something about unfinished business."

"You can't let him stay in there while everyone escapes," Lucida said. She went to push past Harry, but Sarah pulled her backward.

A quartz halogen flared, throwing light on the uneven ground. Figures froze, then sought cover.

"It's Bruick. The idiot!" Sarah spat. "Come on. Lucida, *forget* your friend." She dragged Lucida after her.

A cannon laser scattered Bruick's gang. Clouds of burst mortar jumped from the ground as bright red photons raked the air.

They had barely covered the open terrain to the shelter of the nearest building when a solar flare bathed the area in white light. Lee appeared then, a maniacal figure spraying laser fire at the spotter. It winked out even as cannon fire picked him up and dropped him dead.

Dario ran to where Lee lay sprawled.

"Leave him. He's dead!" Sarah yelled. She cursed the impulsive kid.

Then random cannon fire churned up the ground. In the flickering half-light, Dario went rigid, then slowly toppled to the ground.

"DARIO!" Sarah screamed but knew it was pointless. She had to run to catch up with the others.

She hadn't quite made it to cover when a staccato report from a submachine gun knocked her off her feet.

"Sarah's been hit!" Welkin cried and rushed to her side.

He turned her over. Blood was seeping through her fatigues. "Too late," she said. Blood gathered about her lips. She shut her eyes and grimaced, her jaw clenched tight.

Someone towered over them. Before Welkin could look up, Bruick said, "Now *you're* the one I was really after, *alien*."

Welkin squinted. Intermittent flashes illuminated Bruick's scarred face. A bloodstained bandanna was wrapped about his forehead. A smile touched his lips. "Pedros! Green! Over here! Look what I've found!" he crowed. He turned for a split second to search for the others.

It took less time for a throwing star to find its mark. The sliver of metal caught Bruick across his throat. He jerked backward in shock and clutched at the sluicing blood, his face suddenly contorted.

Lucida rushed to Welkin's side. "I killed him, didn't I?" she asked. Her eyes were shocked.

Gillian suddenly appeared from the night. She looked at Lucida with new respect. Perhaps the colonist wasn't as useless as she had first seemed.

"You saved my life!" Welkin exclaimed. He shook her. "Come on, Lucida. Help me with Sarah."

Lucida tore her eyes from Bruick's convulsing body.

They hefted Sarah between them and staggered off in search of the others. Gillian fanned her weapon in a wide arc and followed in the rear.

Behind them, Bruick stanched the blood from his throat with a rumpled bandanna.

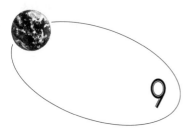

9

Con had forced them to march all night long and into the next morn-ing, taking turns to carry the crates of food and the improvised stretcher on which Sarah lay, her wound lightly poulticed by Efi with herbs from her own emergency kit. He was aware that the *Colony* people could ill afford to be out in the open when day broke. It would take some of them many months to become accustomed to harsh light.

They rock-hopped across a bubbling brook fed by the Yarra River, which arose in the foothills and flowed through the city and out into the bay. Once a flourishing river, now parts of it were thick with sludge, occasionally given life by torrential rain. Farther upstream they could see raging smudgy waters as they leaped over craggy rocks. At one point they came across a curtain fig tree, whose descending aerial roots fell from its strangled host tree, which had long since rotted away.

"It looks like some swamp thing," Welkin said; then quickly re-alized the Earthborn wouldn't even have heard of their own comic monsters.

They soon entered a pocket of ghost gums and climbed an escarp-ment. When they reached its zenith, they looked over acres of semi-burned bushland.

"Fires," Gillian said. "Mundine—the gimp I learned from—used to say it's a natural process. Nature's way of sweeping the ground clean so that eucalypti, bracken, and ferns can regenerate. That right, Sarah?"

Sarah's eyes indicated a smile. "You've been *reading*, too," she said proudly. Most of all she wanted the kids to read and write. It was the one ability that would place them above the likes of Bruick.

Con pointed at something. Flying low was a pink-breasted galah. The parrot screeched loudly as it disappeared into the foliage of a towering palm.

"What is it? What is it?" the *Colony* kids squealed in unison.

"Dunno," Con said helplessly.

"Colorful food," Gillian joked, and they all laughed. "I bet Sarah knows—"

She looked back. Sarah had fallen asleep. "Sarah's got a library hidden in a basement back in Melbourne. When we can, we'll come back and take it to the Dandenongs. We'll know everything then," she said naively.

During the next hour they were no longer surprised to see wonderfully colored birds. Crested bellbirds with their white faces and black breast bands, Gilbert's whistlers with their distinctive cinnamon throats and black lores, and rufous-bellied flycatchers all flew across their path.

Dumbfounded by all these new experiences, they kept going until daybreak.

Sarah slept for most of the trip, tossing fitfully and moaning from time to time. Angst-ridden, tortured cries. Welkin had not been able to understand her and wasn't sure he wanted to. After a time the outbursts stopped and she fell into a trancelike sleep. Con announced with firm conviction that she was going to pull through.

They bedded down in what Sarah had deliriously described as an old barn. The long-deserted homestead was actually a huddle of makeshift huts. Rusting corrugated iron flapped wildly whenever a gust swept through the rotted timbers.

Despite Sarah's earlier warning, Con lit a campfire to heat water to bathe Sarah's wound as well as to cook some of the pilfered food. While Gillian would not usually disobey her sister, she was quite happy for him to do so this time. Sarah was in no condition to complain; she needed the warmth more than anyone until her fever broke.

The leaping flames fascinated the *Colony* kids for hours. Zedda and then Efi managed to burn their fingers despite Budge's warnings not to get too close. They sucked furiously on their wounds and went back for more.

Despite the many wonders Earth held for them, the Skyborn were drawn inexorably to Budge. He held them captivated for hours on end with stories about life on Earth. They were simply fascinated by his bulk and stammering. Zedda, Sarah noted wryly, seemed to have developed a crush on the big kid.

On the second day, as they sat inside the shell of their makeshift shelter, Zedda suddenly sneezed. "Oh no!" she squealed. "I think I've caught something!"

Con turned about and grinned. "It's called hay fever. Change of season—it's the pollens in the air."

"Are you sure?" Zedda wiped a cuff across her nose. "It's making my nose tingle."

Con laughed when he saw her eyes. They were red and puffy from irritation. "The way you Skyborn look right now!" he hooted. "Believe me—sneezing's going to be the least of your worries on Earth."

"Just blow your nose, Zedda," Sarah said kindly, passing a piece of cloth from a pocket of her utilities. "Try not to rub your eyes. You'll get your revenge when Con catches his next cold. He'll look like death warmed up."

"Not me," Con said merrily and started whistling tunelessly.

It took another day for Sarah's fever to break and several more before Con decided it was safe to move on.

"Since when do *you* give the orders?" Sarah gruffly asked one morning.

Con shook his head. "I don't. I'm just doing what I know you'd want us to do."

"You're right," she softened. "And I think it's time we all assessed the situation." She turned and faced the *Colony* refugees. They had made a decision while she recovered. "So you're going back there?" she asked resignedly. "And there's no way I can talk you out of it?"

"It's something we have to do," Elab said. "Your plan to rebuild things is wonderful, but it needs people to make it work, trained people. Well, there are other gangs still on *Colony*'s lower decks. We didn't have time to contact them. So we're going to do our bit." He looked to Harry, who nodded confirmation.

Sarah wasn't surprised. Since she had been delirious, the *Colony* kids had begun holding secret meetings. No doubt, Sarah believed, questioning the wisdom of them throwing in their lot with the Earthborn. She didn't think much of their chances back on *Colony*, but what could she do? Sarah knew it was best for them to go their own way, whatever the risk. There was only one fly in the ointment and she fretted about it alone.

"With the supplies you've provided from *Colony*, we can make a go of it," Harry said.

Sarah gratefully and gently patted her chest. "I wouldn't have made it without your medic's help."

Efi poked at her shirt pocket. "Paid in kind. *Efharisto*—thanks, for the sunglasses." She smiled.

"It's a small price to pay for what you've given us," Sarah said. Then, turning to Welkin and Lucida, she said, "You two going or staying?"

"Someone has to look after you Earthborn," Welkin said. Sarah snorted.

"I've been putting a lot of thought into your transceiver needs," added Lucida.

"Yeah?" Sarah barely held back a cry of exultation.

"Well, you'll need an oscillator, a crystal that gives you a signal at a certain frequency, an amplifier, and a tuned circuit to generate a signal from your microphone—you do have a microphone, don't you?"

Sarah laughed. "We'll dig one up."

"Then there're shielded cables to connect things up, like your antenna—what do you have for an antenna?"

"We've got a satellite dish from a wrecked carrier. We've got it stashed down in the valley; shouldn't be too hard to retrieve."

"You'd better let me look at it before transporting it," commented Lucida. "Besides, there might be other equipment we can salvage. Preamplifiers and boosters—there might even be gearing to steer the dish—" Sarah raised her hand to interrupt her but Lucida was in full glow. "Oh! A signal analyzer to see which bits of junk are still working." She frowned. "No, you probably wouldn't have one of those. But it doesn't matter! Most of all we need power to run it."

"Really?" Sarah queried in mock amazement.

"Of course you—" suddenly Lucida grinned. "You're joking. Right?"

Everyone laughed.

"Yeah, I am," Sarah admitted. "Anyway, we've got sheets of solar cells and rechargeable batteries. You'll have to adapt them to make electrical gear work. We've tried in the past, but it either just sits there and does nothing or it starts to smoke."

Lucida nodded knowingly. "That's because you need to know what the voltage rating is, and which leads are electrical input. Hook power up to the antenna bit and you'll overheat the circuit. Transformers can change the power supply to a rating we can use."

Sarah looked at Con. "Transformers?"

Con looked nonplussed.

"Most of your old equipment had transformers, didn't it?" Welkin guessed.

"*Has*," Lucida reminded him with suppressed laughter. "Their equipment *has* transformers."

"Hey, sorry," Welkin apologized. "Transformers and satellite dishes are . . . are archaic."

"Welcome to the past," Sarah said, not unkindly.

"Anyway," Lucida went on, breaking a brief silence, "we can *make* a transformer. I've read about them," she explained when Welkin looked surprised. "Sure, they're just metal blocks with wire wound around a central core. We can make a transformer—or a transceiver would be better! A transceiver and receiver all in one."

"No point in talking if you can't hear the reply, right?" Sarah said.

"Of course," Lucida agreed.

"That's us occupied for the next few months," Sarah said. She looked out across the mist-shrouded valley to where Melbourne brooded helplessly like some crippled giant. You could vaguely make out the tall derelict office blocks in the city center. "The rest of you will have to be careful back there. Pedros and Green are on the loose, too. It's not safe," she reflected.

Harry looked about him. He and Elab had a team of twelve besides themselves. Veterans of the lower decks.

"We'll take our chances. And hey, when you get the transceiver working, contact *Colony*—we'll listen for you on 121.5 megahertz." He smiled. "We might even answer you."

"That's a date," Welkin said.

But something in Welkin's voice betrayed his thoughts. He didn't expect it to be that easy . . .

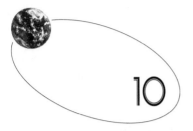

10

Sarah stood back to admire her handiwork. The next moment the ground seemed to be rising up to meet her.

"Sarah!" Before she could topple, hands steadied her. She refocused her eyes, and two versions of Lucida swam before her.

"Sarah? You all right?"

"Of course. Just let me rest a tad."

Lucida sat her down on a tree stump. "You look a bit pale," she said. She felt Sarah's forehead. "And hot. You're running a fever. You should rest. You've been working yourself too hard."

Sarah squeezed Lucida's hand. "You must promise not to tell anyone about this. They'll worry."

"*I'm* worried!" Lucida sat back. "It's the wasting disease, isn't it?"

Sarah wiped perspiration from her face. "I don't think so. I've just been feeling out of sorts lately. It's nothing."

"If it's nothing serious you must tell the others. Gillian at least should know! Maybe she knows of an herb—"

Sarah brushed her objections aside. "Forget it. I'm fine now. It's passed." She stood up slowly. "What do you think of my new invention?"

Lucida looked unhappily at a wooden contraption. "So this is the big secret. What is it?"

Sarah looked over her shoulder and beckoned Lucida forward. "We've been sleeping out in the wind and cold for the past month, yeah? If Budge lets off one more protracted sneeze I'll scream."

Lucida stifled a nervous laugh. "I think he's doing that to annoy you. He's working on a song called 'The Stutter Sneeze.' I can't tell you how funny it is. It's weird—he can *sing* it reasonably okay without stuttering, but when he *speaks* it, he stutters."

Sarah smiled. "He's a riot, all right. Maybe he should sing when he speaks?"

"Zedda was teaching him to stop stuttering. He was going fine until she left. Apparently, it's all to do with concentration, breathing, and confidence. If Zedda comes back . . ."

Then Sarah said in a sober voice, "Never seen anyone moon so long over a lost romance."

"You mean Budge and Zedda?"

"Hmmm. Wonder how the Skyborn got on back there? So tempting to take a peek and see—but much too risky. I'd prefer it if the jabbers think we're dead."

"You have been getting morbid lately," Lucida observed. She wrapped her arm around Sarah's waist. "So do tell—what is that?"

They were looking at a coffin-length wooden structure on four legs with a slanting bark roof.

"It's more comfortable than you'd imagine," Sarah said, climbing inside and demonstrating the comfort by lying down and resting her head on a straw and burlap pillow. "It's a transportable hut. We can make a few and take them with us wherever we go." She peered at the skyline above the thick canopy of branches. "We're not always going to be safe from *Colony*, Lucida."

"Elab and Harry and—"

"They don't have a hope in hell of taking on *Colony*," Sarah interrupted her.

"So you say," Lucida said.

Moments later Welkin was running into the clearing.

"Sarah! Sarah!" he called urgently.

"Whoa! I'm in here," she said. "Take deep breaths from the diaphragm. It helps."

Welkin bent over at the waist, then pulled himself upright and dragged in a lungful of air. "It's Elab and Harry. They're back!"

"Back!" Lucida repeated wonderingly. "All of them?"

Welkin shook his head between wheezing gasps.

Sarah grabbed him by the hand. "Come on. Tell us on the way. Where are they?"

"Down by the river," Welkin panted. "They made a raft and paddled up here. They're pretty tired."

"And hungry, I bet," Sarah said. "Must've taken them weeks." She did a mental calculation. "And they'd have to carry the raft over land part of the way. Doesn't make sense."

By the time they had reached the riverbank, the entire family had congregated. Elab spotted Sarah, and a sudden hush descended.

"You city folk should eat more," Sarah joked, but her stomach contracted in concern for them. Four out of fourteen: Elab, Harry, Zedda, and Efi. All suffering from malnutrition and maybe hypothermia.

Elab hugged her. "We've come for dinner, now that you mention it," he said.

Sarah looked up and Budge caught her eye. "We-we've al-ready arr-arranged it," he said.

"Well come on, everyone," Sarah said. "Let's get away from here. The mozzies—sorry, mosquitoes—are fierce this time of the afternoon. Con? Could you and Budge haul that raft out of there? Hide it under some branches."

"No one followed us," Harry said. He looked to the others for confirmation.

"I'm sure they didn't." Sarah smiled quickly. "I'd prefer it hidden, that's all." She went over to Zedda and Efi. "I'm glad you're both safe."

The girls returned her smile. But Sarah sensed that beneath their warmth there lurked traumas that would take a while to expunge.

The crackling fires cast eerie shadows across those who squatted close to them. Sarah looked over to where her makeshift house stood in the flickering light. Zedda and Efi had curled up inside it and had slept all afternoon and into the night. She was glad Elab and Harry had wakened earlier. She needed to know what had happened. How safe were they here? It was too easy to become complacent. *There's rarely a second chance*, she caught herself thinking.

Sarah waited while Elab licked his fingers. "Wild turkey. I'd love to breed them."

"Then why don't you?" Harry said. He'd commented earlier about the lack of progress. Sarah's family still lacked permanent quarters.

"Because for a while we're going to be nomads, Harry," Sarah said slowly. She knew how the others felt about this. A recurring nightmare was that one day someone would come up with a democratic policy and suggest they vote on the subject.

"*Colony*'s not going to come up here looking for you," Harry said.

Help came from an unexpected quarter. "I wouldn't be so sure," Elab said cautiously. "They have a 'cleansing' regimen." He shrugged and looked directly at Sarah. "When we got back there, the first thing we noticed was that it was so quiet. Welkin had told us about the scavengers—the gimps. Well, they were gone. No sign of them or anyone else."

"They couldn't have gotten rid of everyone overnight," Sarah said. "There were just too many factions. What about the jabbers, the ferals?"

"They did get rid of everyone," Harry said bluntly. "They left bodies strewn all over the place. Probably to carry disease. The place stank of death."

"Lighten up," Elab said quickly as the others gasped. "It wasn't as bad as that."

"So what about Bruick's jabbers?" Sarah turned to Lucida, then cut her off before she could say anything. "I know you say you saw him die, Lucida. But that man has the uncanny knack of springing back up from the grave as though he were Satan himself." She caught herself then, realizing her voice had risen several decibels. She took a deep breath and clenched her mouth shut.

"We didn't see Earthborn—sorry, people," Elab corrected sheepishly, "fitting Bruick's description. No one had rings and pieces of metal stuck in him."

"Did *Colony* get the others, then?" Sarah asked anxiously.

Elab looked to Harry, who nodded. "Well," Elab began, "Marjel came down with something. Then Kaaron did, too. We buried them just outside . . . that place."

"Melbourne," said Sarah. She thought back to the girls. They'd been inseparable. Survivors of the lower decks who hadn't spoken a word to anyone. She'd figured they'd been so traumatized they were incapable of speaking, finding solace instead in their own closeness.

"Came down with something?" Lucida asked, staring meaningfully at Sarah.

Elab almost said something but paused as though he expected Sarah to interrupt. He looked back at Lucida, sensing he'd missed something. "Con said it was probably a fever. Maybe the insects carry it." He shrugged helplessly. "They just lost all energy. We rested for two days, but they didn't get better. On the third day . . ."

Harry took over. "After that, we got ambushed on the way in." He shrugged fatalistically. "I guess we weren't prepared for it. We thought it was safe until we hit the city proper."

"How far away from the Dandenongs were you?" Sarah prompted.

"It was nowhere near here," Harry said.

Sarah was silent. They just couldn't comprehend that they were still in danger out here. More so than ever now that *Colony* had really taken over Melbourne.

"There were only two of them," Harry said hurriedly. "We thought they might just be renegades. Freebooters out to get anything they could."

"Did you see them?" Welkin asked. "Was one of them tall, olive complexion? The other short and stocky with red hair?"

"That's them," Elab said. "How'd you know that?"

"Pedros and Green," Sarah supplied. "You got them, didn't you?"

Harry looked over to Sarah's hut. "They did. Efi and Zedda. Pure chance, really. Elab had only just suggested we really needed flankers, and Zedda and Efi volunteered—almost as a joke. They said it was their turn with the laserlites."

"Remind me to thank them," Sarah said, casting a look over at the portable hut.

"We lost Garth and Gemma," Elab said somberly. "You mightn't remember them, because you were sick at the time, but—"

"I remember all fourteen of you," Sarah said. "If it hadn't been for your help none of us would have made it out of Melbourne alive. I'll always remember you." She smacked her forehead. "I can almost blame myself for this loss. Pedros and Green were my mistakes. I should've gone after them the moment they deserted."

"Th-th-they wan-ted th-th-that," Budge said, forcing out the words.

"It's no one's fault they were there," Elab said. "We were careless and paid the price. If not for them, we might've all been killed by the *Colony* cruisers."

"Cruisers?" Sarah queried, an unusual tiredness in her voice.

"Flying bikes," Welkin supplied. "They normally patrol in fours."

"But there were two teams," continued Elab. "It was hard to tell where they were coming from."

"They make a high-pitched whining sound," Harry said. "The noise from their propulsion units surrounded us. We scattered, but there was nowhere to hide. They've flattened whole blocks. It's like the surface of an asteroid back there. Nothing but fused and contorted rock for miles. They've squashed everything."

"They've got their own city," Sarah mused, thinking of the juggernaut known as *Colony*.

"You never did think we stood a chance of getting back on board, did you?" Harry asked pensively.

"What I thought doesn't matter. It's the trying that does. You *tried*." She looked at the faces directed toward her. Babes in the woods, each thinking perhaps he or she knew better. She needed to set them straight and she needed to do it now, while they were still raw.

"I've outlived most of my generation, yeah? I don't have the degenerative gene." She searched for the right words. "But it means more than that. I'm alive because I know when to duck, when to run, and when to fight. Some of you were on the lower decks for a while. You also learned, otherwise you wouldn't be here. Well, it's our job to make sure everybody benefits from our experience." She paused, but no one spoke. "And age doesn't mean that I'm infallible. A war is coming. And we have to be ready for it. You have the right to choose your own leader."

There. She had said it. An awkward pause followed, which Lucida broke. "You're doing all right, Sarah. I think I can speak for all of us here. We owe our lives to you."

Sarah looked carefully at each of them, then slapped her hands on her knees and got up. "That's settled, then. I'm off to bed. Early to bed and early to rise, will make you something, something, and wise." At their confusion, she admitted that she'd forgotten parts of the quote.

11

"I'm worried about these cruisers," Sarah admitted to Elab the next morning. "Also, we're pretty vulnerable here. If you guys could paddle upstream, I'm sure *Colony* troopers could easily cruise above the river in a tenth of the time."

Elab smiled. "You don't know how much trouble we had taking to the water. None of us can swim. Skyborn have never bothered with it, although we have a sim game designed to accustom us to it. We always figured swimming was hard work. It was the least-used sim on board *Colony*."

Sarah swung down with a piece of timber and drove another stake into the ground. She knew that the ninety-yard-high mountain ash forests with their understory of blackwood and tree ferns provided decent cover from *Colony* craft, but even at this early stage, she was planning to outmaneuver *Colony*. She had no delusions about ever conquering the Skyborn, but maybe, just maybe, she could discourage them. Even now she realized that time was her enemy.

She sniffed the air and seemed to soak in the tangy forest smells. Elab's next question snapped her back to the here and now.

"Looks like they've nearly organized the transceiver."

"Couldn't have done it without Lucida," she said, as she heard some voices cheer. "Soon as we've made enough of those huts, we'll be moving out." She smiled. "Everything's going to be portable, Elab. Even the antenna. It'll mean a shorter range, of course, but we'll be safer."

"What makes you think anyone's left out there?" he asked flatly.

Sarah stared vacantly across at the rolling hills of dense bush.

"There are people out there, Elab. Families, just like ours. They'll hear the call and come."

"Things will never be the same as they were," he said, looking up at her. "You people have lost too much."

Sarah looked at him curiously. "We don't want them to be the same, Elab. Ever." She could have smiled, but an inexplicable melancholy came over her. "Come on. The day's slipping by."

They were just in time to see Con hooking up a guy rope. Another rollicking cheer went up and it echoed across the hills. Sarah could not describe the sense of overwhelming triumph and camaraderie she felt over such a seemingly trivial achievement.

They all craned their necks to see the tip of the antenna that seemed to probe the dark, scudding clouds. It was Sarah's greatest hope that it might one day link the Earthborn globally. Of necessity it was a simple affair: grafted aluminum struts and cannibalized satellite dishes patched with foil tape. Whatever its shortcomings, the Earthborn were temporarily elated by its accomplishment.

Farther down the track, Welkin finished tying a handle to the side of a hut. They'd made five of them now, and he allowed himself a chuckle. They gave the appearance of a row of rickshaws. He had seen a vid of something similar years ago. Maybe Sarah had seen them in some old book? She was always saying that knowledge was power. Perhaps this was what she meant.

Welkin heard the cheers. He was sorely tempted to start on the next hut, but he'd be expected up there. Suddenly he realized that something was worrying him. It was the silence after the cheers. The cicadas and bullfrogs were stilled, birdlife was no longer chirruping. The countless rumblings of the dense scrub had suddenly become silenced. Then he heard something. The crack of a breaking twig.

He dropped to all fours, monkey-crawled to the edge of the clearing, and sat in shadow as the morning mist cleared. He scanned the immediate vicinity, eyes squinting vigilantly.

He rested on his haunches, cursing his aching thigh. "Ohmistars!"

he said, stretching his right leg even as it began to stiffen. There was no way it should still be healing after all this time.

Without conscious thought, he unhooked the bow from his shoulder, withdrew an arrow from his quiver, and strung it. His fingers straddled the bowstring and he bent the bow, testing its power. If *Colony* people were out there, as Sarah feared, he was as good as dead if they found him here alone. He knew better than the Earthborn just how inferior Earth weaponry was.

Steeling himself against the fear of ambush, he scrabbled from under his cover at a quick but limping trot. Another distant cheer went up and he silently wished the antenna crew would rejoice in silence. At the bush fringe, he fanned his nocked arrow in a semicircle before continuing down the trail that meandered partway into the shelter of the scrub.

A wild animal thundered through the undergrowth somewhere to his left. A pheasant or, more likely, a wood pigeon flapped in sudden alarm through the upper branches of a stringybark.

Perspiration soaked his face, attracting a swarm of ravenous biting flies. Damn the insects! According to Sarah, they loved the salt. He brushed them away with his wrist and again cursed their dogged persistence.

He crept silently through the undergrowth. To his own ears each footfall sounded as though some drunken oaf was stumbling across dry leaves; but in fact he moved in silence like a shadow. He had Sarah's tuition to thank for that skill.

"Hiya, Welkin!"

Welkin whirled. His left arm had already powered back to draw the bowstring even as he recognized the voice.

"Gillian!" he hissed with relief. "You could get yourself killed creeping up on people like that."

Gillian laughed. "Sarah's really got you spooked, hasn't she?"

Welkin loosened the bowstring and put the arrow back in his quiver. As well as Gillian, he felt another presence—something else lurking unseen. "You can't be too careful," he muttered through tightened jaw muscles.

Gillian yawned mightily. "You coming up for the celebration? Sarah's asking after you."

"Yeah, I'm coming," he said. He watched Gillian skip lithely along the path.

He smiled at a thought. Whatever made the elders think they could conquer the Earthborn so easily? Look at the way Gillian *glided* down the path. These people were born warriors. Their diet comprised raw foods, full of nutrients, unlike *Colony*'s manufactured tablets that provided its population with sufficient protein and vitamins but were lacking in fiber. Only the elders ate the real food, a point that he had never questioned until Sarah had mentioned it one day. The Earthborn were also considerably stronger in temperament than the Skyborn, because of their tougher lifestyle.

Colony people would be no match for them, if it were not for their superior technology. *Physically, we're stronger*, he reflected. *But how long will that advantage last, now that we're living on Earth with its weaker gravity?*

Welkin's brow knitted. *We.* He still thought of himself as a Skyborn. *But I eat like the Earthborn, think like them, live with them. What does it take to* be *one of them?*

The trail suddenly became dark and Welkin felt mild alarm. He had lost Gillian. He broke into a run. The clouds were gunmetal gray with flecks of black threading through them. Sarah said that winter was around the corner. Now *that* was going to be exciting! Imagine the rain, the snow, huddling up in front of log fires singing songs!

The sense of being watched grew stronger as he rushed after Gillian. If *Colony* was going to come after them, as Sarah predicted, it would have to be soon, before the snow and blizzards arrived. It was most unlikely they would ride their cruisers in dangerous weather.

Welkin stopped abruptly and listened. His hand went to the quiver, but Gillian's earlier teasing admonishment made him change his mind and he let his hand drop. "Gillian?" he called cautiously. He stepped away from the rough-hewn track and crouched down among some ferns.

She was playing a trick on him. Somehow she'd doubled back and at any moment would jump out at him and laugh her head off. He cursed the foolishness of the Earthborn, then cursed his own upbringing that had left him without any sense of humor.

A sudden crash of snapped branches broke the silence. Welkin spun about, his knife already drawn.

"Gillian? GILLIAN!" Heedless, and against his better judgment, he charged through the undergrowth toward the noise. Branches tore at his face and snagged his clothes, but he ignored them. He heard a grunt over to his left, then a short gasp for air.

Welkin swerved past a towering mountain ash and almost stumbled over Gillian and what appeared to be the body of a man at her feet. She straightened as he skidded to a halt. There was blood on her knife, which she wiped clean on the body's shirt.

"Is it Bruick?" Welkin gasped.

"Dunno," Gillian said. "Sarah always kept me away from the jabbers—seen them from a distance, though." She was glassy-eyed with shock.

"Looks like a jabber," Welkin said. "How'd you know he was out here?"

"I didn't. I sneaked into the bushes and doubled back to give you a fright, when I almost ran into him."

Welkin frowned at Gillian. It was easy to see that Sarah had trained her well.

Welkin looked down at the body. The kid was maybe twelve, with livid scars across his face—Bruick's idea of tattoos. Earrings and nose studs pierced his skin like dirty pins in a cushion.

"It was him or me," Gillian said, indicating the machete that was still firmly gripped in the kid's hand. "I've never killed anyone close-up before."

"You did good," Welkin said. He searched the body for valuables but found none. The machete was useful, and he pried it from the dead fingers.

"Do we bury him?"

"I don't think so," Gillian said. "Sarah will want to check him out."

When they arrived back at the clearing, Sarah knew immediately that something was wrong. "What's happened?" she asked, then saw the machete.

"The jabbers," Gillian said. "They're here."

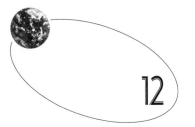

12

It had taken the best part of a month for Sarah to make contact with the families spread out across the width and breadth of Victoria. It had seemed simple enough at first, spreading the word that a large self-sustaining community existed, that it intended rebuilding a law-abiding society, that it offered safety in numbers, an end to loneliness, and the promise of a future.

When weak signals were finally received, Sarah was disappointed at people's reluctance to make contact. It seemed inconceivable to her that families would want to remain isolated and vulnerable. It seemed that the long years of fear had taken a toll.

There was a real need to contact the smaller families, those that wouldn't have access to transceivers. She'd sent Budge, Con, and Welkin back into Melbourne's outskirts to retrieve her books and CRCs. Luckily, most of the cellars hiding her treasure were still intact.

She laid out her precious dog-eared map of Victoria and marked with a small cross any location that housed a transceiver. It took several days to identify locations of the old townships where others might be living.

Sarah chewed her fingernail pensively. If she could work out where they were likely to be, then *Colony*, with its sophisticated tracking equipment, would have pinpointed them long ago. It also made their position in any one spot very precarious.

She called a meeting of the family. "There's an ancient rule of war: divide and conquer. Cut your enemy into small pieces then wipe out the pieces. Well, we've done the dividing for our enemies, which means we're easy prey. We have to build our family, and build it fast. To do this, we need to somehow motivate others to join us. If they're happy where they are, they won't risk uprooting themselves on the advice of some stranger. Any ideas?"

"It's good belonging to a family," Con said. He looked about him and at once felt safe. Back in Melbourne, there had been only a handful of them. It had made the going tough. "It's obvious," he added. "We all help one another out."

"But if they feel they have nothing to be afraid of, why should they move? More mouths to feed is the way they'll look at it." Sarah searched the faces of the Skyborn for an answer.

Budge took a deep breath and swallowed a couple of times. "Do the-they kn-know 'bout *Co-lony*?" he stammered.

"Telling them about *Colony* will only frighten them more. We have to reduce their fear." Sarah returned her attention to the map. She looked up with an expression on her face that suggested she had discovered something of significance.

"Maybe they're afraid of *us*," Welkin said. "We could be planning a trap."

"How to convince them of our good intentions?"

"People trust what they *see*, not what they *hear*. We have to prove we're trustworthy," Welkin insisted.

Lucida looked thoughtful. "We could establish a network of trade routes with them, exchange goods, and create a market for scarce items. And we could take care of families that are having hard times. We could give them food, find them medicines for their children."

"Why would we do that?" Con asked, puzzled.

"Because that's what a family does, it takes care of its own."

There was a long silence. Most of those present had difficulty with this idea; they had lived most of their lives in perpetual danger *because* resources were scarce, where a person had to steal to stay alive. The notion that to do more than "stay alive," to live like a human being, perhaps meant *sharing*, was startlingly new and even a little frightening.

Sarah was staring at Lucida in wonder. "You're right! What's the point of telling them we're a family if we don't act like one?"

"That's it!" Welkin said.

"But what do we trade? Or . . . give away?" Con flinched at the words.

"Anything we have that they don't," Lucida said. We can plant vegetable gardens, harvest fruit, and hunt wild pigs. We have to become *farmers*."

Con wiped his glasses. "I need a new prescription. You lot are starting to look attractive!"

Sarah cuffed him. "I'll put an order in with the first optometrist we meet."

"I guess there's no telling what the other families have," Con said.

"Warm clothing, I hope," Welkin said. Everyone knew the Skyborn weren't yet acclimatized to Earth's conditions. If they suffered from the cold down in Melbourne, they'd probably perish from the biting climate in the hills.

It was a laborious job, but they all knew it had been worth the hardship when they saw the first of the families arrive at their agreed meeting place.

They came like wraiths through the fern gullies and the tablelands of densely tufted prairie grass and vine thickets; they came along the broken asphalt roads as though totally unaware of *Colony*'s sinister presence.

Sarah had designated six rendezvous points. At each site she left a scout who was to reroute the travelers. This was to ensure that *Colony* didn't lie in ambush and net the entire united family. At worst Sarah knew she could lose several of their number, but that was an unavoidable risk.

The six meeting points spread out like a wheel, encompassing what was formerly a town called Kallista. It had long since fallen into disrepair, its heavily timbered houses having succumbed to white ants and wood rot.

Three months after Sarah's family had left the city for the Dandenong Ranges, a couple in their teens, who introduced themselves as the O'Shannesseys, arrived at the base camp, having been sent on from one of the meeting places.

Sarah spent a day and a night with them, sharing information. She sent them back with a wheelbarrow full of fresh produce, as well as some medical supplies and spare radio parts.

It took some time for the O'Shannesseys to realize that Sarah didn't want anything in exchange, and when they finally departed for home, they did so puzzled but grateful.

A week later, Sarah, Welkin, and Lucida sat around a small log fire.

"*Dry* wood," Welkin said, dumping a stack of twigs and branches beside the crackling fire.

"Because green wood makes smoke," Lucida added.

Sarah's face flickered orange and red as the flames danced in the wind. "You're both doing well. Everyone here has you guys to thank for the success we're having contacting people."

"Because we're exotics. From *space*," Lucida said, making a spooky sound. Welkin laughed.

"A bit of that," Sarah admitted.

"They get a bit disappointed when they first see us," Welkin said. "Remember that first family—?"

"The O'Shannesseys? They came hurrying up to us and asked where the Skyborn were!" Lucida burst out laughing.

Sarah snorted. "And you idiots told them that the Skyborn had just beamed back up to the mother craft for a quick snack and—"

"—that they'd be back down shortly!" Lucida bubbled with laughter.

"Dear me," Sarah said, holding her face and shaking it. "The look on their faces. Anyway, on a more serious note, the transmitter wouldn't have been possible without you. Let's just say we owe you."

Welkin rubbed his hands in front of the fire. He'd seen that done so many times on *Colony*'s vids and had always wanted to do it. Even now, though, he couldn't for the life of him figure out *why* people rubbed their hands in the warmth of a fire.

"It's just amazing how many people have met on the trail and discovered other settlements that thought *they* were the only survivors!" Lucida said.

"Homing pigeons," Sarah mused. She threw another log onto the fire. "Of course, the larger settlements are merely sending representatives—they're still much too wary to commit themselves."

"We'll have an army soon," Welkin predicted.

"Welkin *loved* war vids," explained Lucida.

"I did not!"

"You did."

Sarah held up her hands. "We have forty-five seniors and at least eighty-five younger kids." She smiled as children's voices babbled incoherently in the background. "Little horrors never stand still long enough to count them!"

"But it's wonderful to see them having fun," Lucida said pensively. "Everything on *Colony* was work, work, work! Even sim games were designed to sharpen reflexes and brains."

"It's not *all* fun for these kids," Sarah reminded her. "They get to know their parents for only a few years. Even after all this time, most of them can't understand why their parents die so young. They somehow know it's wrong, but it's so hard to explain it to them." She sighed.

The three stared into the fire. Every now and then gum exploded and embers spat into the air like misguided rockets.

"You know," Sarah said, "before all these people came here, I'd forgotten about smithing, weaving, pottery, a lot about herbal lore." She frowned. "So many trades that other settlements had a smattering of. Now they're all here, sharing their knowledge."

"Let's just hope that some of the more cosmetic fads don't catch on," Lucida said.

"Like those people who dye their cheeks and lips with elderberry juice," Welkin put in.

"Or the bleached blonds," Lucida added, making a face. "Why do they do that?"

"And how?" Welkin wondered.

Sarah cleared her throat. "Celts used stale urine."

Welkin and Lucida looked at Sarah with their mouths open.

"As for *why* they do it," Sarah went on, "that's anyone's guess. You might ask them."

"Not me," Lucida said slowly. She fingered her own natural blond hair.

Welkin nudged her. "One of them asked me how you got your blond hair so evenly dyed."

Lucida looked at him coldly.

"I told them you swim in the creek a lot."

"They didn't believe you," Lucida said. "They still stink."

"Okay, you two," Sarah said, getting up, "it's time for sleep. *Colony*'s more than a little peeved at our existence. One of the teams said they spotted *Colony* cruisers in the foothills yesterday. It means they'll be up here shortly. The real fun is about to begin."

Two days later, Gillian, Welkin, Harry, and Elab were hunting pheasant.

"Make more noise—really hit the scrub," Gillian called to the beaters. She turned to Welkin and shrugged. "Unless they make a lot of noise, the pheasants aren't going to take wing, are they?" she queried.

"They're making enough noise to bring *Colony* down on us," Welkin grinned. "There goes one!"

Four arrows sped through the air. One hit its mark and the bird fell to the ground with a thump.

"I got it!" Gillian screamed excitedly.

"If it's a yellow-feathered arrow, it's mine!" Elab called as they rushed to where the bird had fallen.

They never reached it.

A *Colony* cruiser skimmed across the grass, flattening it. It launched a missile that ploughed a hole across their path.

"Down!" Elab screamed.

The explosion sprayed rocks and dirt into the air, sent a shock wave rippling through the ground.

Weaponless, the beaters fled into the surrounding forest. That's when the jabbers caught them in crossfire.

"Ohmigod!" Gillian cried.

Welkin tackled her to the ground just as the cruiser brushed her head.

The high, whining propulsion units of other cruisers rose and fell all around them, flattening the grass. Four to a team. One or two teams. Could be eight of them, Welkin calculated.

"Go for the jabbers!" Elab cried urgently.

"What's he saying?" Gillian shouted above the whining cruisers. She loosed an arrow and cursed when it snapped on the cruiser's fairing.

"Come on!" Welkin steeled himself to charge the jabbers who were now lobbing arrows at them from a thicket eighty yards away.

He stood quickly and launched an arrow. It didn't find its mark, but the jabbers lost enough of their enthusiasm to halt their attack.

Elab and Harry stood then and fired point-blank at the circling jabbers whose slivers of metal ornaments shone in the morning mist.

Then they were among the jabbers. Elab and Harry were lethal in close combat. They had slashed two jabbers within moments of closing with their ranks.

Gillian plunged her knife into one who barreled into her. She felt the hot, sticky blood as it ran down the haft of her knife. She staggered then, dazed, wondering whether it was her blood or the jabber's.

Welkin tugged her around and pulled her along. Someone screamed in pain, but it came from beyond the field where they'd been ambushed. Ten minutes later, they stopped beneath a stand of stringy-barks.

Between short, frantic breaths, Gillian gasped, "What-what happen-happened to the cruisers?"

Welkin crouched down and sucked air noisily. "They were there one minute, then gone the next," he said, not comprehending what had happened himself.

"May-maybe the mist was too dense. Or they weren't prepared to find the jabbers on the ground?" she wondered. It didn't make sense.

The troopers could have landed a short distance away and finished them off with their laserlites.

"Can't figure it out," Welkin said at last. "But I think Elab and Harry got away . . . They're so *good* at it," he added.

"Killing?" Gillian looked quizzical. "You're no softie yourself," she said and pulled him to his feet. "Come on. We have to find them."

Welkin frowned but said nothing. *Softie.* He hadn't heard that term for a while. Now that he thought about it, no, he wasn't a softie anymore. He lengthened his step. He was a hardened veteran of the Earth wars.

Some skirmishes did result in major losses to Sarah's burgeoning family, but she fought back with a tenacity that for a while halted *Colony*'s probes into her territory. One tactic was to hit the Skyborn on their return from an attack. Few complete combat teams ever returned intact from deep probes.

That year winter whitened the slopes and made traveling into and out of the Dandenongs almost impossible. These were the harshest times for the Dandenong family. Fresh food was always scarce, and they were particularly vulnerable to the *Colony* cruisers that made daring raids whenever they found evidence of Earthborn activity.

It worried Sarah. The reality was that no matter how many families joined the settlement, they would always be vulnerable to *Colony* attack. They simply couldn't defend themselves adequately with bows and arrows against modern weapons. And the occasional weapons they did score from downed Skyborn were either badly damaged or at best out of power, which was not easily replenished. Even the cruisers they sometimes salvaged would run out of fuel, and the methane converters that Welkin jury-rigged made the cruisers dangerously unstable.

Their first major contact with the *Colony* cruisers occurred one winter morning. Striker One, an outreach radio contact base farther down the slopes, had had time to warn them that they suspected *Colony* had homed in on their transceiver, and that Family One should cease transmission for now.

"We wouldn't do anything so stupid," Sarah retorted.

"*Colony*'s on its way, Sarah," Con said. "We're not ready for them. Welkin reckons—"

"Yeah," Sarah said. "He's told me all about their firepower." She closed her eyes and thought for a second. "Call the others. We'll have to work fast." She looked at the darkening sky. "They'll not get here till early morning at the earliest. It means we'll have to work through-out the night. But it'll be worth it. Keep transmitting in code. Warn the others not to reply—just caution them. *Colony* might have decoded us."

They worked all the night. Sarah called a halt just before daybreak, as the mist was clearing from the ground.

"You've all done well. You all know what to do. Any questions?"

"Do we take prisoners?" Zedda asked seriously. A roar of approval went up and she nudged Budge to stop his braying laughter.

"Calm it," Sarah called, although she couldn't help grinning. "Play it by ear, guys. Just try not to damage their hardware. We need the cruisers intact and especially any weapons they are carrying," she said optimistically.

An hour later Sarah's planning bore fruit.

"Four cruisers," Sarah called. "They're moving pretty fast and low to the ground. As Welkin said they would." She passed the binoculars to Lucida. Uncharacteristic worry lines etched a frown into her sun-freckled face. She held a yellow bandanna aloft just in case anyone should jump the gun. It was imperative that they wait until the last possible moment.

The high-pitched roar of the cruisers was audible now. It sounded like a thousand buzzing bees. The noise gained in volume, and it wasn't until the flying bikes—as Sarah called them—were directly overhead that Sarah snapped the bandanna back and forth.

Tall, elastic branches snapped upward as restraining ropes were cut. The thick vine webbing that was strung between them whipped up to snare two of the cruisers. A third swerved to the left at the last possible moment; a fourth rider, luckily for him, was inexperienced and as a result was too high to get caught.

One of the damaged cruisers exploded in midair. Thick, curdling smoke followed it to the ground where it exploded again on impact.

The other was snared in the webbing, its throttle stuck on high, its revs screaming hellishly until its rider could disentangle his injured hand from the handle. He flailed about for several precious moments, not sure whether to abandon the craft or sit tight.

Gravity decided the issue, and he fell headfirst through one of the web's gaps. Sarah turned away as his body hit the ground fifteen yards below.

Welkin's eyes hadn't left the remaining cruisers. They circled the transceiver hut warily, irritant insects unsure of themselves. Welkin knew their anxiety. He'd ridden those cruisers a thousand times in mock sims, though rarely on Earth and never in combat. He'd been relying on little experience.

Welkin let his hand fall.

Shrubbery was tossed aside. Twenty-odd Earthborn led by Zedda stood with their feet wide apart, their captured weapons trained on the sky. The remaining cruisers were going for the transceiver now. They hadn't had time to release their missiles when the Earthborn fired at point-blank range.

One of the cruisers erupted into a fiery ball and fell apart long before it hit the ground. The remaining rider jerked to one side as laser fire seared his shoulder. His cruiser wobbled furiously for a moment as he fought to control it.

Those beneath the cruiser prayed he would lose control, but somehow he didn't. The rider's right hand was useless, but he simply reached across with his left hand and controlled the throttle in the same gear.

They watched bitterly as the cruiser vanished from sight. Sarah kept watching until its black vapor trail had dissipated and its screeching motor was no longer audible.

"We did well," she said brightly. She always inspired optimism, whatever befell her family, although she was devastated that only one cruiser would be retrievable. If they could get it down safely from the netting!

Welkin was silent for a moment. "They'll come back. Maybe with a ground force."

"We won't be here," Sarah said. "Dismantle the antenna. We're out of here. Now, have you been working on that cloaking device for me?"

A secret dread of Sarah's materialized. Bruick had indeed survived his "slashed" throat. He had also survived *Colony*'s purge of the city. Nor did it surprise Sarah to learn that he had taken up residence in an old monastery the jabbers called the Stockade. It was an old bluestone edifice over at Diamond Creek. And according to Sarah's spies, the O'Shannesseys, it housed all the rabble that refused to join the united family.

Bruick's jabbers were growing in number, and it was rumored they now numbered at least a hundred, including children.

Sarah's family had had several skirmishes with them, and each side had suffered casualties. In the meantime, Sarah consoled herself with the fact that their transmissions had reached several new settlements and they had made personal contact with like-minded people. Her own family had grown by another thirteen older kids and several children in the past week alone. Whereas she welcomed new members to the family, she was only too well aware that half of them were loners with no history. As she had infiltrated Bruick's camp, she knew he had done the same to hers.

And the biting cold didn't let up. Their food supply had dwindled, and they relied more and more on Gillian's knowledge of food gathering.

Sarah had relented on several occasions and allowed the growing family to take up residence in old settlements that they found rundown and overgrown with weeds. In several of these they had found established tenants, who seemed nonplussed that there were other humans around.

"My main problem with staying here is that everyone will get too comfortable," she told those gathered about her. Besides, she thought bitterly to herself, she couldn't achieve anything just sitting in a camp day in and day out. Maybe she was being selfish? Then again, she was grooming both Welkin and Elab to take her place should her malady get worse. That sort of tuition had to be done in the field, not hanging around a homestead all day.

"Being too comfortable doesn't seem to bother Bruick," said a lanky kid with blond hair.

"No, it doesn't, Lars," Sarah said. He was one of the newcomers. Most of them had been decent kids, in need of Sarah's discipline and organizational skills. Others, like Lars, were more rebellious. He'd been in charge of his own little group and was reluctant to give up his authority. Nothing she couldn't handle, she told herself. Besides, he was a strong, able-bodied kid with natural skills others found hard to master. His bowmanship was second to none, as was his ability with the laserlite.

"So why don't we stay here for a while?" Lars asked. "We can't keep sleeping in *boxes*." A murmur of agreement rippled through the gathering.

"I'm coming to that." Sarah took a look at each of their expectant faces. "We're all agreed that the *Colony* troopers will be back. Yeah?"

They nodded. Confirmation had reached them early that week over the radio. Already Sarah had set up a relay with three other families, all of whom had had minor run-ins with the Skyborn. *Colony* was on the move, and now that winter was fast retreating, Sarah knew it would be only a matter of time before ground forces would march on them.

"Intuition's a fine thing." Lars was about to interrupt her, but Sarah held up her hand. It was an unwritten law that her raised hand meant silence. "Bruick's a crafty bugger. He'll have something else going for him. He wouldn't be stupid enough to hole up in a stockade. His fortifications might be safe from us—we'd never breach their walls—but *Colony* would wipe them out in five minutes flat."

"Then why hasn't it?" asked Devan, another recruit.

"I rest my case. But if you need it spelled out to you, he may have wrangled a deal with them."

"What would Bruick have that *Colony* would need?" Devan asked contemptuously.

"That's what we need to find out, but history's full of strange bedfellows," Sarah replied. She got up and stretched her aching limbs. "It's getting late. Lucida's crew has set up the antenna again. Reckons it'll be fully operational by the morning. We'll broadcast for a couple of days and move on. Any problems?"

"Yeah," Lars mumbled.

Gillian's eyes blazed. It was a hereditary fire that Sarah recognized instantly. "That's settled, then," Sarah said before Gillian could say anything.

Gillian joined Sarah outside. Gillian's cold stare followed Lars and Devan as they walked off.

"Don't be angry with them," Sarah said mildly. "They feel as impotent as the rest of us. Devan's not a bad cook, either." She patted her stomach. "He's been looking after me."

Sarah's words brought Gillian's head around slowly. "It's mostly Lars," she said bitterly. "Him mouthing off like that spreads doubt. Why doesn't Con or Budge or *someone* have a word with them?"

"Bully them, you mean?" Sarah chided.

Gillian's face creased in frustration. "You *know* what I mean. Why can't they just see that individually we're just so many annoying bugs to be smashed underfoot, but together we're something more?"

Sarah's lips formed a smile. "Habit of a lifetime. Can't change it overnight."

"Other habits need changing, too."

Sarah frowned. "Such as?" she asked.

"I reckon we've been on the defensive too long. We should think about taking *Colony*."

"Attack *Colony*?" Sarah was genuinely shocked. "We wouldn't stand a chance, Gillian. You know that better than anyone." She stared at her sister narrowly. "This isn't about *Colony*, is it?"

"You may have the others tricked, but not me. Something's wrong. You've not been eating that much, you're always going for naps, and you've been pushing a few of the others really hard. Especially Welkin, Con, and Elab. Like maybe you're not going to be around much longer." Tears welled in her eyes and Sarah dabbed them away for her.

"I thought I was hiding it pretty well," Sarah observed. She'd even padded her clothing to hide her emaciated body.

Gillian shook her head. "You look awful. Everyone knows something's wrong. Why do you think that idiot Lars is being so cocky? He's so stupid he probably thinks he's going to take over the family in some power struggle."

"I think my chosen few would have something to say about that," Sarah said.

"Two of them are Skyborn," Gillian reminded her. "Lars, Devan, some of the new people—they don't trust them."

"More fools them," Sarah told her. "Are you sure you don't like Lars?"

"*Like* Lars?" Gillian said incredulously. "*Him?*" she added scornfully. "I'd rather die."

"Hmmm," Sarah mumbled. "Just making sure, girl."

"Welkin's the one for me," Gillian said firmly. "He's cool, he's smart, and he's going to live a long time."

"But he's rather backward in coming forward?" Sarah suggested wryly.

"It's just his culture. Skyborn kids his age don't think about . . . well, you know. But we do. Now that we're safer, we should think about breeding."

Sarah hugged her sister. "I can see it's time to tell you a few things."

"Sarah! I know all about *that!*"

"I know you do. But what I've got to say is much more important than what you're thinking." Sarah smiled at Gillian's frown. She brushed her hand across her sister's spiky hair and led her off into the night.

Sarah called a secret meeting of the committee. Her once tanned face was now sallow and gaunt, her eyes like glazed marbles, her mouth shrunken as though her teeth were missing. It had been barely three weeks since her first attack of disorientation and nausea. And a week after her night-long talk with Gillian.

"Cancer," she self-diagnosed. She shrugged at their communal gasp. *Cancer my foot*, she thought, looking briefly at Gillian. It was more like the wasting disease, but different. Maybe she'd caught whatever had killed Marjel and Kaaron. But she had darker suspicions than that.

"Sarah—"

"Hold it!" Sarah held her hand up until the committee fell silent.

"It's just another wasting disease. I've been watching friends die for I don't know how long. I've lived longer than anyone. So now it's my turn. At least I still have my senses, my faculties." She took a lingering look at each of their distraught faces. "You kids are the best, and I've pushed you all hard this past month, for good reason."

Lucida sniffed loudly. "We don't want you to go—"

Sarah pulled Lucida to her and held her firmly. Lucida closed her eyes. "The family needs new blood. And you guys are it. You'll need a firm hand to control things. And I want each of you to promise me that you'll stand by one another."

"We will," they said as one.

Sarah held up her journal. "I'm entrusting Con with this," she said. *It'll keep him out of harm's way, and make him feel equally important.* "In it are a great many things, chief among which is our history." She gave a self-conscious shrug. "I've written down a lot of herb lore and stuff that shouldn't be lost with my passing."

Ceremoniously she passed the journal to Con. "I know you'll look after it, Con. It's important that you do, and the person next in line, and the person after that."

"I will," Con said humbly. "You know that I will." He held the almost legendary book reverently.

It was during the ensuing awed silence that Sarah took her leave.

The next morning she was gone. Gillian was the first to sound the alarm. The entire family spent the best part of the morning scouring the neighboring forest for her, but it was useless.

"Just like that," Gillian cried against Welkin's shoulder. "She didn't even say good-bye."

"She did. Last night," Welkin soothed. He wasn't ashamed to admit he'd wept bitter tears that morning while searching for Sarah. It was hopeless, of course. After all, it was Sarah who had trained him to track, and the pupil wasn't likely to best the master, especially this one. And no amount of knowledge in the journal equaled the real thing.

"You know, animals go off to die. I read that," Gillian sniffed. "They're too proud to die in public, so they find some secluded spot and die peacefully."

"That sounds like Sarah," Welkin said quietly.

"Bloody Bruick," Gillian said and her eyes narrowed as resentment welled up inside her. Cancer hadn't got him! She bit her lip at the thought. But there were no whys when someone died.

Welkin gazed forlornly into the surrounding woods. An unfamiliar lump kept lodging in his throat. He'd never felt this bad before, not even when his mother had died.

Lucida stormed into the room then, her face flushed with excitement. "Guess what?" She stopped and looked at them both. "Sorry, I didn't mean to intrude."

"It's all right," Welkin said.

"Look, we just heard news over the radio that there's been a mutiny on board *Colony*!"

"What?" Welkin exclaimed, disentangling himself from Gillian.

Gillian rushed forward and grabbed Lucida by the shoulders. "Is it open? Can we go down there and—"

Lucida held her hands up. "Hey, it's never going to be as simple as that," she said flatly.

"So what's the excitement about a mutiny?" Gillian demanded.

Lucida looked openmouthed to Welkin then back to Gillian. "You don't understand—"

Welkin took over. "A mutiny would be a terrible shock, it might even destroy *Colony*'s social fabric. It wouldn't be lost on the Skyborn that this is the *second* mutiny, that the first happened a hundred and fifty years ago. It's possible everybody now knows Earth isn't a lethal planet full of bloodthirsty savages and bacteria. That could change things in a big way."

"With enough luck, a rebel group could decode the city's defense shields and sensors and slip out under the cover of night."

"So what?" Gillian asked. "It just means there's another gang out there."

"Not necessarily," Welkin said.

"Where would they go?" Lucida pondered. "Somewhere *Colony* wouldn't follow, a place where there were no families to worry about. An Eden away from anyone or anything that might threaten them."

"You're not suggesting we go looking for them?" Gillian said. "They could've gone *anywhere*."

"Especially if they escaped with shuttle craft or cruisers," Welkin admitted.

"Who sent this information, anyway?" Gillian asked, suddenly suspicious.

"It came from Striker One. They've been pretty accurate in the past. There's something else," Lucida added.

Something in her voice made both Gillian and Welkin go very still.

"Rumor says that since *Colony* landed, the jabbers have the answer to longevity."

A stab of alarm flared in Welkin, then died. "That's not possible," he said. "Bruick just couldn't—"

"Not unless Sarah was right all along," Gillian said ruminatively. "Remember she was always saying he had something up his sleeve. An *edge*."

"It could explain why *Colony* leaves Bruick's Stockade alone," Welkin added. "There was always talk of the labs developing a longevity drug."

"But what does Bruick do for them?" Lucida wondered.

"He spies on us—" Gillian began.

"No." Welkin shook his head. "*Colony* can keep track of us without his help."

"*Colony* just wants to lure him into a false sense of security. Divide and conquer, like Sarah said. Once they've finished us off, they'll know where to find his little nest of nasties," Lucida said.

"I think he'd be more valuable to them than that," Welkin said. "But idle speculation isn't going to help us. What we do know is that once the rest of the family gets to know this, most of them will go over to him, and why wouldn't they? To have their lives extended threefold would be enough to tempt almost anyone."

"It wouldn't be long before the entire united family would be over there in the Stockade," Gillian realized.

"One big, easy target," Welkin added.

"And the only reason Bruick hasn't let this out already is that *Colony* is dishing out only enough for his inner circle." It was easy to fill in the gaps. And it didn't take Gillian long to make up her mind on a course of action.

"I'm going to pay Bruick a visit," she said firmly. "Find out if there's truth in any of this."

"You can't do that," Welkin said with less authority than he intended. "You're Committee. You'll wreck everything that Sarah worked for if word gets out you've gone there."

All expression left Gillian's face, all except a brief glint in her eyes that Welkin caught fleetingly. "Don't tell me what to do, Welkin."

"You'll never make it alone," Lucida said tightly. "And we can't afford to lose you."

"I'm going," Gillian persisted. "We can't let Bruick hold a trump card like this," she added defiantly. "He'll make sure there's never enough to go around. Only his favorite cronies will get longevity. The rest of them will be his playthings, relying on his generosity just to live past eighteen." Her eyes blazed. "There'll always be more of them begging for his favors, doing whatever murderous acts he wants just to get a hold of that drug."

Lucida was shocked at Gillian's venomous outburst.

"I'm not going to live in Sarah's shadow," Gillian added. She swept past them, heading for the door.

"Even if you destroy Bruick's supplies, what makes you think he can't get more?" Welkin asked.

"Bruick won't be around," she said ominously.

Lucida joined Welkin by the door and watched Gillian lope off down the track. They were still standing there some time later when a speck of rain splattered against the dusty veranda.

They went back inside and closed the door against the rain that was soon drumming on the corrugated iron roof.

"I'll have to go after her," Welkin said, watching the sheet of rain through a grimy window.

"Then you'd better get a good night's sleep," Lucida said, stoking a fire. "You'll need it."

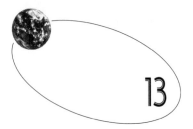

13

Gillian joined a small family as they wound their way down Yarra Spring. They had been the first to answer Sarah's invitation; they had recently visited Sarah's family a second time and were now heading back home after a successful bartering.

"So you're off to seek your fortune?" Patrick O'Shannessey said. His thick brogue was a mixture of Highlander accent and an old form of pidgin English that was currently sweeping through the Earthborn families.

Gillian could understand it all right. But she almost giggled when she remembered the first time Welkin had heard it.

Patrick's partner, Mira, trudged ahead, machete hacking scrub from their path.

Gillian set her face mischievously. "Since the united family came together, we've discovered that there's more 'out there' than just isolated pockets of survivors. I wouldn't be surprised if big cities have come to life somewhere. There's a giant sea that separates us from other continents," she added, repeating Sarah's teachings. She pictured the Silvan Reservoir and marveled that once her ancestors had traveled across a sea mass a zillion times larger than the reservoir. In the glory days the Silvan Reservoir had supplied water to whole suburbs, maybe even Melbourne itself!

"You'd be best to forget them fool notions, girl," Patrick said. He heaved a sigh of despair. He was eighteen and dying of old age. "There's monsters in the deep—anyone'll vouch for that."

Reality snapped back at Gillian. "Haven't seen any monsters in these parts," Gillian contradicted.

"They been cleaned out long time since," Patrick said authoritatively. "Bigguns they were, heard tell." He thought for a moment. "In water where there ain't no humans, reckon there'd be monsters big as these trees," he said, looking up with wonder on his face. "Bigger, maybe."

Sometimes she felt like screaming. She had her sister's keen mind but lacked Sarah's book-learned experience. There *had* been monsters, but they dated right back in Earth's preholocaust history. To fight the false beliefs of most families, she needed to know everything Sarah had, and more.

Gillian swallowed her annoyance. Her silence seemed to spark a hope in Patrick. He shrugged to rearrange his backpack. "So what are your plans, girl?"

"My plans are my own," Gillian said. She doubted Patrick would be a spy for Bruick, but the Committee believed they had been infiltrated. Despite their considerable care, *Colony* still managed to find them, though they no longer believed that *Colony* homed in on their transceiver signals. This had worried Sarah until the end.

Despite her own suspicious nature, Gillian remembered how close the O'Shannesseys had been to Sarah before her disappearance. If her sister had trusted them, then that was good enough for her.

"Sorry. It's just that I'm still working things out."

"You're right, and you're wrong," Patrick said. "Your business is your business and I've no wish to interfere, but the family needs you. That's a responsibility not lightly cast aside."

Gillian reached out her hand and laid it on Patrick's shoulder. "You two got to know Sarah pretty well."

Patrick nodded slowly. Mira stopped abruptly, and Gillian felt a tension rise between them. "So?" Mira asked. It sounded like a challenge.

Gillian filed it for future reference. "So," she said casually, "you should know where I'm coming from. I need to follow my sister's example. I need to experience life . . . *then* I'll be useful to the family."

Mira seemed to think this over. Patrick gestured for her to continue hacking a path, but she shook her head vehemently. "Nay, Patrick." Her face hardened. "You say you're off adventuring, girl. I see no provisions. You'd be ill equipped even to reach Ferntree Gully across the way."

"Mira, it's a Committee person you'd be defaming. Mind your tongue, girl."

Mira took a step forward. Her sharp-edged blade was now menacingly close to a strike position.

Patrick barred her path. "She'd nay be of Bruick's lot. She's Sarah's kin, for God's sake." He sounded horrified at Mira's lack of respect for someone for whom he felt admiration.

"Then of all the families leaving for the plains, why'd she choose to travel with us? And going east, not north like the others?"

Patrick looked quickly over his shoulder. "I can't see it's any of our business, Mira." Nonetheless he looked pleadingly at Gillian to explain.

"She has no answers," Mira said curtly. "Because she's going to the Stockade to report to Bruick." Her eyes glistened with malice.

The sudden turn of events struck Gillian as odd. Something wasn't right. "I might ask you the same questions. Why are you heading east? No one comes down this way."

Patrick and Mira exchanged quick glances. Mira's eyes went wide, but she said nothing.

Patrick squared his shoulders then, and the backpack fell from him. He took a step back and was immediately aware that Gillian had similarly unhooked her pack.

The three stood in a silent tableau for several seconds. Something scuttled in the underbrush and made a high piping sound, but none of them moved.

Finally Patrick said, "We'll not budge another step till you tell us why you teamed with us rather than any of the others."

Gillian looked from one to the other. Patrick's earlier reaction had obviously been a bluff. She almost laughed when she thought back to when she had first approached the couple, asking to travel to the bottom of the trail with them. It was united family policy to assist fellow members in any difficulty whatsoever.

Patrick had nearly choked. He'd warned her they were "blazing a new trail," that she would be better off traveling with a better-equipped family that wasn't hell-bent on hardship.

She now realized this was no normal family. Her gut instinct was that Mira loathed Bruick with an almost obsessive hatred. This fact became apparent whenever Bruick's name came up. What were the odds of stumbling across a family with motives similar to her own?

"Speak now, Gillian," Patrick said. His voice had turned cold.

"By virtue of my Committee rank I am not bound to answer your questions, Patrick." She looked meaningfully at Mira. "Sure, I have my own agenda. As I now know you have."

"You'd be a mind reader to figure that one," Mira said scornfully. Her knuckles were white on the black haft of the machete. "Go from us." It was almost a plea, Gillian noted with surprise.

"Bruick . . ." Gillian said thoughtfully. She looked up at the darkening sky. "You deliberately left the more accessible trail down the east slope to make the going tough so I'd leave you." The thought hit her like an avalanche. "You haven't deviated from your preferred course that much, just enough to make the going tough."

Mira and Patrick seemed to share a silent communication. Mira's affirmation was a barely perceptible nod of her head.

Gillian had been ready to flee. She could possibly take out Mira with a well-aimed knife throw. She felt the reassuring cold steel flush with her calf-high fur buskin. But Patrick would be a hardier combatant. Weaponless, Gillian didn't fancy her chances at unarmed combat against the more powerful Patrick.

A look of dawning understanding flickered over Patrick's face. "You'd not be Bruick's eyepiece at all." He crinkled his face sheepishly. "Fool's talk, you'll understand. But what then?"

Gillian chewed her lower lip. She tossed up whether to lie or simply give them the facts.

"I'm finishing the business my sister started out to do," she said. She dared either of them to laugh. Her teeth closed tightly. "She'd have wanted that."

"I see," Patrick said. "And this business—would it be to do with the villain Bruick?"

Gillian waved the question aside. "Bruick's going to outlive all his contemporaries." She had never seen the man close up, but her sister's description of him flashed through her mind. "He's devil dealt and now has to pay the price."

"And you'd be settling that score by yourself, like?" Patrick's voice held doubt. For the first time he seemed to collect his thoughts, and he looked about him as though expecting to see an army of family materialize from behind every bush; even Mira altered her stance.

Alarm made Gillian look up and catch sight of someone fading into the mottled green foliage high up on the slope. It could have been a trick of the light, and she dismissed the thought as she returned her attention to the pair. Neither seemed to heed her scrutiny of the slopes, as though they didn't want to give weight to her suspicions.

"Alone," Gillian said simply. "It's Snow's End Festival." She lifted her hair, which still fell in clotted knots. "I'll pass as one of the jabbers." She looked at Mira. It struck her as odd that she hadn't spotted it before. Mira too had opted for an unfashionable style. Bruick material, she thought with wry amusement.

Patrick looked fleetingly at Mira, then directed his attention to Gillian. "I'll not ask about your quarrel with Bruick. But me and Mira aim to settle an old score." He shook his head slowly. "Just don't get in our way, girl, is all I ask."

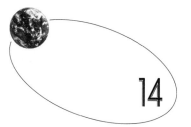

14

The exuberant voices of children at play were joyous. No matter how long Welkin lived on Earth, he would never fully get used to children having fun. At their age, he had been learning the rudiments of quantum physics; slightly older, he was being strapped into sims to battle ever-increasing odds in order to ascertain his full potential as a fighter pilot. Ironically, if he and Lucida had remained on *Colony*, they'd possibly have been in the combat teams strafing the Earthborn.

Welkin remembered trying to explain time dilation to Budge.

"You see, Budge, four hundred years of Earth time would be like only, say, one hundred years our time." He laughed. *Colony* physicists would have been appalled at his bumbling maths.

"Th-that's cr-cra-crazy," Budge had said. He had looked across to Sarah for confirmation. Sarah had poked her tongue out meditatively and considered the little she knew of time dilation.

"Something like this, Budge. In space, only three generations would have elapsed on *Colony* in the same time span as twelve on Earth."

Budge had smiled as though he believed they were razzing him.

Unperturbed, Welkin had pushed on. "You see, according to relativity . . . let me explain on a different level." He'd closed his eyes in concentration. "*Colony* was traveling at something like fifty thousand miles per second, which would have had a time-altering effect on the people traveling at that speed, relative to, say, people here on Earth. If you could have seen us while we were moving, say, from five years out, you would have noticed that everything, including our clocks, had slowed down. We would have appeared not to have aged as much."

"Sh-sh-sure thing," Budge had said and laughed at them for being fools.

"Enough of relativity theory," Sarah had said, closing the discussion.

Welkin grinned. Dialogue like that seemed to flash in and out of his memory. How Sarah had become so knowledgeable was beyond him. Maybe that's why she'd been so special.

He felt rather than heard the presence of someone beside his hut.

"Hiya," Lucida said in the Earthborn vernacular.

Welkin rubbed his leg and winced. It still sometimes gave him hell. He bent and stretched it several times. The tightness dwindled to a dull throb. He dragged himself up and shook his head. "You were right. I really needed that sleep."

"I left it as long as I could. Everyone's asking where Gillian is. So I guess she's gone."

"I guess." He rubbed his stiff neck and winced as a headache grew more acute. He turned to face Lucida. Right now all he wanted to do was go back to bed.

"You can't do this thing alone, Welkin. You know that, don't you? I suggest we attack the Stockade, with everything we've got. They won't be expecting it."

"It's too soon to launch an attack on them," Welkin said firmly. "It's too heavily guarded." At Lucida's pleading expression he turned abruptly and pulled aside the door flap. "Look out there, Lucida. What do you see? Tell me straight."

Lucida put her arm around his shoulders. "I see a lot of people who are free of tyranny. I see happiness, Welkin."

"What I see are a bunch of young kids and a few older kids who think of themselves as adults who are too immersed in their everyday lives to look beyond tomorrow. Sure, it's what Sarah wanted. To have a united family with no worries beyond what to cook for dinner . . ."

"We've fought *Colony* and Bruick these past six months, Welkin.

Don't ever forget that. We've lost too many friends to sweep that aside."

"And you're asking a lot more people to participate in something that's not their concern. They came to us because we offered security and freedom from hunger."

Lucida blinked, taken aback for a second. "And that's what we've given them."

Welkin massaged his temples. The last thing he wanted right now was an argument with Lucida. She'd always been the smarter of the two.

He tried to fight his bewilderment but couldn't. "What crazy scheme have you come up with now?"

Lucida smiled. Welkin was so funny when he couldn't think straight. "I've set up a Committee meeting."

"When for?" He sounded bored with the idea.

"Now."

"I hate it when you do this to me," he grumbled as he pushed past her into the eye-numbing glare.

Welkin sent Lucida ahead. He needed time to gather his thoughts. He paused by a water pail and splashed icy cold water over his head, and immediately felt wide awake.

People parted for him as he made his way to the shack in the middle of the settlement.

His hair was still dripping wet when he opened the door to the Committee room. It was no grander than the rest of the dwellings the family used, but it had a wooden door rather than a canvas flap.

Everyone looked up when he entered. They'd been discussing something without him, although he didn't resent that. No major decisions could be made without a full hearing. Efi sat at the head of the table and waved to him when he entered the room. *"Yia."*

"Hiya," he returned and nodded to Elab, Harry, Zedda, Budge, and Con. He observed how old the two Earthborn had become lately.

Finally he acknowledged the newcomers: Lars, Devan, and their latest recruit, Zocky.

"Sorry I'm late. I just couldn't get up." He glanced out through the window. "Seems like everyone's expecting some major change. Quite a crowd gathered outside."

"*Ta nea kikloforane gligora*—sorry, news spreads fast," Efi said. She concentrated. "Word is that Gillian has taken several families with her. To start afresh somewhere."

Welkin regarded her alertly. "It's always been our way to tell the united family our plans. Why in Space would they—"

"Because a few things have happened lately that they've been unaware of," Lucida reminded him. "Since Bruick's control over the Monbulk area, we've decided to keep some things secret. His spies could be anywhere."

Even in this room, they all thought, but no one voiced the opinion.

Zocky leaned forward across the table. Her long blond hair, squared-off features, and powerful body made her popular among the people. Beside her looks and intelligence, she had charisma, so much so that she had been appointed the Committee's spokesperson.

When she spoke, the others listened. "Since Sarah's death, the united family has dwindled alarmingly. This is agreed. Yes?" She swept the congregation with her wide blue eyes.

There was a murmur of assent.

"It is common knowledge that shortly *Colony* will resume its raids. Which is why many of the smaller families have fled even though a lot of the passes are still snow blocked." She waited for any objections to her assessment, but the others kept silent.

"Therefore, we need to give confidence to the remaining families, let them see that we're doing something, that we are protecting them. We need to hit back at our enemies!"

Several voices rose in agreement. Welkin rapped the table twice for speaking privilege.

He stood up and leaned on the table, while Zocky sat back and watched him. "If you're planning a raid on Bruick's Stockade, I can tell you we don't have enough people for it." He looked pointedly at Lucida. "Similarly, a raid on *Colony* would fare even worse. It would be a case of lambs running to the slaughter."

Zedda rapped twice then. Her knuckles made two hollow sounds like clacking sticks.

Mildly annoyed at being cut short, Welkin sat down as Zedda pushed herself from her chair. "Zocky means that we should hit back at *Colony*, not attack it. Sabotage is a more effective weapon for guerillas like us. We can move fast, we know the terrain, we can strike and disappear before it can respond in force. We should go to Melbourne."

Welkin could see that the others agreed. "They will know it's us. They'll strike us here harder than before."

"We figure we've got nothing to lose," Devan said. He had been admitted to the Committee a month before. Despite his pigheadedness, he had a sharp wit and had proved himself in combat with the Skyborn. Wiry and quick-footed, it had often been suggested that if Sarah's family had had a thousand more like him, they would take both *Colony* and Bruick down. It was a pity he would probably never have children like himself to carry on the fight.

Welkin stared at Con. "Surely *you're* not involved in this conspiracy?"

"It's not a conspiracy, Welkin," Con said defensively. "Anyway, I can't go." He looked down at Sarah's journal. "My eyes . . . it's hard enough now for me to keep track of everything for the journal."

"Well, then," Welkin said. "Sounds like you've all made up your minds, doesn't it?"

"Welkin, come on," Lucida said. "Nothing's decided without a vote."

"Okay, then." There was an edge to Welkin's voice. "Who's going to lead this expedition? You know I can't. I have something else to do."

There was an awkward silence during which each Committee member looked fleetingly at Efi. She took in a deep breath. "Elab was nominated and accepted. Or would you prefer someone else?"

Welkin felt restless and tired all at once. His headache had gone, but other worries preyed on his mind. "Without wishing to state the obvious, I assume the party will be seeking the Skyborn who supposedly fled *Colony* after the mutiny."

"If such a group exists Elab will make contact with them, *ne*— yes?" Efi said slowly, gathering her thoughts. "*Colony* may still be pursuing them. If so, Elab will be authorized to offer them help in return for sharing of their skills."

"A reenactment of Bruick's dastardly deed, eh?" Welkin stated wearily.

Before he knew it Lucida was at his side. "Welkin. What would you have us do? We're always shifting to elude *Colony*. We constantly play a game of hide-and-seek. The normal life span of the Earthborn is so brief that it seems their entire lives are fraught with danger. If it's not *Colony*, it's Bruick or their wasting disease; if not that, it's famine." She waved her hands in exasperation. "I'm fed up with watching their misery, knowing damn well we can help if we push ourselves that little bit harder."

"You're asking Elab to go and risk his life, Lucida." His words weren't spoken harshly. They all knew Elab had agreed to do it, because the Committee had asked it.

Efi stared at Welkin and rapped the table. "No one knows for sure just where the *Colony* mutineers went. They may have found somewhere this side of Melbourne."

"There are a lot of 'maybes,'" Welkin said. He was surprised at his calm tone. He sounded as though someone had just told him Elab was going down to the river to do some fishing.

"I think of it as a pilgrimage," Elab said at last. "Spread the word of Sarah's family here in the Dandenongs by 'bush telegraph,' as Sarah called it. Tell families throughout Victoria that we are gathering in the hills. We need to do this, Welkin."

The whole idea created turmoil in Welkin's mind. The one overriding factor was that at last they would be in a position to attack for a change. Perhaps spreading Sarah's teaching would keep the memory of her alive a little bit longer.

"I guess you'll need volunteers," he said when he realized they were all staring at him expectantly.

"We're basically it," Harry said. "Lucida will stay behind with Zedda, Budge, and Con. The rest of us are going with Elab."

"Good luck," Welkin said and left them.

When he closed the door, silence fell over the Committee like a shroud.

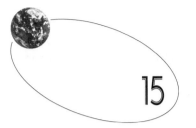

15

Gillian, Patrick, and Mira had made slow progress until the time the three had settled their differences. They had agreed to an uneasy alliance, since their goals were mutual.

Patrick now took the lead, and they headed back along a well trodden track. They didn't walk directly on the rutted, weed-strewn asphalt path but rather stuck to its ill-defined borders, where at least there were no tangled trees and thick vines sticking through the tar. Patrick seldom had to use the machete, and more than once he simply made a detour to bypass some hulking obstacle like a fallen copper beech.

Each kept to his or her own thoughts at first. Mira cursed their bad luck. They'd deliberately left early so as not to attract attention, but Gillian had had similar motives. The Committee girl was cute, if somewhat headstrong, and smart. Mira knew that despite his reservations, Patrick had taken a shine to her. But even he couldn't ignore the fact that a Committee person traveling alone seemed out of place. The united family cosseted its Committee, which comprised mainly personnel chosen by Sarah herself. Why would the girl want to travel with two itinerants out here in the scrub where it was everyone for himself? Her last thought on Gillian ran deep in her subconscious. She rued their earlier admissions to Gillian regarding their plans for entering the Stockade.

Mira rested her hand on the empty scabbard where she normally housed the machete. Gillian's appearance was certainly a spot of bad luck.

Patrick's thoughts were less hostile. He counted Gillian as an extra ally with whom to fight a cunning foe. Their plans had now changed quite dramatically. Maybe they could sneak into the Stockade as people down on their luck, forced to beg or steal to live. They had been there before on many occasions, of course, but had remained as inconspicuous as possible. With luck, this one last time, they would arrive unnoticed.

Once inside they would separate, giving Mira and Gillian a chance to pretend to be girls of easy virtue to gain access to Bruick's private quarters. Even so, his bodyguards might prevent their leaving when and if the girls managed to kill him. Patrick's mind was in a constant turmoil as to just how far he and Mira could trust Gillian.

Patrick's eyes sought the slopes in the middle distance. Maybe he and Mira should tell Gillian everything. Just sit her down and tell her the facts. He cursed his indecision. What should he do? "Play it by ear if anything goes wrong," Sarah had said.

"All very well," Patrick mumbled to himself, but what if your intuition is wrong?

Gillian could sense their unease. It would be best for her to abandon the couple when they were within bowshot of the Stockade. She could disappear into the scrub and take her chances. But this turn in thought made her feel selfish, even treacherous.

Gillian's mind was in turmoil the three days it took them to reach Bruick's Stockade. On more than one occasion she suspected that they were being followed. Patrick and Mira had laughed off her suspicions. Nonetheless, she remained alert to any possibility.

The Stockade looked forbidding etched against the last dying rays of the sun, a huge, bleak monstrosity of ill-matched bluestone and mortar that seemed at odds with any beauty that remained in its proximity.

It had been here that Franciscan friars had built their fortified winery against an increasingly violent populace round about 2110. They hadn't stopped the virus that had attacked the vines and withered the grapes before they ripened. Later, they turned their hand to building a self-contained society, but they had deserted the castle when their vineyards were laid waste. It had then become a rural retreat, so the hand-me-down stories said. In the early twenty-second century the castle had been laid siege to by various roaming gangs shortly after the Great Whiteout.

Assisi, as it was then known, had fallen into disrepair. It had been pillaged and its precious artifacts removed. But now, as Gillian's eyes took in the towering turrets and the bleak shingle roofing, she thought Bruick had restored it to its former glory. She pondered that thought. No, he'd probably taken it away from those who had done the restoration.

"It's the festive week with much partying going on," Patrick said beside her. "They'll be nay looking too closely at the likes of us."

As Patrick and Mira started to move on, Gillian reminded them to disarm, as no one was allowed inside the castle walls carrying arms.

"Aye," Patrick said uncomfortably. He unslung his bow and quiver and disappeared into the foliage. Mira followed him.

Now was as good a time as any for Gillian to slip into the Stockade. But something held her back. Perhaps it was best to stay together.

Gillian waited awhile. It was evening and the air was fragrant with the scent of eucalyptus. There was a distant rise and fall of the sound of voices and musical instruments. It seemed the jabbers were reveling in the festivities.

Gillian suddenly became alarmed. She had been daydreaming. "Patrick?" she called. "Mira?" She cursed herself when she realized that rather than deserting her, they had simply left her behind!

She moved quickly then. If Patrick and Mira had been spies for Bruick, she would have little hope of eluding the gate guards, but there still might be time.

She slowed as she came within sight of the portcullis guards. They looked exactly as Sarah had described them. A rough lot: dreadlocks, pieces of metal hanging from every conceivable piece of skin, gross tattoos etched across their faces. The two guards at the gate seemed particularly loathsome, wearing rank leather jackets that could at any moment have climbed off their backs and walked away.

One guard stuck out his tongue provocatively at Gillian, who pretended to ignore him. One jump sideways, left knee raised just so, a straight jab, and her foot would wind up five inches into his stomach. She itched to do it but kept walking.

On the surface the garrison seemed happy enough. The mall resounded with laughter and the cries of vendors advertising their produce. Gillian paused before entering the melee. She noted the western wall where she figured Bruick might reside. It seemed the most imposing of the Stockade's dwellings: a two-tiered affair of bluestone slabs, narrow leaded windows, and solid double doors that were reached by climbing flagstoned steps.

There were no guards on the towering, crenellated wall girthing the Stockade; the battlements themselves seemed insurmountable. Gillian noted the single exit—there was no back door to this place. But there was a certain complacency in the air that could prove to be the Stockade's undoing.

Dusk had arrived. Thick, scudding clouds had darkened the sky, and already the generators were being fueled for the coming night. Lights flickered on uncertainly, and a cheer went up.

Gillian scowled enviously at the opulence Bruick enjoyed. Not for Sarah's people the extravagance of electric lights and immunity from *Colony* attack. In her at that moment burned an all-consuming rage that propelled her forward with a determination that would later frighten her.

She was jostled the moment she entered the throng. Every available space was used by vendors selling everything from earthenware jars to precious foodstuffs, trinkets, and bolts of fabric. The sight kept Gillian's rage at boiling point. Sarah had tried so hard and these people had simply opted for Bruick because he wasn't troubled by *Colony* constantly attacking him. Bruick enjoyed immunity because he had betrayed the Earthborn. And these people here with him were no better.

Surprised at her own vehemence, she strove to put on a cheerful face. A sad girl amid so much merriment might cause suspicion. She was only too well aware that she might be recognized. Sarah's sister would be a great prize.

Her first port of call was obviously the tavern. It had a most unsavory reputation and was unsafe for any girl to enter unaccompanied by a man; that much she had heard. But she needed to get the feel of the place before she carried out her plan.

She stood on tiptoes to see above the crowd but soon gave up trying. She'd been pushed into the mud twice already and nearly trampled to death by people either too unfeeling to care or sadistic enough to kick someone when she was down.

Either way, she used her elbows more than once to force her way to the edge of the square. With her back against the rough-hewn walls she finally circumnavigated the marketplace and almost fell into the doorway of an alehouse. She ducked back as a potbellied taverner waddled past with a wine barrel slung precariously across his shoulder.

The tavern was like nothing she had ever imagined. The clientele was bawdy, with men shoving one another while others staggered around with flushed faces, leering at the skimpily dressed girls. Several girls about Gillian's age flounced about, seemingly oblivious to the jeers and taunts of the male patrons.

The people here were everything Gillian had been brought up to despise in humans. The fumes of acrid smoke and the reek of stale sweat assailed her; the urge to gag was strong.

" 'Ere," someone said, and Gillian was wrenched around and pulled roughly into the barrel chest of a leering bearded man. His foul breath made her pull back as far as his grip would allow.

Gillian smiled uncertainly. He was as likely a provider of information as any in this foul place, although she knew an urgent desire to knee him in the groin.

"What's a lovely like you doin' 'ere, then?" He smiled a toothless, rancid smile. His fingers twirled her matted hair and drew her forward so they were nose to nose.

Lifted slightly off her feet, Gillian strained to maintain her balance. "Bruick," she said brusquely. "I've been bonded to Bruick."

The man flung her from him as though she were a snake. He looked around hastily to ensure no one had seen their brief exchange. "You're in the wrong place, girl. He not be seen in the likes of this 'ole." He nodded to the great oak door that was slightly ajar. " 'Cross the square. Joint called the Maiden Flower." He laughed and looked her up and down appreciatively. "Foxy thing, aintcha?"

Gillian gave him a wisp of a smile and backed out of the room, but not before suffering several insults from foul-mouthed youths.

"Sweet meat!"

"Giz a bit!"

"New talent I bet!"

Gillian gasped and fled the tavern to roars of laughter.

Flushed and enraged, she staggered against a railing. Even out here the square was filled with thick smoke from the myriad cooking fires. Pigs were being turned on spits over giant forty-gallon drums; musicians were banging on any tin they could scavenge. The music bore no resemblance to anything she had ever heard, a sporadic banging of rock on metal, or blocks of wood being bashed together in some parody of a percussion band.

Gillian hated these people at that moment. The desire to lash out almost overcame her reason. She blundered through the press of bodies until she came to the nearest wall and crouched down in its shadow, forcing herself to breathe slowly. As a semblance of calm returned, she felt the inside of her buskin. The blade was still there, hidden inside the leather lining. She stroked it for reassurance.

Well, better now than never, she thought. She took a deep breath and got up. She edged her away around the square and down an alleyway beside the Maiden Flower.

She had no plan beyond ridding the world of Bruick. That he could be easily replaced by someone just as vile hadn't entered her mind. All she knew was that her sister had died trying to bring peace to the world, while Bruick had brought nothing but misery. Well, she planned to bring some misery of her own tonight!

At least she didn't feel conspicuous as she was swept along with the tide of carousing merrymakers. It was no hard task to swirl to one side as she passed a doorway and slip inside. When the door closed behind her, she realized she was in the kitchen. The smell of cooking oil was strong, the aroma wafting from a giant stewing pot. She stepped beside it and twirled the wooden spoon, which moved sluggishly as though through thick soup.

She was suddenly reminded that she hadn't eaten for a day now.

She quickly ladled a spoonful out, blew heartily, and swallowed. The broth wasn't as bad as she had expected. She'd swallowed three more mouthfuls when a voice behind her made her start.

"There ye be, wench. Git a move on, will ye,'fore the lord flails ye alive."

Gillian regained her composure and turned with wide-eyed innocence. "But I'm new t' th' job, master," she said in slang. "There's been naught instruction on me chores."

The chef closed his eyes in exasperation. "The plates, girl. Take the plates an' take 'em up yonder stairs. Ye knock first, ye hear? Else ye'll lose ye hand sure as that," he said, making a chopping motion across his wrist.

"Aye, master," Gillian whispered timidly. Her heart was pounding heavily as she was ushered past the guard at the base of the stairs. She felt the eyes of the patrons appraise her as she swept past the top stair and halted at the first door on the right.

She glanced around, then banged resoundingly on the door. A muffled voice bade her enter. She balanced the tray of steaming broth with one hand and turned the wooden knob.

She had taken only two steps inside before the tray was taken roughly from her hands and she was knocked sideways.

She crashed against the wooden paneling and bounced headlong onto the floor. The side of her face went numb and a ringing filled her ear; the rest of her was beginning to paralyze with the shock of what had hit her.

"Aye, Master Bruick. That'd be the wench," said Patrick O'Shannessey.

Despite her reeling vision she managed to scramble up into a crouch, but firm hands clamped down on her from behind. "Traitors!" she spat.

"Watch her!" Mira warned.

Hands went straight to her left buskin and withdrew her knife. It clattered across the floor to where Patrick and Mira moved from its path as though it were a striking snake.

Gillian saw a man in his late teens hitch his pants and move slowly toward her. He was the ugliest person she had ever laid eyes on. A crucifix had been crudely tattooed on his forehead, and there was a livid scar etched across his throat. Pieces of metal hung from his cheeks, lips, nose, and ears like fishhooks. He had a sharply cut black goatee that had straggles of gray in it. His clothes were threadbare and held together by a patchwork of safety pins.

"Me Bruick," he said mockingly. "What's *your* name, my little pretty?"

Gillian snarled. She looked past Bruick to where Patrick and Mira stood well back. They had no doubt guessed at her deadly intent as she scrambled to her feet. She exhaled sharply as hands like claws dug into her shoulders and her arm was twisted painfully behind her back.

"It's her, all right," Patrick said from the corner. "Gillian. Sister of Sarah."

"You're dead," Gillian said icily. "All of you. Dead."

Bruick smirked. This gesture was an invitation for the others in the room to share his pleasure. Gillian counted five, plus maybe two behind her. She noted with fleeting satisfaction that Patrick and Mira appeared worried.

"Dead?" Bruick said. "I hear your big sister is dead."

Gillian writhed against the hands that restrained her. Her knife was tantalizingly close, but it might as well have been in the next galaxy.

Bruick frowned. He reached out and pinched Gillian's chin and brought her face around to catch the candlelight. "Yeah, I do see a little of your sister in you," he said. "The eyes, mostly. And maybe the nose." He followed her gaze to the knife on the floor. " 'Course, the temper speaks for itself, don't it, Gillian? Bad-tempered little thing. Like your dead dumb sister."

Gillian shook her head free of Bruick's hand. Her now swollen cheek began to throb. "You wouldn't know a thing about her," she said. "She was always too good for your sort."

Bruick's eyes widened and a smile touched his thin lips. "Is that right? Your sister and I go back a long way, little girl. Before you were even dragged into the world."

Gillian's heart began to thump. Earlier, he had seemed to be toying with her, but now his mood had suddenly changed. His pupils narrowed to points, like those of a predator.

Held totally immobile, she could hardly twist her head to one side as Bruick kneeled down and came close to her face. His breath blew in short, ragged snorts that stank.

Gillian was aware of the metallic taste of her blood as it leaked from her lacerated cheek. She figured she'd lost a tooth, too.

Bruick ran his fingertips across her face. Then, as though having lost interest, he stood up. "Of course, now I have the problem of what to do with you." He turned to the others, firing off questions. "Why did she come here? Who sent her? What shall we do with her? Is she any good to us alive?"

His men muttered various replies.

Bruick spun back to her, plainly excited. He licked saliva from his lips. "The jury can't reach a unanimous decision. The judge decrees you be placed in the dungeons till I'm good and ready."

Gillian was yanked roughly to her feet and swung about.

"Don't damage her too much," Bruick warned her captors. "She hasn't been found guilty. Yet."

She spat blood at him, but it fell short. Her arm exploded with pain as it was jerked behind her back. Clawing hands grabbed her hair, yanking her head back and exposing her taut neck.

What Bruick did next filled her mind with a seething red mist. He laughed. She could still hear the sound of his triumph as she was dragged through the tavern and into the cellar below.

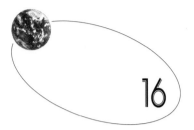

16

The crowd had been waiting expectantly for Welkin to emerge from the Committee room. When he closed the door behind him it was something of a letdown. Instead of the usual speech after an important Committee meeting, Welkin simply smiled thinly and headed straight to his hut.

Elab watched the door close behind Welkin. No one said anything. After a moment, Zocky got up and went outside to make the customary speech. She was good at it.

Before Elab knew it, the others had left the table and he found himself pondering his team.

There was Devan. Elab had watched him grow these past few months. He was cautious, part Asian and stubborn as a mule, and once he'd made up his mind about something, that was it. Not a likable trait in a team member, but, like Gillian, it seemed the kid was often right.

There was Lars. Now Elab could easily have done without him. Quick to anger, he was nonetheless the strongest of the team and a damn good shot with the bow. He'd accounted for eight troopers and one heavy already, nearly "ace" status by Elab's reckoning. If he could just keep Lars busy, he'd be an excellent addition to the expedition.

There was Zocky. She was a little headstrong, like Lars, but with a fierce determination to prove herself better than any man. Elab smiled. She'd be constantly at odds with Lars, and that wasn't such a bad thing.

Then there was Harry, good, old, reliable Harry. It was hard to believe they'd been enemies in *Colony*'s lower decks. Without a doubt, he was the best man to have watching your back.

Within two days of the Committee's decision to send him to Melbourne, Elab squatted on the floor of his hut, surrounded by his team. He'd already drawn up a rough map of their journey as he perceived it. Sarah's few maps had been incomplete, often illegible, and extended only as far north as a place called Albury.

The faces he saw about him were eager enough. In fact they had shown signs of restlessness lately. They were anxious to get out past Melbourne before the first of the spring raids on their camp.

Because Sarah's map was irreplaceable, Elab had taken the precaution of sketching out the first leg of their journey. The lines he had made in the hard-packed earth resembled a kid's scribbling, but this was a serious business and no one cared.

"This line," he said, pointing to a broad horizontal band, "is what was called the Great Dividing Range. According to the map it's just like the Dandenongs, but I think much bigger." Judging by the map it was once the backbone of the eastern states. But the Hum Highway used to go right through it. He shrugged off any doubts. "No telling, but I think before the Great Whiteout people used to go there all the time, which means it's not going to be inaccessible."

"Doesn't look that far away," Zocky said absently. When she saw the others roll their eyes, she said, "By cruiser, of course."

"Yeah," Lars said sardonically, "I seen you ride one once. Didn't sit down for a week if I remember right." He nudged Devan, who grinned.

"Did too!" Zocky snorted.

"Okay," Elab interjected. "Committee's going to provide us with a laser—"

"One?!" Lars said incredulously. "We've recovered a dozen still charged."

"And we're four and the family is over a hundred." Elab shook his head. "They've got kids to care for, Lars. Besides, we'll be well armed." He looked at them each in turn. "We're possibly the most able-bodied group in the family."

With his knife Elab gouged out the route he intended taking.

"The Hum Highway," Zocky guessed correctly.

"Maybe it sang," Devan joked.

"It's a bit of a hike to get to it," Elab said thoughtfully. "But according to the map it will take us right through the range."

"Will it be safe?" Devan asked. "I mean, we usually keep well clear of the old roads. *Colony* seems to use them as reference points."

"*Colony* won't be looking for us any farther than this," Elab said, pointing to a large bend in the Yarra River. Once we're across that we'll just be another small family wandering about. Sure, if they see us we'll lie low till they pass."

"What if the river's still swollen?" Lars asked.

Before Elab could reply, Harry said, "We'll build a raft." A smirk creased his features. "Piece of cake. We've done *that* before."

They sat there all afternoon discussing the pros and cons of their journey. By dusk Elab figured they'd all worked through the various options, as well as Lars's numerous objections. Whatever their chances of finding *Colony* mutineers, he couldn't imagine doing it with a finer bunch of kids.

"I guess that's it, then," he said. The others stood as he sheathed his knife. "We move out in the morning. I'd suggest getting an early night."

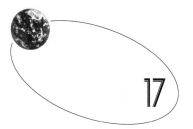

17

Welkin was annoyed at the predicament he found himself in. He ran a hand through his knotted hair and smacked himself reproachfully on the forehead.

After trekking through the bush for three days, he now crouched outside the walls of the Stockade. The mottled gum tree he hid behind was no windbreak against the fierce gusts that tore across the range grass. He shivered in his misery and wondered how long he should wait until going in after Gillian.

It would be only a matter of time before he was discovered. Just this morning he'd seen a small party, ten strong, leave the fort at a trot. At first he thought they were looking for him but then realized they had simply been secretive and therefore wary of anyone knowing their movements. They'd dispersed at the forest's fringe and regrouped farther inland.

Welkin had followed them for a short distance. They seemed to be heading west, either toward the united family or maybe beyond. *Colony?* It wasn't such an unlikely guess.

He felt a strong urge to follow them, find out where they were going and why, but he couldn't leave without making sure Gillian was okay.

Then he spotted Bruick in the group, and the doubt returned. Could he possibly be planning an attack on the family? Surely he would take more fighters with him? So it must be *Colony*. Welkin was tempted to get Bruick right now, and his hand even went mechanically to his quiver to find an arrow.

But something stayed his hand. Memories of Gillian, her gamin smile and sometimes laconic nature. "Damn," he cursed and held his head down until the smell of the grass made him sneeze.

He'd been waiting out here a day and a night, reconnoitering. His stomach was knotted tight, and the few insects and berries he'd managed to swallow had made him feel ill—so much so he reckoned it safer not to eat anything.

The festivities in Bruick's Stockade had quieted down. The sun had sunk beneath the horizon, leaving behind it a red sky marked by dark angry clouds.

He didn't intend staying out here another night. Being a Skyborn had its disadvantages. His stocky legs were a dead giveaway, and he had no means of covering them right now. He'd considered joining revelers as they entered the Stockade, but that was too risky.

The gates were closed every night and guards posted. He was confident of dispatching the guards easily enough, but the locked gates, now that was another matter entirely.

His weathered face creased in concern. Why in Space had Gillian gone there in the first place? But then, just about everything about the girl confused him. No chance she'd ever want to bond with him, of course—she treated him much as Lucida did. Even so, they'd slept side by side and shared a lot of good and bad times. He felt an ache in his stomach at the prospect of never seeing her again. And he got really anxious when he saw her talking to Lars or Devan.

Welkin took a deep breath and forced himself to relax. He shook his head, undecided how to proceed. Most of the mounting tension slipped from his face. He unclenched his jaw muscles and knew right there and then that tonight was the night to be Starbound, or Earthbound, or whatever happened to the Skyborn who died on Earth.

He waited an hour after the great creaking iron gates were closed and the sentries lit the torches that cast flickering shadows. He then moved stealthily forward.

Much closer now, Welkin scanned the defenses. He knew that climbing over the razor wire that clung to the parapets like poison ivy was suicidal. That left the front gate with the sentries.

His mind made up, he sneaked forward.

Gillian glared at the guard as he deposited a bowl of gruel under the cell door. Unappetizing as it was, Gillian knew she needed to maintain her strength if she was going to get out of this place. She could expect no help from the family. She'd gone on this one alone, and that was the way it would end.

The green gruel in the basin didn't look as if it held much nutrition, but it was better than nothing. She settled herself against a wall, groaning. Every movement woke a pain in her. She'd come through the ordeal reasonably well, so far. She had a tooth missing and miscellaneous aches and pains, and she knew she had a black eye.

She'd gone over every brick in the dungeon, examined the solid bluestone foundation, and found nothing. There was no way out. The guards never once came into the cell, so any hope of overpowering them was out of the question.

Gillian had tried to make conversation with the various jailors who had brought her food, but they'd maintained a stony silence as though they were somehow afraid of her. None of it made sense. She brought the bowl to her lips. She'd taken a quick sip before realizing that the guard was staring at her.

He grinned a toothless grin.

Gillian would have loved to have had the luxury of throwing the food at him, but she needed it too badly.

Unable to get a reaction from his captive, he pushed himself away from the cell, and Gillian listened as he stalked off into the darkness.

It wouldn't be long now before one of her visitors was Bruick.

She'd contemplated robbing him of any joy by committing suicide. But she quickly discarded that option. No matter how dire her predicament became, she wouldn't give up life until her body gave it up for her.

She held her breath and upended the bowl's contents into her mouth. It slipped down her throat like slime—a continuing length of connected fluid that passed along her throat like a gelatinous snake.

It made her gag a little, but she was determined to hold down the food. She dry-retched for a moment, but the food stayed down.

She paced the dungeon for the rest of the afternoon. Each step was a sharp reminder of her injuries, but she knew she couldn't just sit still and wait for something to happen. She never was one for idleness.

Gillian raised her head at a muffled sound. It was hard for her to tell the time, but it was late at night, the middle of the night, maybe, when she heard a scuffle along the corridor. It sounded like someone being dragged along the straw-strewn cobbles.

Gillian clenched the bars and peered into the dark. The door at the top of a short flight of stairs swung open and a body was shoved through. It rolled limply down the steps and sprawled in the muck at the base. She knew how *that* must have hurt. The guards had tossed her down the same stairs.

Two dark shapes detached themselves from the doorway and bustled down the stairs.

"Gillian!"

It was Patrick's voice. The other figure had to be Mira. Gillian stepped back from the bars. It had to be a trap.

"Gillian! Quickly, girl. Where you at?" Patrick whispered anxiously.

"She's in here!" Mira called to him. Her voice sounded strained and afraid.

"What's the matter with you, girl?" Patrick admonished. He held a ring of keys aloft and tried inserting the wrong key. "Which key?" he demanded.

"Come to finish off the job?" Gillian asked through her cracked lips.

Patrick gave her a quick, questioning look. "I've no time to explain meself to you, girl. We did best we could under the circumstances." He rattled the key ring. "What do you say? Which one?"

"It's the diamond-headed key," Gillian said. She managed to keep her tone neutral. No telling what to expect from this pair.

The door swung on rusting hinges. It was Mira who came in and placed Gillian's arm over her shoulder and gently helped her to the door.

Patrick had already hefted the limp body of the guard and thrown him on the bunk, draping the burlap bedcloth over him.

"Won't keep the jabbers guessing long," Patrick said when he reached them. "But time enough for us to make good our escape."

Gillian went rigid. "I'm not going from here until I've settled a score."

Mira's grip on Gillian tightened. Gillian didn't have the strength to resist.

"If it's Bruick's death you're after," Patrick said, "he's gone."

"You're lying."

"No," Mira interrupted. "He left this morning at first light. Took a party of ten. No telling what path they took once they got in them trees."

Gillian's temper erupted again. "All this for nothing," she croaked.

"Not if we get him out there," Patrick said.

The coldness of his voice chilled Gillian. "We'll never catch up to him if he left this morning," she said.

"And we'll nay catch him on his way back if we lark about in here," Mira reminded them.

"I can't move too fast," Gillian replied in a choked voice. Every word she uttered through her split lips was a fresh torment.

"They're animals is what they are," Patrick said with venom. "It's blacker than sin in here," he cursed. "Hold that lantern so, Mira," he added. Satisfied, he moved them on up another flight of stairs that led out to a narrow winding corridor. Despite their efforts to move silently, their footfalls on stone rang like muffled shots.

Mira swung the softly glowing lantern toward Gillian and gave her a quick look. "Your mouth's a mess. And you've black coals for eyes. But they've nay treated you too badly."

Gillian smiled grimly. Sleep deprivation, malnutrition, and being incarcerated in a dank and dark dungeon seemed bad enough to her.

If Mira had been expecting a reply from Gillian, it wasn't forthcoming.

A gushing wind whistled through the rafters as rain fell on the shingled roof. It started as a light patter—like the feet of tiny birds scrabbling about—then the deluge came, a sudden roar that drowned out any attempt at conversation.

Patrick led them to a great oak door, unlatched the bolt, and pulled the door slightly ajar. Looking across the curtain of rain, they could see the portcullis. It was all that was separating them from freedom.

Patrick ushered Mira and Gillian forward. "Quickly now," he said needlessly.

Welkin stretched his elbow back as far as it would go. He knew there would be no second chances. He released his fingers, and the bowstring vibrated as it snapped taut.

The arrow went true. Even as Welkin watched the man spin in a confused circle and fall, he was nocking the second arrow and pulling back the string.

He followed the line of the arrow and veered the bow to the left. The other sentry had taken one step forward, completely bewildered, then dived for cover.

Welkin released the arrow. It sang through the air as the clouds opened up. It was hard to see, but Welkin knew either the man had stumbled or his arrow had caused him to fall to one side.

Welkin gained the shelter of the Stockade wall as torrential rain hit. Bad timing on his part. There were two bodies, and he dragged the larger of them under cover of the awning and removed the man's cloak. The oilskin wasn't a good fit, but it would have to do—he needed protection from the rain.

Welkin peered around the corner to seek out more sentries, and he thought he could see shadowy forms flitting about in the poor light. Flattened against the wall, he wished all this was over. His teeth chattered, then his pulse quickened at a new sound.

First it sounded as though someone was in the guardhouse. The door squeaked shut, then someone cursed beneath his breath near the gate, rattling the heavy metal latch that resisted being opened without a key.

"Guards," called an angry voice. "Open up the damn gate. Let us out, for God's sake. We've urgent news for Bruick and must overtake him tonight!"

Welkin glanced down at the two bodies. He withdrew his dagger. Hands clutching the guard's keys, he stepped up to the gate.

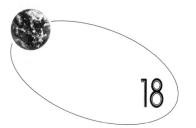

18

Elab watched his breath vaporize as he waited for his team to assemble on the path from the settlement. The last snow was melting into the ground, leaving only pockets of slush as evidence of its passing.

"So I'm late," Lars announced carelessly.

"Don't start," Zocky said.

Elab held up his hand. His team quieted. He surveyed each of them: Lars, Zocky, Devan, and Harry. They seemed too few for such a formidable mission. Elab wondered for the briefest moment whether they knew what they were volunteering for. More important, did they know how few of them would return?

"It's all downhill from here," he quipped. "Let's move out."

Few saw them passing. The Committee had in fact let it be known that Elab's team would be leaving the day after next. The last thing they wanted was for Bruick to be able to lay an ambush for them in the foothills.

Each in turn looked back at the settlement as they left its precincts. None had any commitment other than the survival of the family. They were the loners, and although their passing would be missed, each knew his or her place would be easily filled.

They left via well-used trails that meandered through the scrub-covered hills. From the outset Elab had allotted each a position in the team. Lars was to go forward and sniff out problems that might arise, Devan was to follow up at the rear, both Harry and Zocky were flankers, while Elab acted as backup should any problems arise.

It took several days for the team to reach the base of the mountains. Elab was pleased with their progress. Lars had been the only worry to date. Since he was up front, he'd made it plain to the others that he should determine the routes they would travel.

As it was, Elab had given the laser to Lars. He'd figured Lars was the most capable and he was leading the way, so that was fair enough.

"We follow the map," Elab said. His eyes were flint hard. He could stare anyone down in seconds. It was a trick he'd learned back in the lower decks of *Colony*.

Lars glared at him. Then he turned to the others. "The map's *old*." The last word wasn't lost on Elab or the others. "And things change, Elab. There are rivers here now that aren't on the map, for chrissake. So you have us wade through swollen rivers rather than find alternative routes. It's crazy, guys."

"You'd rather have us go farther and farther north and wind up weeks away from where we're heading?" Elab asked. "Just so you don't get wet, Lars?"

"We got drenched last night because we were out in the open when we could've been farther west and maybe found shelter."

"Maybe," Elab acknowledged. "Maybe not." He held up his hand to silence Lars's obvious retort. "There's good reason for following Sarah's map. Its chief purpose is to save us time. If it leads us astray every now and then, I reckon it's nothing compared to what'd happen if we went off without firm direction."

That should have ended further discussion, but Lars still hounded Elab from time to time. "Just to keep him on his toes," he told the others when they complained of his behavior.

While Lars proved to be a minor nuisance, the others got along well with Elab. Harry had clearly put a lot of forethought into their journey. He'd brought along several strands of wire that he'd fashioned into fishhooks. He also made a couple of fishing rods with fine gut and a sapling.

"Hooray!" Zocky trilled one morning when Harry's line hauled in a wriggling mottled gray shape.

"It's only an eel," Lars said. "I'm not eating that."

"More for us," Zocky replied.

Lars sneered as they watched it thrashing in the green water, its mouth torn jagged by the makeshift hook.

Harry jerked the rod up and the eel landed squirming on the muddy bank. Zocky pounced on it and sliced off its head. She held the limp eel for all to see. "Our first kill of the season!"

Encouraged by their success, Devan and Zocky took turns sharing the other rod.

Within the hour they had snared three eels and something that looked vaguely like a trout.

"It's all fished out," Zocky announced triumphantly. She'd laid out the fillets on a large frond.

"We'll salt what we don't want right now," Elab said. "Dig in."

"Bon appetit," Devan said. When the others laughed he felt his cheeks flush. "What's the matter? Did I say it wrong?"

"You did well," Elab said through a smile and a mouthful of fish. "Better get some of that trout fast—Lars reckons it's the best."

"Just don't like raw eel," Lars said moodily.

They rarely cooked anything, for fear of alerting renegades. If they'd had more time, Elab would have shown them how to cook in the ground, creating little telltale smoke, but it was simply a chance that they could not afford to take. Besides, they had all eaten worse food than raw fish.

The dense bush made for slow progress. Elab caught glimpses of the others as they filtered through the towering she-oaks and eucalypti that now studded the foothills. They'd long since given up the customary waving to one another.

Elab had forgotten how fresh and green the slopes could be once spring arrived. In winter the ghostlike white, mottled trunks of the red-spotted gums made a beautiful sight. Soon, as spring followed winter, their midgreen, lancelike leaves would start to bud. Already the various acacias were in full flower. Their pale lemon and golden blossoms bathed the slopes in a blaze of color. Elab pondered deeply on the wattle's significance, but try as he might he couldn't place it. The fact that it was the floral emblem of Australia had been forgotten by the Earthborn a generation ago.

They'd had no trouble coming down the slopes. Zocky had reported three skeletons she'd found strewn around a long-dead camp-fire. Under other circumstances Elab might have spared time to investigate, but Zocky had assured him that whatever fate had befallen the trio, its cause was long gone.

Apart from the fish they caught Devan had been lucky enough to fell a wild boar. Devan insisted that they roast it, and his adamancy fired the others. Elab relented when he saw their anticipation of a good cooked meal and allowed them to roast it. They were out of immediate danger now, due to the coverage that the trees on the lower slope afforded them. Higher up anyone with powerful binoculars could have followed their path day by day, plotted their course, and had time to organize a welcoming committee had they been hostile.

The party encountered few fellow travelers. They would exchange polite greetings as strangers do, but since Sarah's disappearance a certain wariness had crept back into the smaller families.

As night fell Elab apologized as he kicked out the fiercely burning fire. The pig was just about cooked anyway, but they could not afford to highlight their presence. The smell alone would carry well into the night on the strong northerly wind that had picked up late that afternoon.

It was left to Lars to cut up the meat and hand out sections of it to the others. He had a skillful way with knives that sometimes worried Elab. As the dying embers of the fire lit their faces, Elab could see the glimmering of a smile on Lars's face as he sliced through the meat with his keen blade.

That night Elab lay awake, listening to the mournful wind as it rustled through the trees. Somewhere farther afield a feral cat yowled across the valley. It was joined by another and another. If the screaming woke any of the others, they didn't show it. Probably couldn't hear it above Lars's snoring, Elab reckoned.

He looked up at the night sky and traced where he imagined the Southern Cross to be etched against infinite space. One thing for sure, he'd never be up there again. He was surprised to realize that he had no desire to travel into space again. He'd found his home here on Earth.

He wished so much that he could let the *Colony* people know how much the elders had deceived them. He desperately wanted them to smell the pollens in the air, feel the brisk breeze as it swept over the range grass, to know adventure and friendship. Most of all, he wanted them to know the thrill of uncertainty. That was the biggest buzz of all. To be unsure what the next day would bring.

They woke early next morning. Elab wasn't in the least surprised to see Zocky cuddled up hard against Harry. They were opposites in personality and stature, but they certainly went well together.

What did surprise Elab was the way Lars regarded the couple. He seemed to be brooding. He then saw Elab appraising him and got up. "Been a long night. Almost fell asleep a couple of times. But Jeez, it's cold."

Elab said nothing. They woke the others and, after a hurried cold pork breakfast, they set off.

They followed the map north and were glad the landscape finally leveled out east of Melbourne. They had some miles of climbing to do now, but it marked, at least in their minds, the real beginning of their trip. They were no longer in family territory.

The sun made an appearance, dispelling any fears that it might rain, despite the dark clouds overhead.

"You could easily get lost out here," Zocky said. Her quick smile indicated it was only a thought and not to be taken seriously.

"Not if we follow the map." Elab's voice was firm. "We know Melbourne's over there," he said, pointing west. "Basically all we need do now is go forward."

"And we keep going until there's nowhere else to go," Lars said.

"That's what you volunteered for," Elab reminded him. He scanned the others for further comment. No one responded.

As they set off, Elab fell into silent melancholy, wondering why he had volunteered for this expedition. If the Skyborn renegades *had* fled *Colony*, there was no telling where they had gone. Why, if they'd had enough fuel and supplies, they could have left the continent altogether.

What then? No one had the desire to cross a sea in the kind of flimsy ships their present level of technology could produce. It was going to be bad enough rafting white waters if the Yarra was over-flowing.

Elab had pulled in the flanking scouts and brought Devan up from the rear; in this terrain it would be easy to lose contact with one another. They followed long forgotten roads where possible and left them only when they deviated from their chosen course. Quite often they came upon the same road some hours later after having hacked through a mile of bushland. It made Elab wish fervently that they'd had street directories as well.

It was well into late afternoon when Lars, who had gone on ahead, came crashing back through the dense bracken. It was so sudden that Zocky and Elab instinctively strung their bows and reached for their arrows.

"There's a settlement down there!"

"So there's a settlement," Harry said, sighing heavily. "Ohmistars, Lars, you almost gave us heart failure, rushing back like that."

Lars straightened up. "So why don't *you* lead the way, Harry?"

Harry shrugged. "Will if you like. But don't expect me to get all excited about finding a family. Bound to be heaps about."

"Not like this one," Lars said. He gestured back the way he'd come. "Go see for yourself."

The settlement was a haphazard affair of tiny shacks built into the slope. Their corrugated iron roofs were specked with rust against the yellow clay background. There were about eight of the dwellings, varying in size, mostly made from rough-hewn wood and bark. There was little sign of agriculture and nothing to indicate human presence.

"Don't see anything too odd about it," Harry said. He sought confirmation from the others. "Can't see anyone. That's not too strange."

"They're not hiding," Lars said somberly. He pointed to the left of the largest building.

Harry's right eye twitched as it normally did when he was nervous. He wrinkled his nose. The air was laden with a smell he couldn't place. And deathly quiet as though nature itself had fled. He wished Lars would stop his game and tell them what he'd seen.

Zocky was the first to respond. "Bodies?" Her skin goose-pimpled.

"There're a dozen of them," Devan said uneasily. He moved forward like an automaton. "Everyone's been killed."

"Maybe not everyone," Elab warned. He alone remained calm. "Keep it down. Whoever did this might still be around." He pushed Devan to the left and Harry to the right. They responded sluggishly to his command, then slowly took up their battle positions. Zocky nodded in reply to Elab's silent order to tail them.

Elab and Lars moved down the slope. The hair on Elab's arms and head bristled. He had the distinct and unpleasant feeling that he was walking to his death.

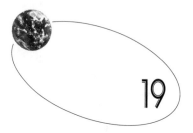

19

Using the guard's key, Welkin unlocked the gate of Bruick's fortress from outside. Fortunately for Patrick, he hesitated a split second before thrusting his knife toward the three emerging figures. Patrick spun back and bumped into Mira, who seemed to be supporting the third figure.

"Gillian?" cried Welkin. She had on oilskins identical to the sentries and looked deathly pale. Even with poor visibility Welkin could see the bruises on her face and caked blood around her lips. "What have they done to you?"

"There's nay time for talk," Patrick said urgently. He'd recognized the Skyborn immediately. But already a dog was yapping intermittently above the thrumming downpour.

Welkin stepped forward and took over from Mira. Gillian collapsed against him as he supported her full weight. He bent down and lifted her with both arms. He nodded for Patrick and Mira to get going. They paused and locked the gate behind them. The jabbers would no doubt have a spare key, but it should hold them for a bit. No one moved about much in the rain unless he absolutely had to.

Patrick spent precious moments locating their weapons while the rain increased in force.

It was little comfort to Welkin that the rain had lost some of its toxicity over the years. The Skyborn had estimated that it would take at least fifty years from the time of the global war for the water to become pure again—at the present time it was only just drinkable.

By the time they had traveled a mile from the Stockade, the rain had dwindled to a light shower.

Gillian's aching limbs tortured her. The pain was almost unbearable, but she knew they could not stop. They needed to get across the bridge farther north. That's where Sarah's family usually posted its outlying sentries.

They reached the Kerry River by first light the next morning. To Gillian's surprise the old railway tracks were still intact. It seemed that no one had attempted to sabotage the ancient bridge, probably because all sides needed to have access to it. Still, the way things were going, it was hard to predict who would do what anymore.

They crossed the tracks in the slackening drizzle. The rusted rails and sleepers were slippery, and Welkin reminded them not to look down. The Kerry River rumbled beneath them. Rocks like jagged teeth appeared stark against the white waters as they fled the Dandenongs.

Patrick and Mira argued that they should live off the land for however long it took Bruick and his party to come back this way.

"I've been trying to live off the land for the last two days," Welkin said wearily. "There's not much sustenance to be had."

"The devil take the food," Mira spat. "We'll ambush him and get plenty of supplies!"

"That's ridiculous," Welkin said. He looked at Mira inquiringly. "You're serious, aren't you?"

Mira nodded tersely.

"I can't go on indefinitely without a rest," Gillian said. She was already staggering and was only too well aware that she was shifting more weight on to Welkin. She felt the world was spiraling in crazy circles.

"Patrick, maybe we should wait alone?" Mira said. She clutched at his arm. "Hit and run. The Stockaders would never catch us."

Patrick shook his head. "Welkin's right. There's nay telling when Bruick'll come back this way." He shook his head dispiritedly. "Our chance will come again, lass."

Mira pulled her hand back and glared at the three of them. Welkin suspected that the poor woman had been emotionally disturbed by something that had happened to her.

"So be it, then." She swung around, but before leading off she said, "I'll be back for him. Make no doubt about that."

The four left the tracks as soon as they reached firm ground. They were totally exhausted by the time they made it back and rested for two days before facing the Committee. Gillian felt ashamed at having failed in her mission to kill Bruick.

She'd learned from Patrick and Mira that Bruick had been aware of her plans from the start, so they'd had to quickly improvise. It seemed that the safest thing for them to do was inform him that it was Sarah's sister who had infiltrated his Stockade. It was either tell him that or be killed. Besides, they guessed rightly that Bruick would treasure a captive such as Sarah's sister.

Gillian was visibly disturbed when told the news that Elab had led the others on an exploratory expedition. It seemed inconceivable that the Committee would allow them to go on such an impossible mission.

"Desperate times call for desperate measures," Lucida said. "Isn't that why you put yourself and the others in jeopardy by going over to Bruick's Stockade?"

Gillian hung her head. She hadn't exactly *wanted* the others there, but her rash act *had* almost been their downfall and, worse, it had set a poor example to others in the family—even if some of them considered her mission heroic. Despite two days of decent food, neither Welkin nor Gillian felt capable of following the search party at this time.

Lacking several members, Trask and Denton had been temporarily elected to the Committee. They had been close friends of Gillian's, but now responsibilities made them more distant. They had even upbraided her on her recklessness.

Gillian said in a low voice, "I just want to say it should have been done long ago. I'm not going to justify my actions, but we've left a snake in our backyard, and the snake is getting bigger and stronger every day. Now we have two enemies instead of one."

Trask acknowledged what she said but added, "It should have been a *Committee* decision."

Welkin looked up. He had been sitting there quietly, saying little. Now he leaned forward and stared intently at the gathering.

"We should have dealt with Bruick before he got established." He smiled at the others' discomfort. "Instead, we let his original gang of ten become the army it is today. We could have had him several times, but Sarah thought that we shouldn't lower ourselves to fight on his level. Sarah was wrong. Sometimes to protect the whole, you must eliminate the disease." He didn't realize he was echoing words used against him not so long ago on *Colony*.

"*Den E-ho-me*," Efi said emphatically. Then, "And we haven't! *Fthani pia!*—I give up!"

Welkin held his hands up in mock defense. "No, we haven't. But all our problems today can be traced to letting Bruick live." He looked over to where the dejected Gillian had slumped in her chair. He knew she was feeling guilty and yet he also knew she *needed* to feel guilty. Growth came only from pain; sparing someone her pain simply kept her a child.

"We're not murderers," Lucida pointed out.

"No, we're the victims," Welkin countered.

"*Pro-spa-thou-me na to fiaxome*—we're trying to rectify that—" Efi started.

"—by sending out five family members on a hopeless mission?" Welkin interrupted. He coolly appraised each of them, almost daring them to contradict him.

They did, of course, all at once. The buzz of accusations lasted until Efi banged her fist down on the table. "*Sioi!*—quiet!" Her knuckles were white, her hands clenched tightly.

"*Ftani pia!* Enough! You know as well as any Committee member, Welkin, that united we're something, and divided we fall. This is why Sarah instigated the Committee. The core, she used to call us. Remember?"

Welkin nodded slowly. He knew where Efi was heading. He'd even predicted she would get up from her seat and begin pacing the room as she spoke her thoughts on this issue. He was glad he'd taken the pressure off Gillian. No matter what transpired in this room today, his and Gillian's destiny was already mapped out.

"Elab is a major part of that 'core.' *Sinfonisame?*—agreed?" Efi directed her words at the Committee yet managed to keep her eyes mainly on Welkin, as though reading his thoughts. "We can spend the rest of our lives fighting both *Colony* and Bruick's Stockade and never achieve anything. Or we send volunteers into the wilderness on the off chance we achieve something but without risking the whole family." Efi spoke brusquely. She was obviously upset that Welkin couldn't see the point she was making. Or maybe she was annoyed that he had risked himself to save a person who acted selfishly and without thought for anyone else.

"Remember Sarah's dictum: 'You've got to kick goals sometimes.' And that's what we're after here. A goal."

She seemed to grope for words, then after a few moments of silence simply shrugged.

"I just don't know what you think you would've done in our place, Welkin. Here's a chance for us to become allies with a faction of Skyborn." She frowned when a thought hit her. "A rebellious faction just like we were. Why, they may even be looking for us."

Efi returned to her chair, a look of surprise on her face. "Look." She clasped her fingers and rested her chin on them. "Let's not kid anyone here. The united family concept was good. *Sinfonisame?*— agreed? With Sarah at the helm we had a figurehead. I sometimes suspect that Sarah knew she was dying a long time ago and wanted the Committee as a bulwark against the united family's collapse."

She sighed and leaned back in her chair, pausing as though rallying her thoughts while the others waited expectantly. "*E keri alazoune*— sorry, times change. I think we're all agreed on that."

The others murmured assent. But Welkin said, "That's why Gillian took the course she did."

Efi gave an exasperated sigh. "Imagine if everyone just got up and did everything off his or her own bat. What's the use of a Committee if its policies are not followed?" She pointed outside to where she knew the family was gathering expectantly.

"Just what do we tell those people out there who have come to rely on us? That we don't know what Gillian intends, or why Welkin has disappeared, or what the rest of us really stand for?" She shook her head. "It was *aprosehtos*—careless, thoughtless, and I'm disappointed you can't see all this for yourselves." She looked from Welkin to Gillian with a quizzical expression on her face.

Gillian had been staring at the floor. Now she raised her eyes and stared directly into Efi's. "We do understand what the Committee's all about," she said. She ran her hand across her newly shaved scalp, momentarily forgetting she was rid of her dreadlocks and their incumbent nits. "But if I'd been successful in killing Bruick, I'd be held up as a role model for the family to copy."

Trask spoke up next. He seemed certain of himself in his new role as a Committee member. "No, you wouldn't," he said. "And if you were, that would be an even greater danger to the family in the long term. We don't need that kind of model. When all is said and done, if you'd killed Bruick, any number of people could have succeeded him. And the Committee would have lost you." He broke off for a second. "You do realize that you didn't have a hope of getting out of there once you'd killed Bruick?"

Gillian cocked her head, a defiant light in her eyes. "A small price to pay," she said at last.

"For you, maybe," Lucida cut in harshly. "But you have no right to throw your life away to the Committee's detriment."

"It's my life!" Gillian flared.

"And ours!" Lucida returned. She leaned forward across the table and challenged Gillian's glare. "We're a community, Gillian. A *family!* We do things together, and we *decide* together. That's how it has to work, otherwise what do we have? Anarchy. And isn't that what the family was created to bring to an end? Wasn't that Sarah's dream?"

The truth of Lucida's words hit Gillian like a slap. She hadn't thought of it like that, but of course that was exactly what Sarah had always strived for: an end to the long, dark years of ignorance and tribal warfare, and a restoration of human society . . . and human responsibility. For a long while after this Gillian felt very small and alone, as if it had been *she* who had left Sarah and not the other way around.

"Okay, we officially tar and feather Gillian tomorrow and run her out of town," Welkin said. The image of tarring and feathering the diminutive yet feisty Gillian brought out several rueful smiles and eased the tension. "Where's all this getting us, huh?"

"Better to have these things said than left unsaid," Denton said.

Everybody nodded, even Gillian, who was still smarting from Lucida's perceptive words.

Welkin pushed himself away from the table. "I think we should call it a day. Gillian and I are beat."

"Then let's reconvene tomorrow," Efi said. She got up and unexpectedly gave Gillian a big hug. Gillian's surprise was almost comical. Then one by one each Committee member hugged her, told her how glad they were that she was back and in one piece. Tears flowed down Gillian's face and she couldn't talk past the sudden constriction in her throat.

Afterward, she let Welkin take her hand and lead her out into the midafternoon sun.

"Thanks," Gillian whispered. "Efi was . . . so strange. What were all those weird words she used?"

Welkin ruffled her hair. "The elders banned foreign language a long time ago. Some people refused to forget their heritage. It's probably because of her outbursts in Greek that she was found out and discarded to the lower decks. She babbles that stuff only when she's really angry or frustrated."

Gillian thought about that. "Banning hundreds of languages on a ship like *Colony* makes sense, huh? But it'd wipe out all diversity—make everything uniform. Neat and tidy."

Welkin cocked his head in contemplation. "*Colony* couldn't afford the luxury of risking different cultures, the possibility of racial tension. It was okay for the pioneers, because they intended to terraform Tau Ceti III. But when the long journey home began, the elders started on the Great Purge."

Gillian tightened her grip on Welkin's hand. The more she knew about the colonists the more confused she became.

20

Elab paused beneath a deodar cedar. Hidden behind its gray trunk, he scanned the tree's lofty branches and considered climbing them. Its gold-tipped foliage would present good cover, but he didn't feel like climbing through its needle-sharp leaves.

He glanced over to where Zocky was crouching behind the gray-green foliage of a mugga ironbark. It seemed inconceivable that anything so horrific as mass murder could have been committed in such an idyllic setting.

With a start he realized the others were waiting for him and Lars to move forward. He gave the signal and advanced warily at a half crouch. He could sense rather than hear Lars behind him. Each footfall dislodged perfumed pollens into the air. Someone sneezed, and he waved frantically to them to keep quiet.

Overhead a kookaburra cackled raucously.

"Damn bird," Lars mumbled. "Reckon I could hit it from here."

Elab stopped, glad perhaps for the chance to break his morbid train of thought. "What on earth would you want to kill a kookaburra for?" he whispered. "There'd be less meat on it than a rat."

Lars pulled his lips back in a tight grin. "Rat ain't so bad."

Elab shook his head. Lars was one of those people who have an irresistible urge to rile anyone and everyone; the type who badger you just to see how far they can push you.

They reached the first outhouse without trouble. Judging from its solitary location, Elab figured it must be the community's toilet. A loose sheet of corrugated iron banged against the rafters. The intermittent rattling noise was a welcome relief from the township's sullen silence.

In more normal times, Elab knew there might be dogs frolicking in the long grass, children playing in the field, buildings going up or coming down, babies wailing for food.

"What's taking you so long?" Lars hissed. "There's no one here but us and the bodies."

"Shut up, Lars," Elab snapped. "Just shut up."

Elab knew he wasn't looking forward to getting up close to those decaying bodies. Already a northerly breeze was sending the stench of putrefaction across the small paddock. Tiny black dots covered the severed limbs, and Elab fancied he could hear the buzzing sound of frenzied blowflies.

"We could always detour, boss," Lars said laconically.

"You should be so lucky, Lars," Elab said between gritted teeth. "You're going on burial duty as soon as we scout the place."

Before the other could answer, Elab loped off toward the next building. It was one of a row of decrepit pine-log settlers' huts. Farther afield he could see what appeared to be a sandstone and mud-brick church. It looked as deserted as the rest of the settlement.

He waved the others on. Slowly they reached the innermost part of the town. Elab felt the tension leave him when they finally converged on the town center. A wooden wash trough lay upturned on an untrammeled garden bed. Abutting the church building, an unruly boxthorn hedge was spreading its limbs like a porcupine's quills. It all looked just too normal.

"Nothing," Devan broke the silence. "Looks like they just up and went."

"They didn't 'up and went' anywhere," Lars reminded them.

They heard Lars stomping across a wooden veranda. He held up a crust of bread. "Wouldn't want to eat it, but I'd guess it's only a couple of days old."

"So they got out in a hurry," Elab pondered aloud.

"If anyone was left," Zocky said. She still had her bow strung and held firmly in her left hand. It was a reassuring sight. If the going got tough she was a good one to have around. Elab twisted around to tell Lars and Devan to dig a burial pit. He gasped as pain tore at his kneecap.

"You all right?" It sounded insincere coming from Lars.

"Fine," Elab said curtly. "Just twisted my knee joint. Look, you and Devan find something to dig a hole with. We can't leave those settlers out there. Even animals deserve a decent burial."

"Sure, boss," Lars said. He threw the laserlite across his shoulder and nodded for Devan to follow him.

Elab turned to Zocky and Harry. "I guess the rest of us may as well conduct a search. There has to be food that's salvageable."

"You reckon it's safe to hang around here?" Zocky queried.

"It's getting dark. At least we'll have shelter for the time being. Sure beats sleeping under the stars and getting rain soaked." When no one challenged his statement, he went off in the direction of the church that dominated the town square.

The church appeared to be the only sturdy structure in the township. Its slanting, rusted roof had been patched in recent years, and the galvanized iron sheeting reflected the sun's late-afternoon glare.

Its facade was a jigsaw of bluestone, mortar, and mud-brick. The folk around here had obviously gone to some effort to maintain at least one symbol of belief that something was right in the world. It was strange how, no matter what else vanished or was forgotten, the systems of belief that had maintained human society for more than two thousand years always survived. Or perhaps it wasn't strange, perhaps religion was the one thing that dark days always nourished . . .

The one glaring mistake the settlers had made, Elab thought to himself, had been to establish a permanent settlement so close to Melbourne itself—and close to *Colony*. This thought troubled Elab as he conducted his inspection of the building. How had they endured so long? Surely *Colony* would have known of their existence. Had they struck some sort of deal with the Skyborn? That made sense. *Colony* would have needed to communicate somehow with the Earthborn at some level. Information from computers was all very well up to a point, but it needed to be supplemented by data gathered on the spot. He'd learned that particular fact a long time ago.

Elab looked at the two narrow leaded windows that had long since been boarded over with mismatched plywood. Someone had gone to the trouble of painting the patches with intricate patterns in various dyes.

Easily defended, Elab thought, although the clergy of this diocese had never intended them to be used for that purpose. He looked back at the ornamental wrought-iron gates and the surrounding picket fence. The gardens had once been well tended. The weeds that now grew in clumps could have come up as recently as two weeks ago. The populace had apparently been in no fear of attack from *Colony*.

Elab followed the gravel path to the entrance. Its front doors were made from some hardwood that had once been painted green. Elab was tempted to knock on the doors, but instead he pulled them open and they swung on well-oiled hinges.

A skylight in the roof provided most of the daylight. Dust motes swirled in lazy motion across the bar of light that shone through.

Some sixth sense told him something was wrong, but he couldn't quite put his finger on it. He sat in a pew and rubbed his head. It was damn hard to think of anything very much when so many questions were bombarding him.

Elab heard gravel crunching and judged by the swift steps that it was Zocky.

"Hiya," he said. "Skyborn never say prayers. But you can, if you want."

Zocky smiled briefly. "Lars reckons the left ears are missing off those bodies. He says the remaining ears look weird, too."

Elab lost his smile. "What the hell would anyone want ears for? And what does he mean 'weird'?"

"Devan reckons they've been taken for trophies. Harry said something about people collecting *scalps* once upon a time. That's not right, is it?"

Elab knew as much Earth history as any other Skyborn. "Scalp hunters," he said slowly. He ran a hand through his hair. "They used to sell the scalps as proof to collect . . . *bounty*."

"What's bounty?" Zocky asked. The deeply troubled expression on Elab's face caused her heart to quicken. "What's *bounty*, Elab?" she demanded.

"It's money, Zocky," Elab said in a hollow tone. "Or something of equal value."

Zocky cocked her head quizzically. "Who'd pay for *ears*? You're putting me on, aren't you?"

"Nope." Elab headed for the door where the last of the daylight was fading. Outside he could see Lars and Devan tossing soil into a pit. Devan had a scowl on his face. Lars was talking a lot. Probably giving Devan a running commentary on how ears could be lopped from heads. He was one sick boy, Elab concluded.

"So who would buy *ears*?" he heard Zocky demand stridently.

"The Skyborn," Elab said after a moment's silence. Unease crept over him. The Skyborn. Bruick. Immortality. The thoughts tumbled around in his head like dice. Divide and conquer. Key personnel. The fittest. Extermination . . .

Elab found himself beneath the archway. "Hey, Lars. Devan." He waved them over.

"Almost done, boss," Lars called languidly.

"NOW!" Elab yelled. He glanced around and saw Harry look up. A sudden nervousness took hold of him and he started to walk back. Then he was running. Lars and Devan had stopped shoveling and, almost as though Harry's unease was contagious, they too began to walk hurriedly over.

"Elab?" Zocky said, her voice tight.

Elab waved his hand for quiet. He was listening for something. It was hard to concentrate with everyone jabbering. Then he heard it. Harry had stopped and cupped a hand to his ear.

Lars gripped Devan's shoulder, and the pair stood motionless while they searched the darkening sky.

The thin whistling sound soon became a thick roar. The Earthborn identified the noise as belonging to propulsion thrusts. The realization galvanized Harry into action. He ran back to where he had left his knapsack, swooped it up in midflight, and had reached the church before Elab had pushed Zocky back inside.

"In!" Elab called. "Lars! Get in here. *Now!*"

Devan loped ahead of Lars and they cleared the leaning fence as two cruisers swooped low over a rooftop and landed somewhere out of sight.

Elab slammed the great doors shut. He bolted them and with his elbow smashed two pieces of plywood from the leaded windows. He took a quick look outside, then pulled his head back behind the wooden frame.

"What are they doing?" Zocky said over his shoulder.

"How many?" Devan wanted to know.

Elab swung on them, ready to tell them to shut up for a moment. But their frightened faces reminded him suddenly of their youth. Lars was the only one not intimidated by the cruisers. He was cradling the laserlite as though it alone would save them from whatever it was that fate had in store for them.

"Settle down," Elab snapped. "I think there's only a couple of them out there."

"They'll radio for backup," Lars said. "They always do when they're outnumbered."

"Keep thinking that way, Lars," Elab said. "You'll die an optimist."

"You got us into this mess, boss," Lars began.

"You call me 'boss' one more time, Lars, and I'll wring your—"

"Guys, cut it out," Zocky said. She strode between the pair as they took a step toward each other.

Devan took Elab's place beside the window. "Nothing happening," he announced.

"Why should it?" Harry said. "They could starve us out if they wanted."

"They won't do that," Elab said, keeping an eye on Lars. "No need. With their cruisers they could reduce this place to rubble in a matter of minutes."

"Then why haven't they?" Devan asked.

"They want our ears intact," Lars said pointedly. "Have to dig through too much rubble if they buried us."

"Lars—" Elab began, but Zocky swiped her hand through the air to indicate silence.

"The ear lopping mightn't have been the Skyborn," she said, glancing furtively at Elab. "Lars, why are you such an idiot?"

Lars gripped the laserlite closer to his chest. "I'm not the one who got us trapped in here," he said. "That right . . . *Elab?*"

"You want to take your chances outside, Lars, you go right ahead." Elab grinned. "We'll follow you if you get past that first building across the square."

"You're all heart," Lars said. "But you're the fearless leader. I'm just a foot soldier."

"Remember it," Elab told him.

Before Zocky could intervene again, a booming, electronic voice seemed to emanate from within the room. The clarity of that voice even fooled Elab into thinking someone had sneaked inside the church with them.

The team sprang into defense postures. In one fluid motion they each swung around and down, presenting as minimal a target as possible. In that same movement, they had drawn their bows and were sweeping ready-cocked arrows to and fro across the room.

"You are surrounded," the voice said dispassionately. "Discard your weapons and come out with your hands raised in the air. Do it now or we shall commence firing."

"That's *so* weird," Lars said. "That voice seems to be coming from right out of the air next to me."

"And me," Devan added uneasily. "Whoever he is, he sounds angry."

"Really pissed off with us," Zocky said as though in a trance.

"You have one minute before we commence firing," the voice said firmly. "We'll bury you heathens."

"That's spooky," Harry said.

"Heathens? You'd think he'd have noticed we're hiding in a *church*," Devan said indignantly.

"There's only two of them, right, Elab?" Zocky said. "And five of us."

"Numbers don't count," Lars said. "Weapon power does."

Elab ignored their chatter. He went to the back of the church. There was a rear door, all right, but it was bolted tight. The Skyborn weren't to know that, though. So one would be guarding the front door, while the other would be out back. Elab tried to picture the rear. Probably an empty paddock, with nowhere to run. Out front was the square, but it was girthed by sheds and huts. They wouldn't all make it, of course. But some of them might.

What would Sarah have done? Damn, he cursed himself. If Sarah had been leading them, this would never have happened. She'd always been such a clever strategist—none of them would ever fill her place. She'd have scouted the entire area before chancing being boxed in; she'd have known precisely what was outside that rear door and how far it was to cover and in which direction. Elab would too, next time. If there was a next time . . .

When he realized the others had stopped talking, he made up his mind without too much thought. Sarah had always said follow your gut feeling. So he'd learned at least one thing!

"We create a diversion at the back door. Lars will punch holes through it with the laser, make them think we coming out that way. Then we make a break for it out the front," Elab said. "We can vote on it if you like," he added. "No? Okay. Lars, on my signal, start blasting. Then get back over here and cover us with the laserlite. That window gives you a pretty good view of the square."

"And what about me?" Lars asked. "You gonna run out on me?"

"Don't be an idiot," Zocky said.

"Stop calling me an idiot," Lars threatened.

"Shut up," Zocky snapped back. "Once we make it to safety, we'll cover you. Right, Elab?"

"Goes without saying," Elab agreed.

"Yeah, right." Lars glared at them then crossed to the rear door. He squinted through the viewfinder and set it on automatic. He nodded with satisfaction. "Do my best, boss," he said.

Elab gave him the signal and Lars opened up, drilling red-hot holes through the heavy door. Seconds later he was back at the window, jamming the laserlite against the frame for support.

"Okay. Go for it. Straight out, then break in different directions!" Elab jerked the front door open and they charged forward, fanning out exactly as he'd told them to. Laser fire sizzled through the air, making a sound like water on hot metal. Elab waited for the stabbing pain, or at least the bright flashes that would herald death, but none came.

He realized, as he skidded to safety, that the others had also reached cover without mishap. "What the hell?" he mumbled to himself as pain flared in his leg.

Ballistic gunfire erupted from around the tiny town. The muffled retorts sounded like dull explosions compared with the curt, sibilant laser fire.

Someone screamed in pain. Elab hoped it wasn't one of his people. Then he saw Zocky on her knees. She pulled her bow tight, and a second later saw her arrow strike someone.

But it wasn't a Skyborn. Maybe Devan? Harry? His frustration made him indecisive. Had Zocky in the confusion shot Devan or Harry? The fading light made it impossible to tell.

He realized with a start that his position wasn't good. Gunfire echoed all about him. None of his team had ballistic weapons, neither did the Skyborn. Which meant jabbers, or some local variant.

An arrow *ka-thunk*ed into the wooden barrel beside him. He had to pluck his shirt sleeve from the flint. Heedless of the danger, he flung himself onto a veranda and through a doorway as bullets churned up the wooden planks.

He threw himself down and kicked the door shut. It bounced back open, but that was the least of his worries. Splinters had buried themselves into his flesh and drawn blood. For a moment he lay there dazed, thinking he'd been shot.

His knee was hurting like hell. Maybe those ear hunters would have his after all. Then he remembered Zocky saying Devan had called the ears "weird." He grinned despite his pain. Maybe his ears wouldn't be "weird" enough for them.

Thinking of Zocky, what was she up to now? He poked his head just above the windowsill and looked out.

Almost pitch black out there. No way could they come out winners. Not with colonists out there with their heat-seeking weapons. Right now his head could be a green blur on someone's targeting screen.

He pulled his head down, surprised that someone hadn't tried vaporizing it.

It was quiet out there now, the sort of quiet that one would expect from a deprivation chamber, which was all wrong. As if everyone and everything was making a special effort not to break the silence.

What had happened to the others? Was Lars still in the church, or had he tumbled out after them as they'd arranged? Had the others been able to give him covering fire? Who had Zocky shot? Devan? Harry? Maybe someone else. But who? The not knowing was frustrating.

Elab tried to push the tiredness from his face. It sometimes helped to push his facial skin up and roughly comb his hands through his hair, hard against his scalp. He did this several times before feeling that tingling sensation.

His vision cleared a little, just in time to realize that someone had crept into the room. He swung his nocked arrow around and up but froze in midaction.

"Don't," came the single word. The inflexion belonged to a colonist. Too accurate and precise a tone to belong to an Earthborn.

Elab slowly released the taut string, let the arrow glide forward with the slackening bow. He lowered it to the ground. He was dimly aware that he still had a knife hidden in his boot.

"Move away from the weapon," the colonist said. "No sudden movement."

Elab did as he was told. His breathing was coming fast and heavy now. One false move and he'd end up so much charred meat.

"I can tell you straight, Earthborn, that I'd rather just kill you right now and put you out of your misery," the colonist said.

His voice was edgy, Elab realized. It gave him a shred of hope. "But you need me, don't you?" he said.

"As a hostage," the colonist said. His voice was ragged, too, Elab noted. Not just with fear but maybe pain as well.

"Not going to fetch much as a hostage," Elab said lightly. "I don't know who's out there, but they're sure as hell not all mine."

"They're yours, all right. Every last murdering wretched heathen of them," the colonist blurted. He took a tighter grip on his laserlite and raised it a little.

Elab looked down its point. It looked like a strand of thick wire, ridiculously flimsy, but capable of charring him to a cinder.

"They're not mine," Elab said firmly. "We've got one laserlite and the rest bows and arrows." He waited for this to penetrate. "I've heard a lot of gunfire out there. We ran out of ammo long ago."

"You're lying, you scum," the colonist said. But his face twisted in doubt.

"You notice something different about me, Skyborn?" Elab indicated his chunky legs.

"You seem older than the others," the colonist said slowly. "You're a renegade colonist. One of those who betrayed us."

"Trust me, *Colony* betrayed me long before I betrayed *it*," Elab said with feeling.

"You're all contaminated. Just like the rest of the Earthborn," the colonist said. His face was slick with sweat.

"So you put us down like vermin," Elab surmised.

He watched the colonist's face for an answer. The seconds passed.

"You're one of the traitors," the colonist said matter-of-factly. "There is a reward on your head. Instant promotion to senior level."

Elab nodded slowly. "Impressive. I suppose all you need do is slice off our ears and present them. Yeah?"

"You animal," the colonist said tightly. "That's just what you bounty hunters do for drugs, treacherous sons of the space demons!"

"Steady," Elab said when the colonist raised the laserlite. Suddenly Devan's words hit home. He'd said the ears had been "weird." That maybe meant different. Like the Skyborns' ears. They were in fact genetically different. They'd somehow grown closer to the skull, were flatter. And usually unscarred, free of blemishes, because they'd been raised on *Colony*.

"Just shut up!" the colonist said gutturally. He glanced outside via a handheld night-amplifying scanner.

"They're Skyborn, aren't they? The ones who were killed here?" Elab said. "Makes sense." He struggled with thoughts that were too bizarre to grapple with.

"They were colonists, all right," the youth said. "You know that well enough. You betrayed us!"

"Bruick," Elab said. The demons take the man. He'd probably planned every last bit of this entire expedition, had planned on Sarah leading a team down here to locate the renegade Skyborn—only Sarah wasn't in the picture anymore. But he hadn't netted such a bad haul anyway—half of the family's Committee. Bruick . . . He looked out through the window as though he might see him sauntering across the square. "You met up with Bruick? Scar around his neck. Tattoos all over him."

"That's him, all right," the colonist said. "Promised us safe conduct up north in return for more supplies. When he found out we couldn't supply him with more Lurisdicton—a longevity drug—he set us up. Slaughtered everyone."

"Except you and your partner."

The colonist shook his head. "He's out back. They got him, too."

"Now listen," Elab said. "Listen carefully. I'm not one of them. None of my people are. We're from up in the Dandenongs—"

"They're heathens, too!"

"So you've been told," Elab said. He rubbed at his leg to ease a little circulation into it. "We've been fighting Bruick since we landed."

"You're lying," the colonist said. "Everyone knows he's a colonist rebel."

"He's Earthborn," Elab snapped.

"He's older than you! That makes him a colonist rebel!"

"There're pure genetic strains here, untouched by the aging disease!" Elab said angrily. "Understand that if nothing else. We had a leader called Sarah who was older than me. Some of them don't age like the rest. Doesn't mean they're all colonists. And besides, if you're one of the mutineers, don't call me and mine traitors."

The colonist scowled. "We're *pacifists*. We haven't killed anyone. We're nothing like you and the other lower deckers. Don't you *dare*—"

Movement outside made them both duck into the shadows. Elab knew that the colonist's laserlite was still directed at his chest.

He swallowed hard. This was going to be a tough call. The colonist was going to fry whatever walked into that doorway, sure as space is a vacuum. A soft footfall landed on the veranda. It came closer, then he heard someone trying to stifle heavy breathing. Could it be Zocky? Hard to tell when the person was deliberately creeping forward, closer still.

Should he scream out and warn whoever it was? Elab tensed himself for what must occur.

As though reading his thoughts, the colonist shook his head slowly. Despite himself, Elab made himself relax. No way would the colonist miss.

Numbly, Elab watched the colonist swivel the laserlite to the door. He could see the shadowy profile of whoever it was on the veranda. Friend or foe? he wondered frantically.

He tensed himself. He'd make it halfway before the colonist could respond to the new threat. Maybe.

Then the back door flew open.

The colonist was good, damn good. He took a hurried step forward, avoiding the crashing door, swung to meet his new adversary, but whoever had been on the veranda was now coming at him from behind.

Elab uncurled from the floor. He was heading for the colonist when he realized almost too late that the huge bulk barreling into the room didn't belong to his team. He changed direction at the last moment, felt his leg wrench tightly, but kept going. His momentum carried him into the man.

They fell to the floor in a tangle of arms and legs.

Laser fire spat into the air, briefly illuminating the room. Elab saw the pink-edged knife rise and fall. Pain seared into his waist and he let out a muffled grunt of surprise.

He managed to get hold of the knife hand, but the man's brutish strength eased the knife swiftly to within an inch of Elab's throat.

Thwack.

It took Elab a moment to realize that his adversary's body had gone limp over him. He tested his own strength, knowing with rising panic that he'd taken a cut in the side. With effort he heaved, and the man fell limply to the floor.

"Get up," the colonist said. He seemed surprised that Elab was still alive. "There are others out there. We have to get out."

Elab felt his side. His hand came away sticky. "I'm not going anywhere," he said thickly. "I've twisted my leg again. And I've been sliced."

"Do it *now*," the colonist snapped. He straightened his weapon.

"Go ahead and shoot," Elab said. He sat back down against the wall. "Then you'll have Bruick's people *and* mine onto you."

Further debate was cut short. A scuffling noise came from beyond the back door that Elab noted was still locked.

"Clark?" came a suspicious voice.

The colonist pressed hard against the wall, well outside the range of the swinging door. "Yeah?" he responded quietly.

The door opened slowly, but before anyone could enter, a rapid hissing noise signaled an arrow in flight. It thudded into the man's back and he tumbled into the door. His mouth opened wide with a look of astonishment; the whites of his eyes were in stark contrast to his camouflaged face.

Elab pulled his leg out of the way as the man toppled. The arrow had lodged just left of his breastbone. Impact with the floor drove it right through his heart.

Zocky! Elab felt a wisp of hope flare within him. It died quickly enough. He flinched when the colonist retrained the laserlite on him.

"Don't be a fool," he said, surprised at his own bravado. "I helped you just now—"

"You helped yourself!" the colonist hissed.

"You need me to tell who's who," Elab insisted.

Someone ran by outside, and they both flattened themselves against the wall. Farther afield someone shouted. Hurried voices replied. Ballistic gunfire cracked several times but received no corresponding replies. Hard to tell, though. If Lars was still in the picture, his retaliatory laser fire would be inaudible.

"They're pulling out," Elab said. "My people wouldn't go without me."

"So you're their leader?" the colonist said hopefully.

It was then Elab realized he had the matter in hand.

"We're all in this together. Keep that in mind and things will work out."

The rebel colonist calculated swiftly. He could move only forward now. He wouldn't last the day out there in the wilderness. The heathen at his feet was his only hope. His shoulders slumped with this realization.

"It's not surrender," Elab told him, knowing the other's fear for his own. "It's a union of people."

The colonist had one second to answer before a rapid line of laserlite spat through the air and he fell to the floor.

Elab's eyes went wide, yet despite his disbelief he lunged forward and swept the colonist's laserlite from the ground. He barely made it back behind the wall before more slithers of dazzling probes blew away the doorframe.

Elab swung the weapon around the corner of the torn doorway and depressed the firing stud.

Nothing happened. He pressed frantically. The weapon was on empty, or it had been sabotaged. Either way, Elab drew his knife and waited in the pitch black for whatever lurked beyond the doorway.

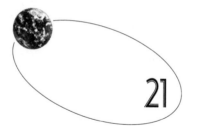

21

The night air was brisk. Gillian rolled over in her sleep and nudged against Welkin. She flapped her arm across his shoulder and sleepily pulled herself closer to him.

Welkin woke and smiled. He had gone to bed alone but wasn't surprised to find Gillian beside him. She'd been having nightmares ever since her incarceration in the Stockade. It might be some time before she put those demons to rest. Until then she seemed to regard Welkin as part of her family—not the grouping that was known as *the* family, but something smaller, more personal. He couldn't quite make out what his relationship with Gillian was all about. They had never shared anything more physical than a kiss and a hug. *Brotherly* sprang to mind. Maybe she thought of him as a kind of surrogate brother, especially since the loss of Sarah.

Even after all this time, he had difficulty adjusting to the fact that the Earthborn were adults at twelve and often dead of old age at eighteen. For him to have a fulfilling life, he'd need to find someone whose life span would match his own. Maybe another Skyborn, though he looked on most of them as friends. But maybe it didn't matter. If you loved someone, then you wanted to grow old with her, even if she grew old faster than you. And it was always possible that Gillian's genetic heritage was one of the pure strains, unaffected by the chromosomal abnormality that accelerated senescence.

He suddenly leaned over and kissed her. She wiped sleepily at her face, as if he'd tickled her. He kissed her a second time.

"Wuh?" Gillian sat up and looked down at him. "What was that?"

"Nothing," he said, suddenly guilty. "Go back to sleep. It's early."
She lay down again and he gently stroked her head.

"It seems early," Gillian mumbled.

"It is," he said and wished he could kiss her again when she was fully awake.

"Is there something wrong? You're acting—"

Welkin quickly clapped his hand over her mouth. They both heard a twig snap, barely audible in the still night air.

"It's probably someone taking a leak," Gillian said, her voice muffled by his hand.

"Someone's leaving camp," Welkin whispered. He quickly pulled on his boots and scrambled to the door flap. Peering into the half-light he caught a glimpse of two figures fading from sight.

"Damn funny time to leave," Gillian said beside him. "Get a load of who it was?"

"Your friends," Welkin muttered. "The O'Shannesseys. Now what's their game?"

"Let's go find out," Gillian said, hurriedly pulling on her own boots. "Bet it's nothing serious, though. Sarah trusted that pair with her life."

"Did she now?" Welkin said. They both armed themselves and scurried from the camp. "C'mon, before we lose them."

They followed the pair for the best part of the morning. At times Welkin suspected they knew they were being followed, for sometimes, inexplicably, the O'Shannesseys doubled back on themselves. Twice Welkin and Gillian were made to separate to avoid being seen.

Morning wore on and with it a sullen sun tried pushing through the omnipresent smog bank. Of necessity they fell back out of view, and by noon Welkin feared they had lost the quarry. The weather was oppressive, and the frustration of recent events was getting to Gillian.

"This is crazy," she stated. "We've come out without provisions. If we keep searching for them much longer, we'll be camping out tonight in the freezing cold. And I for one have had it!"

Welkin dumped his pack on the ground and climbed a eucalypt to scan the valley. Low-flying cloud shrouded the distant terrain and he cursed beneath his breath. He came back down and brushed his hands against one another and blew on them. "They're following the same path Elab and the others would have taken."

"Is that right?" Gillian said cynically. "*I* heard they kept their plans to themselves."

"Which goes to show you don't get to hear *everything*, hmmm?"

She started to speak but reconsidered. "Okay. So why don't we cut out the stealth act and race on ahead? If we stumble on them, then it'll all be out in the open. If not, we run ourselves into the ground because"—she shrugged with exasperation—"we're out here unprepared like a couple of idiots. Just what have you got on your mind?" she demanded doggedly.

"Are you finished?" Welkin squared his shoulders. It made a nice change to hear Gillian asking, rather than telling. It gave him a heady feeling. In fact, he had noticed that her whole manner toward him had changed since the Stockade incident. "I managed to live on berries and fungi, remember. It *can* be done."

Gillian went red. She hadn't quite got around to thanking Welkin for rescuing her. It was one of those things she preferred to leave unsaid. Like maybe thanking someone for saving your life trivialized it. Of course you're thankful. That sort of thing didn't have to be *said*, did it?

"So we live like sparrows for a few days. What then? We sprout wings and fly home and tell everyone we eloped but changed our minds?"

Welkin pouted at that thought. "We're armed," he said. "And I've got a strong hunch Elab might need us."

"But they've been gone *days*, Welkin," Gillian protested.

"And we're not laden down with supplies or hampered by numbers. The two of us should be able to move at twice the speed a party of five can."

Gillian growled with frustration. "I know you guys go back a long way and all that, but this is just ill conceived. You know?"

"Then you go back and tell the others," Welkin said stoically. He grunted when a sudden thought came to him. "I'm doing exactly what you did."

She clicked her tongue in annoyance. "Does that mean it's *my* turn to save *you?*"

"Let's hope it doesn't come to that," Welkin said. With that, they set off at a fresh pace.

They loped along, over the bracken, for the best part of an hour, neither wanting to yield to the other's desire to rest. Finally it was Welkin who suggested they should stop for a breather.

They pulled up just short of a dry creek bed that coiled its way across a windswept plain. Welkin kicked at a clump of spinifex; more of it stretched as far as the eye could see, tussocks of it dotting the ground like weeds needing to be pulled.

Gillian focused on two stunted trees that might have reminded her ancestors of twin goalposts. "Bare as all else. My throat's parched, and I don't see any berries or water," she said reproachfully.

"We'll find stuff once we get off this lunar landscape," Welkin said and wiped at the perspiration that caked the dirt on his face. "Hard to believe artists used to come out here and paint scenes like this," he said. "Scrub, red rocks, and sand."

"Sarah found beauty in this," Gillian said, throwing her arms wide. She looked at him with some confusion. "You Skyborn will never quite get it, will you?"

Welkin smiled reminiscently. "Sarah used to say we'd had all that mushy stuff bred out of us. Not our fault, really."

"Guess not. *Tcha!* You people never would have shared moonlit walks along the beach, or cuddled up on cold winter nights beside a roaring fire."

"Or eloped," Welkin reminded her. "We're just killjoys from space!"

Gillian squinted.

"What is it?" Welkin scanned the horizon.

She shaded her eyes with one hand and pointed excitedly with the other. "There they are! Look, Welkin. You were right."

Through the heat shimmer, Welkin followed Gillian's pointing finger. He could just make out the shapes of distant figures. "Maybe a half mile away. No more," he guessed. He rubbed his eyes quickly and refocused. "Maybe it's not them. There seem to be three of them."

"Two," Gillian contradicted. "I saw only two."

Before he could move, Gillian grabbed at him. "Let me do the talking. I know them."

"Suits me," Welkin said, moving off after her.

They caught up with the O'Shannesseys as they passed through the "goalposts" and were wading through taller range grass and bracken that bordered the basin.

The O'Shannesseys had spotted the pair some distance off. At first they had kept moving, but finally it appeared they'd discussed this new development and had decided to wait for their pursuers.

Within hailing distance, Patrick called a welcome. Welkin noticed that he was carrying a laserlite and that his left arm was bandaged and soaked with blood.

"Hiya," Welkin replied wearily. This last jog had just about done him in. He was the first to admit he did some crazy things. Coming out here after his vigil at the Stockade was one of them. Nor was Gillian in much better shape after *her* ordeal.

"You'd be traveling light," Patrick said skeptically. "Quick, Mira, the water. The pair of them look ready to drop!"

Gillian took Mira's water bottle with trembling hands. She'd forgotten how fresh and wonderful water could taste. She passed the canister to Welkin, who was staring at Patrick's arm.

"Fool me," Patrick said. "Slipped a ways back and slid down into a gully."

"Could've broken his fool neck!" Mira grumbled.

"You left early this morning," Gillian said cautiously. Leaving a campsite predawn was unusual but not against any family law.

"When it was dripping cool," Patrick said heartily. "We like to travel at night, mostly. You'd be best to take heed yourselves, mind."

"You've been following us," Mira said, suddenly annoyed at the charade.

"Mira, quiet, girl!"

"Let her have her say," Gillian said impatiently. She knew she'd get more out of the impetuous Mira than the level-headed Patrick.

"The fool girl's got a fierce tongue on her—" Patrick began, but a new voice interrupted him.

A voice they all knew.

It chilled the blood in Gillian's veins. It made Welkin feel suddenly light-headed, and he might have reeled giddily if it hadn't been for the water he had just splashed over his face.

Sarah rose out of the bracken several yards away and brushed herself down amid a cloud of dust and chaff.

"*Sis?*" Gillian said doubtfully. "I don't believe—"

Sarah strode forward and threw her arms around Gillian and hugged her tightly. Within seconds they were both crying. "It's all right. Everything's all right."

"Sarah—why? When?"

"It had to be. I'll explain it all. Just hold me."

Gillian let the tears come. Her body shook, and within seconds she was sobbing as no one had ever seen her sob before.

"I thought you were . . . *dead!*"

"Everyone did." Sarah stroked Gillian's hair. "That's what I needed them to think," she said.

The five of them stood like that for some time: Sarah gently swaying with Gillian, Patrick and Mira exchanging sheepish looks, and Welkin's mind going through all the implications of Sarah being alive. And healthy! The wasting disease had vanished as though it had never existed. Conflicting thoughts fought for understanding. How could she possibly have conquered the cancer that seemed to be destroying her? Or maybe she'd shammed the cancer and not eaten for two months to mislead everyone into believing she was dying?

And the O'Shannesseys. Where did they fit into all this? Why had Sarah chosen *them* as her confidants?

The sheer scope of Sarah's duplicity was beyond Welkin's comprehension. *He* was still a kid after all, he reminded himself. He held off saying anything until at last Sarah pulled back from Gillian and wiped the tears from her face.

"You've been patient, Welkin. Thanks for that," Sarah said as she retrieved her laserlite from the grass. "But we should talk on the move. We need to reach Elab before it's too late."

"Too late for what?" Welkin asked suspiciously. "Just what's going on, Sarah?"

"I'm not really sure," she confessed. "It's a long, long story."

"And we've got a day or two, I reckon," Welkin reminded her. "Maybe start at A and work your way through to Z?"

Gillian looked sharply at Welkin and realized that under normal circumstances Welkin would never have addressed Sarah in that manner. But right now, it seemed reasonable.

"First up," Welkin forged ahead, "does Elab know you're still alive? And the others?"

Sarah looked sharply at Gillian. "No, Welkin. No one but Patrick and Mira." Sarah sighed wearily. Most of her major plans had their flaws, but most of the time they achieved their purpose. This one hadn't managed even to get off the ground. She knew why, of course. She'd been battling her own sister—a piece of her that was younger and less experienced but every bit as cocky as the older sister. How could she best a younger, more resilient version of herself? It was a part of the equation that she hadn't even taken into her calculations. Silly, silly woman, she chided herself.

"I guess all this began way back when Patrick and Mira told me that Bruick had done a deal with *Colony* for the longevity drug."

"You knew and didn't let on," Welkin said, disbelieving.

"Let me finish," Sarah said. "Then you might begin to understand. Anyway, all his other crimes combined couldn't equal this one. It was treason—the betrayal of all the Earthborn. I knew the family would never sanction an attack on the Stockade, and I wouldn't have wanted so many deaths on my hands, anyway. No, it was far easier for me to go it alone in a more clandestine manner. But then I got sick, so sick I thought I was going to die. My mind made up, I sought the help of Patrick and Mira. Then something really strange happened. After a week of living in the bush, I started feeling better."

"She was being poisoned," Mira cut in. "Probably a Bruick plant—"

"Poisoned!" Gillian echoed.

"Forget it," Sarah said. "We don't know for sure. But anyway, it changed my mind about my future. I made other plans."

"The three of us might have got away with it," Patrick added.

"But things got complicated," Sarah continued. She ruffled Gillian's short-cropped hair. "It was no one's fault."

"But if you'd only *trusted* me—" Gillian blurted.

"—you would have still insisted on coming, and I couldn't have allowed that," Sarah cut in.

"Why not?"

Sarah searched the slate-gray sky for answers. "Simply because the family needs you. And will need you for many years to come, Gillian. It needs the Skyborn, too. You've got to understand these things. Sometimes I feel so damnably *old*."

"So it was your sister's intention to even the sides a wee bit. Get rid of Bruick for starters," Patrick said, summing up Sarah's plans. "We had hoped to give you the slip and adjust our plans accordingly."

"But you're every bit as determined as your sister," Sarah said fondly to Gillian. She looked over to Welkin who was trying to keep up with all these revelations. "I saw Welkin at the Stockade and prayed for him to go off someplace so I could maybe rescue *something* of my plans." She laughed at Welkin's reaction. "It was sheer vanity on my part, Welkin. I wanted so desperately to help you, to be with you, rope you in, but I couldn't bring myself to drag anyone else into this. It was bad enough that Patrick and Mira would have . . . well, maybe gone down with me. Since I thought I hadn't long to live, laying my life on the line wasn't such a big deal."

Welkin turned to the O'Shannesseys. "And what's your stake in all this?" Envy and jealousy were bubbling inside him like lava.

"That be none of your business," Mira said curtly.

Sarah held her hand up to quell what might become dissension. "Mira has her reasons." She smiled briefly. "It's a personal thing, Welkin, to do with Bruick's past . . . crimes. Best left alone."

"So you didn't figure on Elab and the others leaving camp to search for the *Colony* renegades?" Welkin prompted.

Sarah shook her head distractedly. "Now that really threw me. The last thing I wanted was for Elab to take off on a wild goose chase. I could've cried when Patrick and Mira told me about it." She cleared her voice. "There was just nothing I could do to prevent it."

"Would anything have changed your plans?" Gillian asked in a challenging voice that Sarah instantly recognized as so like her own.

"I don't know," she replied honestly. She eyed Gillian and the others speculatively. "It's hard to know what to do sometimes, Gillian. Go with the flow—fight against it . . ." She put her arm around Gillian's shoulders. "I have a hunch we'll know how all this is going to turn out soon enough."

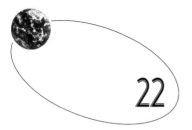

22

It took the best part of the next day and night for Gillian to come around to Sarah's way of thinking. At times, as she watched Sarah organize a rope across a swollen stream, or direct them to higher ground that might cost them time yet afford them shelter beneath broad belts of eucalypti, her resentment slowly abated. It came as a shock to her to realize how angry she'd been at being *abandoned*. It seemed to have awakened some long-lost feeling of terror that she couldn't even begin to explain. And anger had helped her shut the door on that dreadful feeling.

But if it was on Gillian's mind to apologize for her earlier behavior, the gunfire they heard pushed it to the back of her mind.

They were less than a mile from what Sarah's old map described as "The Falls" when the dull flashes of ballistic fire dotted the night. The steady drizzle that hadn't abated for the past few hours did nothing to dampen those sharp reports.

They dropped to the ground when the first shot echoed through the night. None of them was exactly in peak condition. Sarah's forced diet and subsequent erratic lifestyle, Patrick and Mira's ordeal in coping with Sarah's plans while keeping Gillian at a manageable distance, and Welkin and Gillian's tortuous few weeks had blunted their reflexes.

The O'Shannesseys edged forward on knees and elbows. Patrick's movements were hampered by his injured arm. "Patrick," Sarah said, "give Welkin the laserlite. You're no good to us with that arm."

Patrick grumbled but handed the weapon over. Welkin took it, checked the charge, and flipped off the safety. There was something *practiced* about the way he did this. Sarah realized that Welkin had grown up while she was gone.

"Any suggestions?" Sarah asked.

"You move around back, Gillian and I will take the front," Welkin said. "Mira can give us supporting cover. And Patrick still has his knife. He can look for stragglers."

Sarah raised her eyebrows. "Good plan. Let's do it." She became a fast-moving shadow that was soon lost to sight.

Another shot rang out, punctuating the steady rumbling of the falls to their left.

Welkin beckoned Gillian away from the roar of tumbling water. The wind rose, but with it the rain turned to mist. Gillian pushed her way through the gray shroud and found Welkin squatting by a rusting hay barn.

Welkin put a finger to his lips, then pointed in several directions. It was hard to see clearly, but Zocky's Amazonian body in the doorway of a shack was unmistakable. The blond girl rose, drew back her bow, and loosed an arrow. There was a dull *thumk* as it struck home. Then Zocky was gone.

Welkin half rose but paused. Laserlite fire suddenly cut through the veil of mist. Moments later another barrage ripped into a shack close by the hay barn.

Gillian rubbed her eyes. Before she could clear them, Welkin was up and running. For someone who had been exhausted earlier, he had surprising speed. Gillian tensed herself, then went after him.

Another shot rang out and Gillian was relieved not to see Welkin stumble and fall. Instead she felt something rip into her leg and the ground race up to meet her. She hit the packed earth hard, then lay flat on her face. Her left leg convulsed, and try as she might it wouldn't obey her. She opened her eyes and thanked her nameless gods when she saw Welkin reach a stone church building and disappear inside.

When no further shots rang out, Gillian took a chance and moved slowly forward. Her leg throbbed achingly, but she knew she couldn't stay out here. Besides, if Welkin realized where she was, he'd come out to get her. The thought lent her renewed energy and she crab-crawled through the dark. The church seemed miles away.

Welkin cursed inwardly. Gillian hadn't followed him. She was capable of looking after herself, but this situation was dicey. He waited for his eyes to adjust to the darkened hall before examining his surroundings. Feeling his way around the walls he finally stumbled across a body.

Alert, he squatted and rolled the corpse over. Lars. Blood congealing on his throat. No weapon. Welkin's mind took it all in. If anything, Lars would have had a bow. Bruick's men were mostly armed with ballistics. He'd seen them leave the Stockade what seemed like ages ago. Obvious deduction: No one would have taken his bow. Elab was known to have taken a laserlite; Lars would have been the obvious choice to carry it.

He tightened his grip on Patrick's laserlite and sniffed the air like a hunting animal, sensing that something was wrong. He stepped over the body and peered out through the broken window. Across the square stood a lone shack. Zocky had killed someone in there. Laserlite fire had been directed at its front entrance. The laserlite fire, he reasoned, hadn't belonged to Elab's crew.

Then Welkin's heart missed a beat. Gillian was frantically scrabbling across the rutted square toward the shack. All reason left him and he moved quickly to the door, totally unaware of another man's presence.

"EYES OPEN!" Bruick mocked. He launched a roundhouse kick that caught Welkin in the side of the head and slammed him into the wall.

Suddenly the back door burst open as Sarah dived through. She got off one shot that plucked at Bruick's sleeve but left him untouched. Bruick fired, and Sarah's cuff flapped loose. She dropped the laserlite and rolled to her feet.

"Hiya, Sarah," Bruick said.

Sarah had a moment to step back into a defensive crouch, but Bruick was too quick. He broke through her blocking hands and headbutted her.

The impact knocked her sprawling, her eyes swimming in and out of focus. She was only dimly aware of the blood that flowed from her ruptured forehead.

"Long time no see," Bruick spat as he moved forward. He retrieved Sarah's fallen laserlite. "You won't need this where you're going," he said, swinging the weapon toward her.

Welkin scrabbled to get up, and Bruick turned to him and leveled a savage kick at his ribs. Welkin rolled with the impact, but there was no mistaking the audible crack as a rib snapped. His head struck the wooden floor twice. In a kind of slow motion, Welkin saw the laserlite come around and take aim. There was a bright flash of light that almost blinded him and instant searing pain in his shoulder.

"WELKIN!" Gillian cried.

Bruick swung about and fired instinctively. It took him a second to realize that no one was standing in the doorway. His eyes dropped to where Gillian had dragged herself. Her left hand was pulled back. The arrow would go right through him at this range. His mind raced. He slowly lowered the laserlite to the floor. "You wouldn't kill an unarmed man, would you?" he said calculatingly. He kept his hands outstretched, palms up.

"Kill him!" Welkin said, gasping with pain. He pushed himself up onto his good elbow. To his blood-smeared eyes, the room seemed a shifting mass of dark shadows. The laserlite at Bruick's feet was an ugly extension of the man.

"Welkin?" Gillian repeated hesitantly.

"I could've killed you back at the Stockade," Bruick reminded Gillian. He let his hands drop slowly to his side. He risked a quick look at Welkin. When he faced Gillian he smiled. "Your boyfriend's okay."

"Move away from him!" Gillian wailed. Her voice was cracking and her hands were wavering.

In the other corner, Sarah sat up groggily. "Welkin's right! Kill him!"

Then Devan's honey-smooth voice: "It's okay, Gillian. I've got him covered."

"Thank God," Sarah sighed and fainted.

"Uh-uh," Bruick smiled.

Welkin froze. Why would Bruick smile? Unless . . . an arrow thudded into a body. The next moment the room flared with laserlite fire. Someone screamed. Gillian? Welkin felt for his boot with his good arm, then groaned, cursing the laser wound that flared in agony every time he moved. His hand gripped a knife haft. In one movement he had it out and his arm flung back ready to throw.

Bruick, his face a grotesque mask of loathing, with an arrow protruding from his chest, spun around in a lazy spiral before toppling headfirst to the floor.

Two figures struggled in the doorway. Welkin was confused. It was too dark and his eyes were too full of blood to see clearly who they were.

Then a third person joined the melee: Harry! He grabbed a head by the hair. Was it Gillian's? Welkin's mind reeled.

Harry hesitated a split second, then pulled a knife across Devan's throat and stepped back as the boy fell forward.

"Gillian?" Welkin managed. Through a miasma of pain he got to his feet, staggered forward.

"She's okay," Harry said breathlessly.

"My leg's shot to pieces, that's all," Gillian wheezed. She pushed the dead Devan from her.

Harry looked around. "Where's Lars?"

"Don't go over there," Welkin said. "They got him."

"Bloody Devan," Harry said, shaking his head in disbelief. "No wonder he was all for coming down here. He meant to take out most of the Committee in one hit. He was so insistent we light a fire for that pig he shot. A signal to Bruick that we were coming."

Welkin crossed to Sarah and helped her into a sitting position. She was coming to, looking about her in bewilderment. She saw Gillian and reached for her.

Gillian sat down beside her, grunting as pain flared in her leg. "Sarah, are you okay?"

Sarah nodded. "Just a bump on the head. I'll be fine in a second.

Ouch! My wrist! Devan!" she said, staring at his body.

Gillian tightened her grip on Sarah's shoulder. "He was the spy. Devan the *cook*. The one poisoning you."

Welkin gritted his teeth against pain. "Anyone seen Elab?" His insides were churning at the thought of their losses.

"He's with Mira," said Patrick, who had just come through the door. "She's bandaging him up." As an afterthought, he added, "There're bodies everywhere."

"And Zocky?" Welkin asked.

"Devan got her," Harry said quietly. He threw his knife into the door frame where it twanged on impact. "If he'd come after me first, Zocky'd still be alive. I knew Lars would never have given up the laserlite. Not unless he was dead." He shook off Patrick's comforting hand. His eyes glinted.

Welkin moved, then started to sway and had to sit down. The cracked rib made breathing difficult now that the surge of adrenaline had passed.

Sarah recovered first, her head clearing. She'd have a nasty bruise on her forehead for a few days, but she was still alive. She picked up the fallen laserlite. "You okay, Gillian?"

Gillian blinked away tears. "Sure. You go secure the area."

Sarah nodded. "I won't be far."

Patrick went to Welkin. When he looked at his face he cursed loudly, rummaged around in his pack for water, and began sluicing the blood away.

"I'm okay. Stop fussing," Welkin said irritably. "For crying out loud! Can't you see Gillian's been shot?"

"Stay put, Welkin," Patrick reproached. "Harry's tending her. And that ain't no pinprick you got yourself there." He unstoppered a vial and soaked the cloth with an infusion of agrimony, yarrow, and comfrey leaves. Both Welkin and Gillian groaned in unison.

"If it doesn't hurt, it doesn't work," Patrick said cheerfully.

"And you're a bundle of joy," Welkin squeezed out between gritted teeth.

"Och, don't be such a crybaby!" Patrick admonished.

23

At daybreak they lit a fire for the twenty-one bodies they found about the township. Digging a mass grave would have been time-consuming, considering they had only three able-bodied people to dig it.

The most grisly find was that of the colonists' mutilated bodies. Even the dauntless Mira had vomited uncontrollably when Welkin discovered their remains stacked in a tiny cellar.

Welkin worked out the likeliest scenario, and everyone concurred with it. The dissident colonists had been set up by *Colony*'s elders who had conspired with Bruick to lure them out. Because of Bruick's well-known desperate need for the longevity drug, it would have been a simple enough ruse for the elders to use him to draw the suspected pacifist rebels out into the open with a promise of help from the jabbers in exchange for their scientific know-how. Bruick's reward would be a guaranteed supply of the drug from *Colony*'s pharmacologists.

It was now Welkin's guess that *Colony*, after quelling the rebellion, would launch an attack on Bruick's Stockade. That would remove any need to keep their promise to Bruick with the consequent depletion of their precious drug supplies. But now that Bruick was gone, *Colony*'s next move in its relentless conquest of Earth was all too easy to predict.

It took some persuading, but finally Elab and Gillian took the two colonist cruisers to prepare the family for the impending danger and also to share the good news that Sarah was alive and coming home.

As they trudged wearily home, Welkin consoled himself with one fact: Bruick was dead. And if the elders destroyed the Stockade as he believed they would, then one more misery—and one more enemy—was wiped from their lives.

As for *Colony*, that was another matter. One that he and Sarah and Gillian would have to give long, hard thought to. But he already had a glimmering of an idea . . .

For now, he had what he had never had on board *Colony*: a family. The Earthborn. And together they had a proud and dangerous destiny to fulfill.